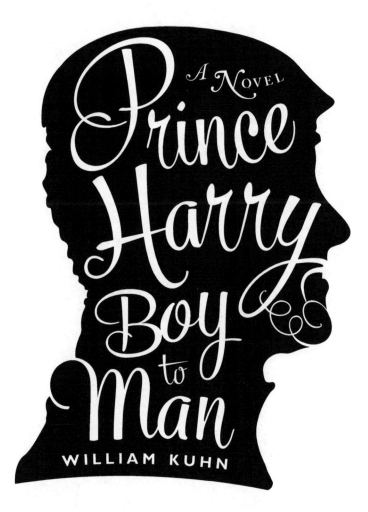

A NOVEL

Prince Harry Boy to Man

WILLIAM KUHN

MONTGOMERY STREET PRESS
BOSTON, MASSACHUSETTS

Montgomery Street Press
Boston, Massachusetts

Cover art and interior design by Jason Anscomb,
rawshockdesign@gmail.com.

With thanks for her editorial and proofreading help to
Marilyn Davidson.

ISBN 978-0-9989170-0-9

For the members of my writing group,

Iory Allison
Michael Cox
Daniel M. Kimmel
Robert LeCates
Linda Markarian
Kilian Melloy
Arnold Serapilio
Jamie Simpson

Part I

The Road
to Oxiana

"Boring," said the young lieutenant with a yawn. "So bored."

"Not in the Household Cavalry," said another lieutenant sitting next to him and not looking up from his book. "Never. Not allowed." They were both at the beginning of their twenties, but both looked young for their age. One had a high red color in his cheeks and freckles across the bridge of his nose. The other had light brown skin and hair so black and glossy it looked as if it had some kind of gel or oil in it, but it didn't. They were leaning back against their packs on the carpeted floor of a nearly deserted airline terminal. "Or that's the way I was trained. Maybe in the polo division being bored's perfectly okay? I wouldn't know."

The first young man narrowed his eyes and looked at the nametag sewn on to the other's camouflage tunic. "Well, Lieutenant Khan, is it? Maybe in the university division,"

he said with a sneer, "you don't say it, but I say it. All the time."

"Do you, Mr. Wales?" said the other. Although they were in the same regiment, they'd only met a few hours before. "What else do you do? When you're swanning around Highgrove and Henley, I mean."

At this Harry snatched the book out of the other's hands. "What's this then? *The Road to Oxiana*?" he said reading from the book's title. "I'll tell you what I don't do. I don't waste time remembering my glory days at Oxford."

"It's a classic. It's nothing to do with Oxford. Robert Byron travelled across Afghanistan in the 1930s. It's about architecture. And antiquities. Don't lose my place."

"Oh is it?" Harry tossed the book across the floor out of reach. "Sorry about that! Pity I lost your place."

As the other young man went to retrieve his book, Harry caught him by surprise. He grabbed him and put him in a wrestling hold. He held his neck in the crook of one of his elbows as he struggled to free himself. "Don't worry. Page 56." Then he tightened his grip and whispered near his ear, "What do they call you at home then, Khan?"

"Mustafa," said the other, unwillingly and under duress.

"Mustafa," said Harry with satisfaction. He put his other hand into Mustafa's black hair and rubbed his scalp with his knuckles. "Oh look. What beautiful hair he's got. All messed up."

"Ow! Get off." Mustafa freed himself and pulled away. He straightened his uniform, smoothed his hair, and looked angry.

They'd been on the floor for the better part of four hours. There had been a breakdown of the military transport

intended for them at Brize Norton. Instead, the army had arranged for their transfer from London to Kabul via a leased British Airways 777 that was supposed to leave at midnight, after the commercial air travel had ended for the evening.

"What time's it now?"

Mustafa refused to look at Harry, but he pulled out his phone from his pocket. "Oh three hundred hours."

Harry squeezed his eyes shut and fell backward on to his pack. He snorted through his nostrils in a combination of frustration and exhaustion.

"No feather pillows for you tonight, sir," said Mustafa, leaning over close to Harry's ear. "What's your thread count over at Kensington Palace? Nine hundred? Maybe a thousand even."

"Don't call me that."

"Sorry mate. It was in the special regulation circular." Mustafa looked down at his phone and began scrolling through several different screens with his finger. "Let's see. Where is it? Oh yeah. Got it right here." He began reading from the document on his screen. "*Lieutenant Wales is a prince of the UK royal family. He is entitled to do his job in the regiment without interference. However, in the ordinary course of duty, recall that his grandmother is head of the armed forces, his aunt is honorary colonel of the regiment, his father and his brother will both one day be king. Treat him with discretion, circumspection, and respect.*"

"What a load of shite."

"Don't let the colonel hear you say that."

"I'm not talkin' to 'im, I'm talkin to you." Here Harry rolled on top of Mustafa and grabbed him just above the waist.

Mustafa made a sound that was in between a laugh and a squeak. He contracted into a fetal position to protect himself.

"Don't let the colonel hear you say that, *sir*! That's how you say it. Don't you?"

Mustafa carried on resisting. He couldn't reply. Harry seemed to know all the different spots that tickled most.

"What's all this 'bout thread counts, then?"

"No. Don't. Stop!"

"I can't hear you! How do you know what I've got to sleep on, then? Dream about my bed, do you? Do you fancy me?"

"No. Stop. I. Stop. Don't!"

Harry leaned back and let Mustafa go. He stretched and yawned. "All in a day's work. Keeping the men happy."

Mustafa squirmed away. He breathed hard and pulled down his twisted camouflage tunic. He was angrier than he'd been before. "I'm not other ranks. I've got the same commission as you."

"Oh, do you?" said Harry. He took a renewed interest and reached his arm around Mustafa as if he was going to start again.

"Get off!" Mustafa rolled out of his reach.

"What's a thread count, then?" Harry looked puzzled. "You mean the bore inside a weapon?"

"No, you're the bore." Mustafa got up on his knees so as to have quicker maneuverability if Harry went after him again.

"I love it when you insult me. It means you really do like me."

"You know what a fucking thread count is."

"Oh, sir? Sir?" Harry turned away and pretended as if he were going to approach their commanding officer, who was

in a distant corner, out of earshot, consulting with one of the flight engineers. "Lieutenant Khan here just said fuck. Shall I write him up, sir?"

"Will you shut the fuck up?"

"He did it again, sir. That's twice, sir."

"A thread count, you moron, is what goes into a sheet."

"I thought a sheet's just a sheet."

"That's cause you don't have a girlfriend who obsesses about it."

"What! You've got a girlfriend?" Harry looked innocent and concerned. "I thought you were gay." He raised his eyebrows sympathetically. "I'm totally okay with it. I mean. You loved it when I tickled you. Your secret's good with me, mate."

Mustafa reached out and gave Harry a slug on the upper arm.

"Ow!"

"What's that necklace you've got on?" Mustafa had noticed that Harry was wearing a chain around his neck with a metal hoop at the end of it. "You're calling me gay?"

"It's not a necklace!" Harry put his finger under the chain and pulled it up briefly above his collar. "It's a man-pendant, see?"

Mustafa was just about to make fun of him for that, when his mobile phone went off. It had fallen on to the floor when they were wrestling.

He leaned out of Harry's range, picked it up, and looked at the illuminated screen. It was a Skype call from his girlfriend. He had the volume down low, so it was impossible to hear what she was saying. "Hi." [pause] "Nope. Still here." [pause] "No, I don't know." [pause] "They're not telling us." Then

something occurred to him. "Hang on, a minute. Hang on." He looked over at Harry. "Guess who's here?" [pause] "No. Guess."

At this Harry sprang forward, put his arm around Mustafa's shoulders, and leaned in his head so he could appear in front of the phone's camera. "Hola, baby."

Although the sound was so low that it was almost set to mute, a small, muffled scream was still audible from the other end of the line.

"See?"

"Ooh, darlin'. He didn't tell me you were bee-you-ti-ful. What are you wearin'? Are those your PJs?"

Mustafa hit Harry on the upper arm again.

"Ow! He hits me all the time. This one does. I'm black and blue all over. And we ain't even there yet."

"Hands off my girl, mate."

"Are you happy with him, then? Cause I've got some gorgeous thread count over at mine. Why don't you come over? [pause] When we come back then? I'm tellin' you the thread count I've got is to die for."

Mustafa laughed. "He doesn't even know what it is."

"Yah I do! And here's somethin' else. Did you know he's gay? He told me. Look!" Here Harry leaned over and gave Mustafa a lick on the ear before he could pull away. Mustafa dropped the phone, rolled away, and made a retching noise.

Harry retrieved the phone. "He loves it. See what I mean? So you and me? We've got to get together when I get back." To indicate friendliness, he used an accent as if he were one of the characters on *East Enders*. He said "got to get togevvuh" before carrying on with, "I'm gonna look after your thread

count, baby."

There was another muffled scream from the phone. Mustafa re-appeared, wiped his hand over his ear, and hit Harry in the ribs this time. Several men nearby, who'd been taking no notice before, began to stand and watch them. One pointed and laughed. Their commanding officer, sensing something amiss, disengaged himself from the engineer and began strolling over in their direction.

The two young lieutenants saw him coming their way and jumped to their feet. Mustafa ended the call and shoved the phone back in his pocket. They both aligned their shoulders with one another to make them parallel. They tucked in their bottoms, straightened their backs, and threw out their chests as if they were on the parade ground and not in Heathrow Terminal Five. They both saluted at the same instant.

The commanding officer arrived and said gently from ten feet away, "All well, gentlemen?" His tone of voice indicated the early hour of the morning and suggested they all should have been asleep by now.

"Yes. Sir." They whispered in harsh unison.

"As you were," said the commanding officer, turning on his heel to return to the opposite side of the departure lounge. The computerized television screens behind him were already beginning to indicate the commercial flights that would begin to depart just before six that morning.

Harry and Mustafa watched him go, and when he'd reached the other side of the room, they at last collapsed back into sack-like positions on the floor.

"That was close," said Mustafa. "Remind me not to sit next to you anymore. They're keeping tabs on you, mate."

"Tell me about it."

For the first time that night Mustafa could see that there was something odd about Harry. When his face was at rest, he looked dejected. He wasn't play-acting. He tried to cheer him up. "You made her night."

Harry said nothing to that.

"It must be useful that. Having a way with girls, I mean."

"I don't have a way with girls."

"Sure you do. I just saw it."

"I don't do anything. They see this," here Harry gave his cheek a dismissive swipe with his fingertips, "and they go wild. I don't do anything."

"Not true, mate. You got the gift. Go with it."

Harry didn't respond to that. Instead, he lay back on his pack, closed his eyes, and crossed his arms. He looked as if he were going to sleep.

"Whatever," said Mustafa. "Go have a sulk then."

Harry said nothing. He breathed in and out through his nose. After a few moments, he really was asleep, gone, just like that. Unguarded, his face took on a bewildered expression. All the mischief and playfulness of before vanished.

Mustafa looked at him and wondered what was wrong.

*

At Atlanta's Hartsfield Airport, four thousand miles away, a CNN team was sitting at the British Airways departure gate. They were waiting for one of the last flights of the night that would take them up the east coast, over Nova Scotia, across the Atlantic, then at length over Ireland, Wales, and the west of England. They'd land mid-morning at Heathrow in time to make a connecting flight that would take them further east. It was a small group of three: a producer, an on-air reporter, and a cameraman. The flight was delayed, and the cameraman was already asleep. He had his feet propped up on his oversized camera case, which he had special clearance from the airline to carry on board. The producer, an old hand in his early fifties, and the on-air reporter, a young woman in her early twenties, were having an argument.

"Look," she said. "The real story isn't in Kabul. That's gonna be guys sitting behind desks."

"Oh, great. No point in doing this overnight flight then? Why don't we just go home and sleep in our own beds?"

She ignored him. "The real story is in Helmand. On the front line."

The older man sighed. "Cindy. We've been over this before. The army moves slowly. They've just about got to the place where they can put women near to front-line positions. Not on the front line, but near it. There's no way in hell they're gonna allow us to embed a female reporter."

"Why not!"

"They're not ready for it. They don't know how to do it. They don't have the capability. They've never done it before. They can't. They won't."

"The army's part of the government. They represent us.

This is 2007, not 1907! They have to change with the times."

"Sure you can say that. But have you dealt with the communications guys in the army? Because I have. For years. They don't move fast. They've just kinda figured out how to update a website. They've got a long way to go before they can put Cindy Lou Who in a tent in Afghanistan with enlisted boys from Arkansas and Alabama."

"If you keep calling me that, I'll report you. For sexism."

"You know the trouble with women at CNN? No sense of humor."

"You know the trouble with guys at CNN? All they know how to do is do what they've always done. Defend the god damned *status quo*."

They both paused a moment because they were angry. They each recognized an element of truth in the other one's charge.

The older man relented a little. "Look Cindy. You've got terrific ratings. You look great on camera. You're a tough reporter. You're not afraid to ask the hard questions." Then he cracked a smile in advance of his own sexist remark. "And everyone loves your hair."

She smiled at him too. He was not a bad guy. He'd given her one promotion after another. He believed in her. He was giving her lots of airtime. He was taking her with him to Afghanistan. He wasn't wrong about the hair. She had a thick mane of dark chestnut hair. The hairdressers at the network could tease it, shellac it with hairspray, and put it into half a dozen different shapes and sizes. She had a loyal fan base that envied it.

"Plus we've already got one guy embedded out there. And a second one going out tonight. He went on the earlier flight.

They're just not going to let a woman do it. You've just got to give up on that. There are other ways for you to make your mark. Even to get into Kabul is pretty big stuff. If we get to a brigadier or an ambassador, ask them some of the right questions, make it look awkward for them, well, Pulitzers have been given out for less."

That's what she liked about him. He didn't condescend to her because she was still in her twenties. He didn't mind dangling the profession's biggest carrots in front of her, even though the chances of their getting one were slim. He was willing for them both to aim high. What she didn't like was his tone. That, she felt sure, was what came with being in his fifties. He was already looking toward retirement. He was already giving up. That was the way she saw it. She still had plenty of fight left.

"The story in Kabul," she said, "is gonna be a bunch of doubletalk from whoever they let go in front of the camera. The real story is gonna be where the Taliban is still strong. Outside Kabul. It's gonna be the local people and what they think of Americans. Why they like the Taliban better. In Kabul they're gonna be full of crap."

He half turned to her sitting next to him. "Look, Cindy," he began. He was using a gentler voice. "You don't have to fight so hard."

"What?"

"You're already in the game with the big boys. You have to learn to tackle smart. Don't always throw your full weight against it. Don't treat it like it's a fight to the death every time. It's not."

"I don't know what you're talking about."

"Here's your problem, kid. You still see yourself as that geeky girl in glasses you were in high school. The rest of us see a gorgeous young woman, self-possessed, smart as hell, and sassy. You think you're going to be left out unless you punch hard, harder than you need to. Nobody's going to leave you out of this game, unless you ruin it for yourself by overreaching. Or making it tough for people on your own side."

"Yeah? Well, you didn't get promoted to where you are because you're gorgeous on camera." She put a mocking emphasis on "gorgeous." "How many senior women reporters have we got out there? Not many. Cause they all get fired when they lose their looks."

"I've told you all along that you have what it takes to make it in broadcast. Not just now, but into the future. You can count on that. You can count on me."

"Well, thanks for your support and all, but I'd rather make it because I bring in a big story. Not because I've got some daddy-o producer lookin' out for me."

"Ouch," he said quietly.

Then she knew she'd gone too far. She briefly ran her hand over his forearm sitting on the armrest next to her. "Look, I'm sorry. I know I hit too hard sometimes. Blame it on my brothers. There were four of them older than me and unless you grabbed for the meat loaf you didn't get any. After college? The only way I got into that media camp without having a reel was by showing up and demanding they put my name down. I had to make them give me an application even when they said I didn't qualify. If you don't push, you don't get what you want."

"Yeah, well try not to hit the people who're trying to help."

"I swear I could fit in with the guys out there. Don't you see? That's where growing up with brothers comes in handy. You clear it with the Pentagon and I'll make sure the guys treat me like one of the gang."

They'd already had that argument. He wasn't going to start it again now. He looked down at the notebook computer open in his lap. It was his way of shutting down the discussion.

Cindy Reed stood up on her patent leather heels and stalked away from him down the carpeted aisle. It wasn't strictly necessary for her to fly in the silk blouse and slim trousers she wore when she was on camera, especially not when she was travelling to a remote location. When they had a cameraman along, however, she thought it was always better to be dressed as though she would have to do some on-camera material. You never knew.

She'd only got a few yards away from where she'd been sitting when she came across a pair of privates wearing desert fatigues. They both had matching caps with long bills, the army's version of baseball caps, pulled down low over their eyes. To this they'd both added aviator sunglasses, though it was long after dark. She stopped in front of them.

They were watching a TV screen above her that was set permanently to CNN. They felt invisible behind their sunglasses and underneath the brims of their caps. The glasses were dark enough to prevent anyone from seeing what their eyes were doing, so they didn't mind letting their eyes check her out. It was as if they were wearing masks. They could see out, but no one could see in.

They'd turned their heads toward her, so Cindy knew they were looking at her, even if she couldn't see their eyes.

"Hey, guys."

"Hey," allowed one. The other one said nothing.

"Just wanted to say thank you for your service." She held her hands behind her back and smiled, as if she were a stewardess ready to get them a cup of coffee if that's what they wanted.

This embarrassed them both. Even though they were temporarily detached from their unit, when they were traveling on the army's dime, they had to wear their uniforms. It had gotten so they could barely walk into a McDonald's without some guy or some old lady walking up to them and thanking them for their service. They'd gotten used to it, but they still wished people wouldn't. They wanted their old anonymity back. The only thing that was unusual here was that she was hot, and hot girls seldom said it to them.

One gave a brisk country nod to acknowledge what she'd said. The other said "No problem."

"Where you guys headed?"

They gave each other a half glance. There might be some room for play here. Women, especially women from the big city, were rarely friendly to them. They almost never started a conversation.

One of the two guys, exaggerating his rural accent, said "Well, ma'am, we'd love to tell y'all, but we can't rightly say."

"Nope," agreed the other. "Operational secret."

"Eye-rack? Gannystan?" she asked them, using the words she expected them to use, as opposed to the ones she'd use on air. They were also the words her brothers would have used, or the guys in her not very good high school would have used, many of whom had signed up to go.

The first one was about to give her a smart answer, when

the second one punched him in the arm. "Hey wait a minute. You were on TV a minute ago. Up there," he nodded his head to the television screen on the ceiling.

Cindy glanced upwards. It occurred to her they might have seen one of the on-air promotional videos she'd recorded a couple of weeks ago. They scrolled fairly continuously through the evening news cycle. She looked back at them coolly. She said nothing.

"Was that you?" asked the first soldier.

"Maybe."

"You wanna interview us?"

"Cause you can't," put in the second soldier. They'd been explicitly told that even though they were returning to Afghanistan via a commercial airliner, they were not to engage with the media in any form or to disclose their eventual destination to anyone.

"No, I don't want to interview you. But I do want you to come with me."

The two young men both leapt to their feet. Had they been looking at themselves from a distance, they would have agreed it was too fast. They both thought it was better to behave around women with a bit less enthusiasm. However, they'd never been propositioned before. That was what it seemed like to them. This woman was not only hot, but also famous enough to be on TV. She led the way down the broad airport corridor. With the exception of the British Airways gate, the concourse was empty at that late hour. They were a pace or two behind her, watching her walk in her heels, and one elbowed the other. He grinned. She came to a men's room fifty yards away and turned to walk in. She gave them both a

direct look before she did.

When they got inside, one of them said "Women aren't allowed in here." He felt sheepish because the rule was so obvious, it made him feel stupid to repeat it. He'd never spoken it before to a young woman who had such a sense of self-assurance and command.

She stopped in front of a full-length mirror in the corner and turned toward them on the tiled floor. "Now, I want you two to strip."

"What?" said one.

The other one was too shocked to speak.

*

Frances de Mornay sat alone in her one-room cottage. Her small roller bag was packed. She wasn't taking very much. A change of clothes. A fleece for cold weather. A pair of plimsolls. She already had a headscarf tied over her white hair. She sat by the window looking out on the street, waiting for the coach from the church. She wanted a drink. There was a travel-sized bottle of whiskey in the top pouch of her bag, but she wasn't giving into that. No she wasn't. Not yet. It was five o'clock in the morning. Good Lord save me from that, she said to herself silently. She could have said it aloud if she wanted. She was

the only one there. As with the whiskey, she'd tried to limit the time she spent talking aloud to herself, even though it made her feel less alone.

It was the whiskey that'd got her there in the first place. She'd decided to move to a village on the west coast of Scotland, not too far from the railway at Oban. It was less expensive there. She had enough money at first for a small house with a garden. People left her alone. The Scots were like that, bless them. They didn't care who you were, or once had been. They gave you your privacy. Then she'd probably had a bit too much privacy. She was just an old lady who'd been unlucky in love. Was that so bad? Who could blame her for taking some comfort from drink? That was the problem, though. Nobody blamed her, because she spoke to no one. The privacy was endless.

She had an accident in her car. No one was hurt, but it was expensive. The court appearance was costly too. The judge's taking away her driving license was a nuisance. She lost track of her money. There were lottery tickets and occasional visits to the betting shop. She liked the horse races, it had to be said. Then there had been the ludicrous agreement she'd signed with her husband. What did she know? She'd only been eighteen when she married him. When he left her, she barely had enough to cover the rental of a flat in Kings Lynn. And no training. Women of her generation didn't. They weren't expected to work. If a friend of her mother's hadn't swept her up and arranged for a place in the Wales's household where would she have been? That was absurd too. She didn't know how to be a nanny. She was already in her forties when she started. She had no children of her own. Her only experience

was to have lived, while still married, in a house that had an Olympic-sized swimming pool. It had attracted every child in the neighborhood. She had been a field marshal of several regiments of under-twelves in their swimming costumes.

Still, she'd rubbed along. She'd managed. She'd made mistakes. And she'd looked after those boys. She'd grown to love them. That was why it had been such a cruel joke when she'd been given the sack. The excuse was the drink. Their mother had made sure to let that out to her friends in the papers, but Frances put it down to jealousy. She'd seen how much the boys loved her. There was no appeal of course. Frances had gone to Scotland afterwards to control expenses, to hide, and perhaps, just a little, to hang her head in shame.

Before she knew it, some people from the local church were picking her up off the floor and helping her sell the house. She'd moved into this tiny accommodation that was all she could afford now. They'd been so kind to her about everything. They'd helped. She was so grateful. They'd even allowed her to get involved at the church, to help in local cases of need, not unlike her own.

That was the first thing in a long time that was more powerful than drink. She felt down near the bottom. Helping someone else who was down there too made her feel good. It was a deep sense of well-being, deeper than the anesthetic of the whiskey. It didn't take much. Delivering a hot meal at lunchtime to a shut-in. Going to wipe up the sick off an old man's jumper who'd been too drunk to get out of his wheelchair. Cleaning out the loo of a local girl who had five children and all of them down with the flu. That was how she could help. Down on her knees in the loo. Yes, Lord. Down on

my knees swilling out the bowl. That's my prayer and that's my thanksgiving. She was pretty sure she had helped, and the girl with the sick children had helped her, too.

They'd let her become a regular part of the church team, seven days a week. It was the one thing that was now hopeful about her life. They'd grown to trust her. She was now sixty-eight, but she still had good bones, good teeth, good hair. Her being in the papers had been forgotten about, or the people who worked at the church pretended not to know. The priest knew, but he hadn't told anyone. He could see how much good the helping was doing her. He'd asked her to join an interfaith church group that was to travel part way with a Scottish regiment that was going to Afghanistan. Fly to London with them. Take them coffee or Cokes. Give them some small bags with treats they wouldn't be able to get out there. Listen to the ones that were scared. Squeeze their hands if they wanted that. They were only going as far as Heathrow. Give them all a kiss and a hug and a warm send-off, and then back to Scotland. That was the plan. Church van to Glasgow Airport. Fly to London Airport. Overnight in a church hall somewhere near Staines. Then fly back to Glasgow late the next evening with another Scottish regiment just returning from Kabul. It was only forty-eight hours, but it would keep her busy, keep her occupied.

"Stop it now!" This she did say aloud to herself. She abhorred self-pity. Self-pity was what led her to the bottle. She had to choke it off before it went that far. At that moment she saw a pair of headlights on the dark street. A battered van drew up in front of her door. She went to go and move her roller bag toward the door. There was a double knock. Then a heavy-set woman with white hair like hers, wearing an

anorak, and a pair of oily Nikes put her head inside the door.

"All right, Francie?"

Frances hated being called "Francie." She also hated when people opened her front door before she could open it for them. It went with the territory, she knew. She was regarded as one of the parish's more hopeless cases. They all expected to find her sprawled drunkenly in the middle of the floor when she didn't turn up somewhere she was supposed to be. Allowing them the freedom to come through the door when they wanted was one of the prices she'd had to pay for their having looked after her as kindly and patiently as they had. With an effort she swallowed back the resentment that swelled up from her loss of dignity and independence.

"Good morning! Yes, I'm fine thank you."

"Did you get any sleep last night? I was all keyed up. About London, you know? Didn't sleep a wink."

Frances switched off the lights and rolled the bag out on to the doorstep. "I slept like a log."

"Well, you see. I've never been before. To London, I mean."

The unworldliness of the others who worked in the church's charity group always surprised her. "Well, the airport is hardly London. And Staines is the suburbs. Pretty grim. It's not London either."

"Oh Francie! You've been to all parts, haven't you? Won't you sit next to me on the coach and tell me about it? How it really is."

Frances didn't like the woman, particularly. Sitting next to her for any length of time she regarded as a punishment not far removed from what Our Lord suffered on the cross. She'd had comfort from her conversion, but Frances's view

of religion was not without criticism or irony. She reminded herself to be grateful. "Of course I will. What fun."

The driver took her bag and stowed it in a compartment in the van's undercarriage. "Mornin' Francie!" He winked at her.

"Good morning, Frank!" Now Frances did like him. His wink made her feel as if she were about thirty-five again. She mugged for him. She went up on one toe and held her waist like a showgirl. "You rogue. I want you to keep your eyes on the road the whole way to Glasgow Airport."

He gave her an exaggerated salute. "Ma'am!"

"That's it. That's the right stuff," she muttered, audible to him, as she climbed the steps into the van. She said hello to the eight or nine others, all of whom she knew. They had all seen her at her worst. There was no pretending with any of them. She said "Good morning, good morning," to all of them, though it was still dark out and no sign of morning or goodness, but their warmth to one another. Several of the women who'd been kind to her reached out their hands to her. She held their hands briefly, one by one, with a look in the eye to each. She came to an empty pair of seats near the back. She slid in and down on to the velour seat, her sciatica giving her a twinge in the lower back as she did so. She winced.

"All right, darling?" The woman who'd come to her front door slid in next to her. She saw the wince.

"I'm all right. Nothing but a few old lady aches and pains."

"I've got a pill for that."

"No thank you. I'll be all right."

"Tell me about London then."

The van pulled away from Frances's cottage. They had at

least a couple of hours' journey to Glasgow Airport, where they'd join forces with aid workers from some other churches. Their first duty was passing out sandwiches to the soldiers whom they'd meet in a staging area adjacent to the airport.

"Oh, it's a long time since I've lived there," said Frances.

"There are millions of people. In London, I mean. Millions. I wonder what it looks like in the dark. All aglow. In the night sky."

Frances reflected on the sinister anti-crime lights of dozens and dozens of sulphur-colored street lamps. She thought of the reassuring rattle of taxis with their glowing "For Hire" signs. She thought of the candlelit dining rooms where once upon a time she'd been welcome. "Yes. It can be pretty. Isn't always."

"You have family there?" The woman had been worried by Frances's having no evident family in the village. She was an incomer and no family ever visited her, at least so far as the woman knew, they hadn't. Frances had an English voice. She sounded like the BBC from during the war, or maybe even before that. Before she fell on hard times, she must have had money too.

"Not exactly."

The other woman laughed gently. "Families can be like that, now. You had children?"

"No," Frances said cautiously. She had a low profile. She wanted to keep it that way. On the other hand, there was a certain confessional ease that came from simply telling the truth. Something about the dark, and the woman's kind, uncritical interest in her made her more willing to speak than usual.

"I looked after two little boys. For a little while. As their minder. That's the closest I ever came. Don't see them anymore, though. I fell out with their parents."

The woman left a tactful pause before she put in, "You must miss them, though."

"Yes, I did. For a while. No, that's wrong. I do. I still do."

Then she reached over to the woman sitting next to her. Frances slipped her hand into the crook of the woman's arm. No, she wasn't her favorite woman in the church group, but she had a beating heart. Of that there could be no doubt. "And I'm so pleased you wanted to sit next to me. To keep me company. Thank you."

*

The army had withdrawn Mustafa and Harry's regiment from the Heathrow departure terminal and moved them into an empty hangar. The Scottish regiment with which they were flying out to Kabul had been delayed in Glasgow. The whole transfer to Afghanistan had been pushed back by twenty-four hours. The men had to make do by bedding down on the cement floor. There were only some old tarpaulins for ground cover. They had to lay out their sleeping bags on those. Since they'd been up virtually all night, they were all

going to be allowed several hours' sleep before being fed a midday meal. This was to be in a makeshift canteen under the wing of a British Airways 747 so ancient that visible rust stains streamed down the join between the wings and the undercarriage. It was unnerving.

There was also the nonstop noise from landing aircraft, as it was now early morning and they were adjacent to an active runway. The men had psychologically prepared themselves for departure from home and going to a war zone. Yet here they were still in a disused corner of an airport next to a plane that didn't look as if it would ever fly again. They were all tired, cranky, and in a bad mood.

A sergeant major, ten years older than they were, approached Harry and Mustafa as they snoozed on their sleeping bags. "Gentlemen!" he said with a swift salute. Harry opened half an eye to see what was happening. When he saw who it was, he scrambled to his feet, kicked Mustafa in the calf to wake him up, and returned the sergeant major's salute. Although they both out-ranked him, the sergeant major was in reality the person who was in charge. He knew what to do. They didn't. What he said was law, even though it was often posed as a question. He intimidated them.

"What is it, sergeant major?" Harry asked, trying to sound as if he knew in advance whatever order that was about to be given to him in the form of a suggestion.

"It's customary, sir, to look after the comfort of the men. Before taking a kip yourself, that is. Sir!"

Harry shot a glance at Mustafa, who was now standing next to him, struggling to give the same impression of unworried competence.

"Of course, sergeant major. Right away. Will do. Mustafa looked at the sergeant major and nodded vigorously.

"Very good, gentlemen. After you, then." The sergeant major pointed the way toward their unit on the other side of the hangar.

Harry and Mustafa began to stride off in the direction he'd indicated. They'd gone no more than five paces, with the sergeant major striding behind them, when Harry broke step.

"Um?"

"Yes sir?"

"The thing is."

"Yes sir?"

"What do they want? The guys, I mean."

"What do they want, sir?"

"Yeah. I mean. What do they want me to do? Exactly?" He pronounced this "exackly," in hopes of getting the sergeant major to relent and crack a smile.

The sergeant major was ready for Lieutenant Wales to be a spoiled, untutored, and undisciplined junior officer. He was looking forward to toughening him up and to making things difficult for him. He was looking forward to grinding his face into the sand a little. It was what all junior officers needed. If the sergeant major's reading of *The Daily Mail* was accurate, this junior officer needed it more than most. He didn't smile.

"Well, sir. You know the drill, sir. It's what you've been trained to do, isn't it, sir?"

"Right, sergeant major. Of course, sergeant major." He looked at Mustafa, whose face concealed what he was thinking. "But could you give us a hint?"

"Well, the flight's delayed. They're tired. They have to sleep

on the floor. They want to be told that everything's under control. And that they'll have something to eat soon."

"So I'm responsible for a typical army cockup then? What am I supposed to do? Hand out airline meal vouchers?"

"Sir! Blaming the organization of Her Majesty's armed forces is unbecoming in an officer. Do you need me to tell you that?" The sergeant major looked from one young man to the other as if they were both hopeless cases. "Shall I call in the assistance of Colonel Arbuthnot? Shall we ask him what to do?"

"That won't be necessary, sergeant major."

"Good, sir."

"So what do we do then?"

"Make sure their sleeping bags are all on top of the tarp."

Harry and Mustafa both lightened up perceptibly. That was something they could do.

"And we're all getting Quarter Pounders delivered at eleven forty-five. Tell them that."

"Right!" said Harry, beginning to feel a bit more cheerful himself. With cheese? He wanted to ask, but thought better of it.

"Oh, and sir?"

"What sergeant major?"

"A little pep talk. That's what the men want." He smiled devilishly. He knew that neither of them was prepared for that. Neither of them had a clue where to begin. "Sir."

Harry gave a gloomy look at Mustafa, which Mustafa returned in the same minor key. They turned and resumed walking, somewhat more diffidently, toward their unit on the other side of the hangar. When they got there they found the

men in disarray. Some were lounging on their sleeping bags on top of the tarpaulin. Others were off the tarp and with their backs leaning up against an aluminum corrugated wall. They looked as angry and dissatisfied as if they were paying customers on a cancelled flight.

"Attention! On your feet, you lot," shouted the sergeant major. "Salute!"

The men got to their feet in surly, rag-tag order. Most of them saluted. Those that didn't received one by one attention from the sergeant major, who threatened them with physical punishment if they didn't salute instantly the next time. They reluctantly joined the others in a salute. Harry and Mustafa watched all this with dismay. They both felt without saying so that the men's disrespect was something they merited and for which they were responsible. When the last of the shirkers had been reprimanded, the sergeant major nodded to Harry.

"Lieutenant Wales wishes to address a few words to you."

Harry looked at Mustafa. "Why me?" He cleared his threat and muttered "Why not you?"

"Lieutenant Wales," the sergeant major reminded him. "Sir!"

"Well, um, hi everybody."

Several of the men looked at each other and smirked at the inadequacy of this beginning.

"I know you must all be as cheesed off as I am ..."

"Sir!"

"I mean as annoyed as I am, that, um, our plane's been delayed."

Harry could see at least three guys nearby him who enjoyed his having been corrected by the sergeant major. He hesitated.

The color in his cheeks became more intense and his ears flushed a reddish orange. This drew attention to the unusual color of his hair. He overheard one of the men say to another, "Gingers don't half get red."

"Especially when they've got nothing to say," replied his friend.

Harry tried to ignore this.

"The thing is. We just have to put up with it and try and be as comfortable as possible. You over there," he said speaking to the men who'd been leaning up against the wall. "You'll be better off with your sleeping bags on top of the tarp here."

"The floor's too hard," complained one of them.

"It's better leaning up against the wall," said another, unafraid. Harry hadn't trained with them, but they certainly knew who he was. They were all looking forward as much as the sergeant major was to putting him in his place. Having grown up in public housing in out of the way corners of the country, many of them, it was a once in a lifetime opportunity to talk back to someone who'd never notice them again as long as they lived.

"No speaking back to an officer!" cried out the sergeant major with a prison warden's menace in his voice.

"Um, I hear you guys."

Several of the men elbowed one another at his addressing them as "You guys." They too had seen the circular about how to deal with him. They had been threatened with punishment if they should ever acknowledge who he was. They'd practically been promised dishonorable discharges if they ever took a picture of him with their cellphones. They were not, however, going to let him call them "you guys" without letting him

know that they were not his guys. General murmuring broke out and two or three of them laughed openly at what Harry had just said.

"Silence!" shrieked the sergeant major. His voice hinted at a hysterical love of harming other people. As the men had trained with him, and knew him to be capable of this, they quieted down instantly.

"The thing is," resumed Harry, "we've laid on some McDonald's. And it's coming soon. So hold your horses."

"I haven't gotta horse," said one. "Not like you do."

"I'm vegan," said another.

"More junk food," said a third, as if it hardly required pointing out.

Harry rouged again. He had no idea what to say to that.

Just at that moment someone at the back sailed what looked like a Frisbee across the heads of the men and hit Harry on the ear with it. Harry at first stepped back as if hurt by something sharp. Then he reached down to his feet to investigate. It was a paper crown, a child's plaything that had come in their last Happy Meal boxes, about six hours previously. It was gold with a serrated edge, decorated here and there with cartoon illustrations of jewels. He picked it up. He put it on his head at a rakish angle. He bent his knees, wobbled his hips to an imaginary beat, and flung out his hands to either side as if he'd just completed a hip-hop step on the dance floor.

A shout went up from the men. Some cheered. Some jeered. Some laughed at his expense. A few of them were more dismayed than they had been before to be flying out to a war zone with a prince who pretended to be an urban gangster.

Some liked being quite close to a major celebrity. Others were sure it would get them into a quiet, cushy, and comparatively easy position once they got out there. The sergeant major folded his arms and didn't see any use in shouting. Mustafa took a step backward and didn't know whether to be pleased or embarrassed at what Harry'd done.

*

Cindy Reed watched the two men undressing in the corner of the Hartsfield men's room. Shedding their clothes made them also shed their toughness. In their sand-colored camouflage and sunglasses, they looked frightening, hard, and impenetrable. They could even have been fierce characters in a military-themed video game. As their clothes came off, she could see that one of them was a little pudgy around the waist. The other had mismatched socks. They both looked more like gawky boys than the faultless military supermen they'd been a moment before. This didn't make her less attracted to them. She liked them more for it. The sight of two guys stripping down to black boxer briefs transferred to her the power and sense of invulnerability they'd possessed only a moment before. In high school she'd worked on the library staff with the other smart kid outcasts. She remembered envying the sovereignty a dozen

football-playing boys had over a mixed high school population of several thousand. These two, she imagined, might once have been part of that shoulder pad and cleat-wearing elite.

Then she grew up. She got into college. She majored in media studies. She did well enough in the screen test at the media camp where she'd talked her way in the door to get an agent. After the agent had completed her makeover, the high school boys would have hardly recognized her, though they'd taken little enough notice of her at the time. In her mind, what she was having the two guys do now was a small revenge of the library staffers, her people, part one.

"Okay. Give me that top," she said to the shorter of the two guys.

"What? I can't fly without it."

"Don't worry. I'll take care of that." To the skinnier of the two she said "And I want your pants."

"These?" he said with a big smile and pointing to his underpants.

"No, those," she said pointing to his camouflage pants in a discarded pile on the tile floor.

"What are you gonna give me for 'em?"

"You'll see. And the boots, please."

They handed her their stuff. She took the things in her arms and stepped into one of the stalls. Its door swung close with a squeak. She latched the door.

"Hey wait! We stripped for you. You gotta strip for us," the shorter one protested. He felt that it would have been more fun in a one-on-one between him and the CNN girl, but as his buddy was there, he was willing to put up with it. They both saw her refusal to take off her clothes in front of them as

breaking an unwritten rule of their adventure.

A little while later the CNN producer, who was still replying to email on his laptop, felt someone slide into the chair next to his. He looked up. He was surprised to find a soldier in sunglasses, ball cap, and camouflage gear. "Hey, someone's already sitting there," he said.

"Howdy," said the soldier.

"Hey buddy. My colleague's just stepped away. She's sitting there."

"Cute brunette? Wandered off down thataway?" The soldier held up his thumb toward the gift shop.

"Yeah, she did." Then with a slight air of apology he said "And yeah she is. But we work together, you know." It was his shorthand way of declining to encourage any description of her looks.

"You like her, huh?"

"What do you mean? Sure, I like her."

"But I guess you wouldn't put her on camera if she wasn't hot, hmm?"

The producer was momentarily confused. Then he noticed the prominent CNN logo on the sleeping cameraman's luggage. The guy in camouflage gear must have seen it too. "You figured us out, did you?"

"Would you?"

"Would I what?"

"Put her on camera if she wasn't hot?"

This was more than he was willing to say. On the other hand, this was a soldier sitting next to him. He thought the soldier deserved some respect. That's why they were flying out to Kabul in the first place. To do investigative journalism,

yes, but also to support the guys who were already out there. So the CNN producer put his voice into a confidential register.

"Well, no. But being hot, as you call it, isn't the only thing. Someone who goes on air also has to have the smarts. They've also got to have the chops."

"But what counts more? Being smart or being hot?"

The producer didn't like the question. He craned around to look down the hall. Where'd she go, anyway?

"Which counts more?" the guy repeated.

"Hey man," said the producer in a friendly voice. "It's great to meet you and everything. But this isn't something I'd usually discuss. You know? Outside the office. The on-air talent is kind of off limits for discussion."

"Oh, c'mon. It ain't exactly a trade secret. Looky here. Some of the girls on your TV show could get jobs walking the bars on Bourbon Street if you all fired 'em."

The producer was just about to protest when two more guys interrupted them by standing close behind them on the carpeted concourse. They were wearing Atlanta Braves sweatshirts and sweatpants, with the price tags still hanging from the sleeves. One cleared his throat. They both held their arms around their chests as if they were cold. The producer looked around at them. One of them was wearing army boots. The other one was in stocking feet.

"Say!" said the soldier sitting next to him, "you got any contacts down there? You know? At the Pentagon."

"No. And why would I tell you if I did? I don't even know you, kid."

"You just look like the kinda guy who'd have contacts. You know? In DC."

The producer was not so insensitive to praise that he was above noticing the intended compliment in this remark. He decided to ignore the strange guys in the Braves sweats. "Look," he said a little more kindly. "I don't. Now, if you'll forgive me, I've got some emails to send off before the flight leaves."

"Cause if you did? You know? Have some contacts in the army, like? Well, I'd sure appreciate it if you could get my buddies back there," here the guy nodded behind him, "If you could get them some new uniforms."

"What? Are you crazy?"

"No, sir."

"Look I work for CNN. You saw that. Right off the bat. I don't have anything to do with the army."

"Oh, man. I'm real sorry, sir. But I watch your TV show all the time. You got your guys goin' out there all the time. Reporters. You know where I mean. The Sand Box? Durkastan?"

The producer looked over at the guy next to him levelly. The producer's glance conveyed lack of interest. "It's been real nice talking to you." The producer said it as if it hadn't been. "But I need you to clear off now."

"So you gotta have guys out there. What do they call that? Is it embedded, or something? Yeah, I think that's it."

The producer looked over and stared at him with hostile eyes.

"So I bet you gotta whole lotta friends in the military."

The producer stared back.

"And you could call one of 'em up. And get my buddies new gear. And you might get 'em out on a flight tomorrow night too. Instead of tonight."

"Hey, wait a minute."

"What now?"

"You know you talk funny?"

"Who me?"

"Yeah you."

"What about it?"

"Your voice. Like it's too gruff."

The guy cleared his throat. "I had a cold a while back. Still gettin' better. Got a ways to go." He coughed.

"No, it's more than that."

"What?"

"You know? Like a woman who thinks she has to drive like a jerk because she's driving in a man's world?"

"What are you talkin' about?"

Here the producer leaned over and took off the guy's hat. A cascade of brown hair that had been tucked up into the cap fell down in luxuriant folds. It looked like a shampoo commercial.

"Cindy!" he said, laughter and reproach in his voice. "Cindy Lou Who," he said more tenderly.

"I told you once already not to call me that," she said in her own voice.

"That was before you started doing your little act there."

"It wasn't an act. I proved I could fool you."

"I knew it was you after about the first five seconds." Here the producer slid down in his chair and gave way to disbelieving laughter.

"I had you and you know it."

The producer continued laughing.

"And I could do it again. In the field. On location."

The producer sobered up in order to close the argument. "In a tent? With a dozen other guys? Twenty-four hours a day? Cindy, you're not even kidding. It's not even a joke. Not even close. What do you take me for?"

"Pardon me, sir?" said the skinnier of the two men standing behind them in the Braves sweats. He now stepped forward to join their conversation. "We do need our uniforms back. If we're gonna fly out tonight. And if we're not, we need 'em tomorrow." He nodded at Cindy with a trace more warmth than he'd used a moment before. "She said you'd take care of it."

"Oh no," said the producer looking at Cindy. "No way. This is your baby. I've got nothing to do with this."

The skinny guy witnessed what looked like the TV girl being shot down by her boss. He put in on her behalf, "And if you ask me, sir? I know you didn't. But I'm just sayin' the guys out there would get a kick out of her. Guys like us. I mean, they might even like it out there a little. Which usually they don't."

The producer swiveled around and glared at him.

"I don't know what the army'd say though," admitted the skinny guy.

＊

Lieutenant Colonel Andrew Arbuthnot had had a year in England after his first posting to Afghanistan. He'd been given six months' leave and then an easy desk job in the Household Cavalry at Hyde Park Barracks. He wasn't afraid of going back to Afghanistan. He'd been in a quiet sector before. He hadn't lost anyone. The Afghans he'd met were generous in their hospitality, especially when they had little enough to offer. They'd at least pretended to welcome development aid and increased security. The Taliban had stayed, by and large, inside their caves. No, he didn't mind the prospect of going back, except that his present routine appealed to him more. He could work all the morning at his desk, then have a pleasant walk across two parks. He'd end up in St. James's Square for lunch at his club. The only small note of sadness in his routine was having to walk every day by the small memorial to the fallen policewoman. It was at the corner of the square. Her name was Yvonne Fletcher. A few years ago, there had been a demonstration in front of the Libyan embassy on the square. Someone from inside the embassy—it had never been determined who—shot Police Constable Fletcher from one of the windows as she worked outside to control the crowd. There were always wilting flowers in front of her memorial nearby his club when he passed. To Andrew that had been the first indication of the change. The UK security forces began to shift their focus away from Russians and Communists. By degrees the new focus had become the Middle East and Islamists as the greater threat to security. He always looked at PC Fletcher's memorial and thought of her. He wondered what she must have been like. It was senseless that any British police officer should die in such circumstances. It touched

him even more that she was a woman.

Inside the club there was no suggestion of mourning. It was all glimmering portraits of men in uniform, framed in gold, and gleaming wooden tables. Quiet triumph was the keynote, though the hint was also that these triumphs had happened quite a long time ago rather than more recently. Clipped box hedges in iron planters stood on the balcony outside the dining room. He would sit at the club table and take his chance with whoever else was lunching, as he was, without a companion. Often they were old buffers who had amusing recollections of dull postings. Or, that was the way they played it, for they would always fail to mention any real difficulties, troubles, or heroism on their part.

After lunch he'd cross the square to the London Library. There he had some volumes of Shakespeare criticism set aside on the shelves where readers could reserve books. He would sit in one of the red leather chairs looking across the square to where he'd just had lunch. The people in the library were different, however. There were no retired officers. Instead, there were screenwriters preparing scripts for the BBC, young people studying for examinations, harassed graduate students on the third drafts of their dissertations, and novelists who'd just stepped in after luncheon with their literary agents. It was unlike the army. That's why Andrew liked it.

He tried to keep up with the state of Shakespeare criticism in the universities. He'd come from an army family. There were Arbuthnots as far back as the early nineteenth century who'd served. He didn't know why he'd thought he could escape it. He'd wanted to read English literature at university. He'd even considered going on to become an academic himself.

He loved the parallels in Shakespeare to modern history and politics. He loved the Lady Macbeth in Mrs. Thatcher. He loved the Shakespearean cadences of Churchill's war speeches. He loved the line of Shakespeare's contemporary, Christopher Marlowe, *Come live with me and be my love.* Written in the 1590s, a recent film production of *Richard III* with Ian McKellen had converted the line into a 1940s torch song. All this had come to him from a mother who'd trained at the Royal Academy of the Dramatic Arts. Instead of reading him children's books at bedtime, she'd given him speeches she knew by heart. She'd do Ophelia's mad scene from *Hamlet,* or Lady Anne's defiance of Richard York, "Vile hedgehog!" He'd wriggled his toes under the covers with delight when his mother said that. That was what had put him in hopes of doing Shakespeare criticism at post-graduate level, but he simply hadn't been good enough. Nor did it fit in with the priorities of academics then. He couldn't find a senior critic who'd agree to take him on. He went into the army instead.

As he was puzzling over a recent book, which had taken structuralist theory and applied it in an abstruse way to *King Lear*, a man in a slim suit approached him. He could see from the way the buttons were arranged on the sleeve—in two pairs, instead of four buttons in a row—that the man was from a Household regiment, though he didn't know him.

"Andrew Arbuthnot! You old fool. What are you doing here? Pretending to be a don again?"

"I'm sorry," said Andrew looking up from his chair. Talking in the reading room of the London Library was forbidden.

"You don't remember me, do you? Alzheimer's is it?"

One of the anxious young dissertation writers said "Ssh!"

from the across the room.

Andrew got up and led the man outside and down the wooden staircase with carpet the color of Pinot Noir.

"I'm afraid we can't talk in there."

"Oh I know. They must have their precious quiet, mustn't they? What about a stroll in the square? You know? Round the statue of good King William?"

The two men walked out of the library, across the roadway, and through the black iron gates of the square. Tall trees cast their moving shadows over the grass. Construction workers and bankers lolled with take-away sandwiches on extended lunch breaks. King William III reared on his bronze horse in the center of the square.

"I can't believe you don't remember me."

"Is it Giles ... ?"

"Taylor! Got it in one."

"We haven't seen each other since, what?"

"I suppose we were eight years old. The Dragon School."

"God, that was a long time ago," by which Andrew meant that he couldn't imagine why on earth someone he'd last known when he was in schoolboy shorts should come and interrupt him in the London Library.

The other man heard and interpreted Andrew's tone of voice correctly. "I won't take up your whole day. The fact is I've been sent to find you by the chaps over at St. James's Palace."

"You're working for them now?"

"I bounce around a bit. Several different portfolios at once, old boy."

"And what do they want?"

"They've sent me to sound you on a tricky mission."

"Tricky missions come from the Ministry of Defense. The palace doesn't call the shots. The last time I checked we were in a constitutional monarchy."

"We are! We are, dear boy. But the M. O. D. and St. James's are in it together on this one."

"And?"

"They want to send out the Prince of Wales's second son to Afghanistan."

"Oh for Christ's sake."

"And they want you to look after him. For six weeks. That's all."

"God damn it to hell."

"Long enough for him to be able to say he's seen active duty at the front and earned a medal."

"A medal? For what?"

"For not having been captured. For not having been wounded. For having only kept Colonel Arbuthnot awake at night for a month and a half. That's adequate. For a small service medal? Wouldn't you say? We're not talking about the Victoria Cross."

"I won't do it."

"A pity."

"No, it's not a pity. It's the most miserable assignment I've been proposed yet. And I've enough seniority to turn it down, if I like. Thank you very much."

"Do you remember when your grandfather came and visited us at the Dragon?"

"What? No. He didn't live far away. He may've come. I don't remember it."

"What I remember is that once upon a time he was equerry to Queen Elizabeth. Bless her. The old queen mum. And he told us funny stories about her. We sat around him on the floor."

"It's possible he did."

"Oh come now. You see the connection, don't you?"

"No." Andrew thought about it a moment. "Oh, hell. Not that?"

"Well, they are related. And possibly your grandfather's having failed to blot his copybook has earned you a kind of recommendation for this assignment."

"I'm still not doing it."

"I see. Well, I'll tell St. James's you said so."

"Good."

"And they'll have to tell everyone else, I'm afraid." The man in the exquisite suit looked up for a moment into the trees as if surprised by the complexity of the over-arching branches. "Won't look good for you in the Household Cavalry, old fellow, will it? Promising careers have foundered on lesser rocks."

Andrew sighed. "Oh, lord."

"I haven't turned you into a rabid republican I hope."

"I read *The Guardian* already."

"I was afraid of that." The other man stopped on the pavement and looked at Andrew. "You won't be too hard on the wretched boy, will you?"

"He's not going to get a blasted medal without earning it. Tell St. James's I said so."

*

Frances rose early from her cot in the church basement. She pulled apart the bedding. She folded the sheets and rough blanket into squares. She left them at right angles on the mattress. Then she climbed the stairs to the church hall and wondered whether she couldn't make coffee for everyone. They were all still asleep, she assumed.

It had been a long day the day before. She and the other church volunteers had met the soldiers with whom they were flying down to London, nearly a hundred of them. They were raw, rough, and many of them uneasy, though they wouldn't say so. It came out in their silence and expressionlessness. They were none of them going to give any of their terror away. Many of them had never been to as big a place as Glasgow before. For others it was their first time on an airplane. The prospect of leaving Scotland and flying to a war no one really understood the point of appealed only to a very small number of them, and they were the off-balance ones.

She and the others had done their best with them. They'd passed out food and drink. They'd stopped to ask about their girlfriends, their wives, and their parents. She'd behaved as much like a white-haired granny as she could, though it was as much of an act with her as their silent bravery was with them. She put her hand on their shoulders and told them how handsome they looked in their uniforms. In her experience most men didn't mind being told that.

They had another long day ahead of them. They were making three hundred more sandwiches for a flight of returning soldiers. Their flight back had to be in the middle of the night so as to avoid their intermingling with holiday-makers going to Ibiza and Tenerife. She felt for the little airline size bottle of whiskey in the pocket of her cardigan. She'd put it there last night. She hoped she wouldn't need it, but it had occurred to her that if she were first up to make the coffee, she might strengthen her cup unseen. Give herself some optimism for the day. That's why, when she walked into the hall and found the young priest from St. Ethelred's in his collar and short-sleeved black shirt, already sitting there with a cup, her heart fell a little.

"Oh. Good morning, Father."

"Good morning, good morning." He smiled at her encouragingly

"How did you sleep, Father?"

"Like a babe. Babe that I am."

He was an amusing man with a lovely sense of humor. She smiled gratefully at him. The room already seemed a bit more welcoming.

He got to his feet and poured her a cup of coffee from the black spigot on the aluminum urn. "Here you are, Your Grace."

"Oh no, Father. I'm not a duchess. You know that. And never was." She reproved him and pretended to be severe, though this was something he often teased her about.

"Oh, but you knew duchesses, though. It's so thrilling. For someone who grew up on the banks of the Liffey, I mean."

"Not all it's cracked up to be, Father. My husband had a big

house. That's all. In the end he had no trouble getting rid of me and keeping the house."

"I can't help thinking ..."

"That in my shoes, you'd have done a better job of it? I have no doubt, Father." The only way to stop him, she knew, was to camp right along with him.

"He was a handsome man, now. I've seen the pictures."

"Father, he was, once upon a time."

"You must've had to do a lot of grand entertaining."

"I don't know about grand. There were always people in the house. It's true. The kitchen went at full gallop the whole time. The wine and whiskey drained away by the cask."

"Oh dear," said the priest more sympathetically. "Was that when it started?" He patted his side roughly where the pocket of his cardigan would be—if he were wearing one—which he wasn't.

She looked down at the pocket of her cardigan. She patted it and felt the small glass bulge. Was it that obvious? Had he seen it right away? She felt a flash of pride and anger. How dare he condemn her?

"I expect you were hoping to get up before anyone else and correct your coffee. Isn't that how the Italians say it?"

She was about to lash out at him when she suddenly stopped herself. He'd helped her. He'd talked to her when she was at her worst. He had time for her. She must be humble, he'd said. She must accept her weakness. She must declare it, not hide it. That was the only road to any kind of peace. Nevertheless, she believed redemption at her age was out of the question. "Guilty, Father," she said with her jaw clenching shut as soon as she'd finished. She looked straight ahead at

him and into his eyes.

He stood up and came over to her. "The good Lord forgives those who struggle, Frances." He gave her a touching look, even though he didn't physically reach out to touch her.

"Thank you, Father," she said looking back at him steadily and more sadly than when she entered the room.

"As we're alone, I'd thought of telling you about something first, before the others have a chance at it."

She said nothing. She raised her eyebrows a little hopelessly. Whatever he had to say wouldn't be able to cheer her up now.

"The church has standing with a British aid group in Kabul. There's a vacancy now. Out there. The pay's not much. But there'd be room and board. It'd get you away for a little while. A change of scene is often good for those like us. You'd be right up against need greater than yours. That'd be a help to you, maybe. In your affliction. You wouldn't have to commit for longer than a month or two."

"Me, Father?"

"Yes, why not?" Here his eyes twinkled as if he might manage a tease out of this. "The trouble is you'd need to go right away."

"When?"

"There's a seat on the military transport going out tonight."

"But that's out of the question! I couldn't go tonight."

"Perhaps not," admitted the priest. "It's far too short notice. It's an impossible job. No one could do it." He looked at her covertly.

"Hang on a minute." Frances might have been feeling she was still near the bottom, but enough of her old fight was with her to feel that he was throwing down a glove. He was issuing

a challenge. If he said she couldn't do it, she'd show him she could.

"You see," said the priest, pretending to change the subject by approaching from a different angle, "it all came up at the last minute. None of the others could take it up right away. They have husbands, or elderly parents, or children to look after."

"I don't!"

"No, that's true." The priest pretended to muse. "You don't."

"If the church could pack up and send me a few of my things. Look after the cottage while I'm away ..."

"Oh, that would be no problem."

"But I'm far too old, Father," Frances said finally.

"You seem all right to me."

"I couldn't possibly. I'm an old lady."

"You've got as much energy as two of the others put together."

"I have rheumatism. Arthritis. Sciatica too. That's just the beginning."

"Well, I won't press you. I'd just mention that whiskey is rather harder to come by out there, if you get my drift."

"Thank you, Father," she said a shade more coldly. "I do appreciate your thinking of me."

Later that same day, much later in fact, after midnight, Frances and several of the other church workers were in the passenger terminal at Heathrow. They were waiting to say goodbye to the men with whom they'd flown down from Glasgow the day before. They were boarding an aircraft to Afghanistan with several other regiments. The other regiments had been housed outside the airport somewhere

and were late to arrive. Frances had collapsed into an airline chair. They still had the flight back to Scotland after that. She'd been up for more than eighteen hours. She hoped the plane was leaving soon as she couldn't take much more. In her semi-dozing state, she sensed some movement in the corridor behind her. She heard a voice. It was an officer's voice. It was unlike the officers' voices of her Scots regiment.

"Have the men form up here, please. We go on board after the 49th Highlanders."

Frances turned her head a quarter of a turn and opened her eyes. The officer who'd just spoken was turning away from her so she couldn't recognize him, but the voice was familiar. She noticed the Household Cavalry insignia on his beret. She was about to return to her doze, though some part of her was aware that their long wait might be nearly over. She might need to stand up soon.

She shook her head to wake herself. She then got unsteadily to her feet. She found the hall and the departure area now full of men getting ready to board the aircraft. As she surveyed all this, she had to shake her head again as if what she saw was in a dream. There he was. She was sure it was him. He had that unmistakable head of Spencer red hair. He was standing at some distance from her down the corridor. He seemed to be trying ineffectually to get some men into order. He had what looked like a sergeant major standing over him with a look of disapproval.

"Harry!" She said it at first to herself. She couldn't believe it. She was about to raise her voice and wave her arm, but then she stopped herself. He was working. He mustn't be interrupted. This was his duty. She mustn't interfere. She

still couldn't really imagine how it'd come to be. They were letting him go to Afghanistan. That must be it. How had he managed to persuade the authorities to allow him to go? It was incredible. As she looked at him more steadily now, she knew it was him. She didn't want him to see her. It would just be an embarrassment for him. What would everyone say if they saw him with an old woman carrying a plastic sack of cheese sandwiches? No, that'd never do.

She turned sharply and walked off in the other direction. She found the priest at the far end of the boarding gate. "Father," she said, "I've changed my mind."

*

The plane had been reconfigured from its passenger service so that it could hold more people than it did ordinarily. Even before this modification, the people squashed into what was euphemistically called the "World Traveller" cabin had about as much room as the men and women on slave ships of three hundred years earlier. Now, the soldiers flying to Afghanistan had even less. The officers didn't have it much better.

They were a motley crew of different nationalities. There were Scots and English regiments. There was an American detachment from Fort Bliss in Texas and another from Fort

Benning in Georgia. There were also Afghan security force personnel, who'd been training with Nepalese Gurkhas in Britain.

Harry and Mustafa were in a special pair of seats. They had been jammed up next to an emergency exit where a partition used in the jet's passenger service had been removed. Mustafa was at the window. Harry was on the aisle.

"You better read the card, mate," said Harry nodding at the emergency exit instructions in a pocket in front of them. "We don't want a Paki bastard holding things up if we have to get outta here quick."

"That's a racial slur, lieutenant."

"Sure it is. I know that. It's cause I like you."

"What'll I call you then? Whitey?"

"Aww. You're gonna give me a pet name?"

Here Harry threw his right leg over Mustafa's left. He leaned in and gave him a kiss beneath his left ear.

"Get off!" Mustafa half rose up and pushed Harry roughly back into his chair. Harry laughed. In his mind, anyone who showed that much anger at a tease, anyone who lost their cool, also lost two points of imaginary score, rather than one.

For his part, Mustafa had reacted a little more violently than he had to because he was over-compensating. He remembered an incident from when he'd still been in school. It had been five or six years ago. He was at home on a school holiday. In those days he'd lived a fairly insulated life. He shuttled back and forth between his boarding school, which was in an eighteenth-century country house in Buckinghamshire, and his parents' place in London. His parents lived in a flat overlooking Hyde Park. It occupied the entire floor of the

building, had six bedrooms, and accommodation for four live-in staff at the back. He knew in theory that he lived a privileged and exceptional life, but he knew so little else that he didn't think very much about it. That's why it came as a shock that night when he was returning home via tube from a party. It had been at one of his school friend's in West London. It was late on a Saturday night.

London could be a bacchanal on weekend nights. People poured into town from the suburbs. Nonstop drinking removed their inhibitions. There were constant crashings of broken glass bottles and crowds of young men stumbled around vomiting on street corners. It looked like the Hogarth etching, "Gin Lane," they'd been studying in his history of art course. He'd never felt much threatened by it all before. It was the spectacle of life in the big city. He liked it. That night, however, he was on the District Line when a group of boys, older than him, got on at Barons Court. They were drunk and loud. They sang football songs and used the noise of their voices to scare people on the train. It wasn't just merrymaking. It was purposeful intimidation. Several people sitting near him moved to the far end of the carriage. Several others, with nervous backward glances, got off and moved to other carriages. Mustafa thought this was an excess of caution. He decided the guys were harmless. Two of the boys had mops of shaggy hair and were not bad looking. He looked on with interest when one of them came lurching by him, opened the door that led between carriages, and unzipped his trousers. He began pissing on to the tracks as the train clanked slowly along between stations. His mates came running over to watch him, hooting and laughing. If Mustafa leaned his head a little

to the left, he could even see the boy's pale, uncircumcised penis, making a tremendous sloppy gush into the darkness. He wished he could do that. It made his own pee look like a dribble. All the other boys were watching too.

That's when one of them turned around, looked directly at him, and shouted "Oi! You! What're you lookin' at?"

The others turned to look at him too. "Yah, poof!" said another.

Although this was a generic insult that all adolescent boys leveled at all other adolescent boys, they said it with particular viciousness because he was different from them. It was not only his skin color, it was also his clothes. His trainers were worn; theirs were bright white. He wore a tweed jacket with a shirt collar open at the neck; they wore branded tee shirts with gold chains. Suddenly their hands were on him and he was being lifted up. They grabbed him out of his seat by pulling up on the lapels of his tweed coat, passed him from one to the other, and ended up by slamming him against the sliding glass doors. He didn't fight back. He knew they were shouting other things at him and that they intended to hurt him, but something in his brain shut down. He was a pigeon grabbed by a hawk. He was no longer able to feel pain, though his adrenaline continued to rush.

Then the lights outside the window re-appeared. They were no longer in a tunnel. The train arrived at Gloucester Road, the next stop. There were groups of people standing on the platform. The train stopped and the sliding doors shuddered apart. The boys dropped him, and alert to his sudden chance, Mustafa scrambled to his feet. He darted out and away from the train. He tore up the stairs and jumped the ticket barrier,

not because he didn't have a tube pass, but because taking it out of his pocket and passing it in front of the card reader would slow him down. He ran the whole way home from there. It was three miles, he estimated. He told no one.

"Harry von Krautheim, how's that for a nickname, pet?" Mustafa suggested.

"Hang on. Where's that from? I'm not German."

Mustafa rolled his eyes. "Sure you are. Hanover? Saxe-Coburg und Gotha? Those are your people."

"That was a long time ago."

"Yeah, well Afghanistan's not Pakistan either."

"Ahf-gahni-stahn!" said Harry, making fun of the three long "ah" sounds Mustafa had just used in his pronunciation. "What a posh bastard you are too."

The irony of the situation overwhelmed Mustafa. Here was one of the poshest kids in the country accusing him of being posh. He didn't know what to say. Since on a short acquaintance he'd been more than once assaulted by Harry, he reached over to hit him hard on the shoulder.

Harry caught him by the wrist before Mustafa could land the blow. "Watch it, mate. Not so hard. We're friends, right?" He reached down and caught Mustafa's other wrist too for insurance purposes. "I've got you now. Tell the truth. Are you really from out there? Afghanistan I mean?" He reverted to short a's. It was nearly an American pronunciation.

"My parents are." Mustafa struggled a bit with Harry's hands, but he found Harry was stronger than him. After a few attempts to get loose, he just let his arms fall.

"How'd they make it to Blighty, then?"

"They took a plane. It's not all Stone Age economics out

there, you know."

"No, I don't know. That's why I'm asking you." Even though Mustafa had ceased to resist, Harry kept his hands on Mustafa's wrists. "So they had a bit of dosh, then, did they? Your mum and dad?"

"Yeah they did. It was theirs. They didn't steal it from the people, like your mum and dad."

"Ah, ah, ah," said Harry, making the universal noise for "no," often used with children. "We're talking about your parents, not mine. Anyway, you're in the Household Cavalry, mate. It's not the Red Brigade."

"Thanks for the reminder."

"How'd you get here anyway? You weren't at Sandhurst."

"No, I wasn't. Maybe I earned my fucking commission."

"Ah, ah, ah," said Harry again. "Quit trying to change the subject. We're not talking about me. How'd you get here?"

Here, once again, words deserted Mustafa. It wasn't only that he had to cope with someone stronger than him. It wasn't only that he'd been thrown together with someone famous as his traveling companion and no one had warned him. It was also that he thought, as much as he tried not to, Harry was kind of hot. He decided on his last stand of resistance. "They parachuted me into the regiment because I'm a Paki bastard."

"What?" Harry let him go.

"Same way I got into Stowe, and they gave my parents a discount on the fees, even though they didn't need it."

"What are you on about?"

"It's because the army wants to say it has a multi-cultural, multi-ethnic officer corps, even in the oldest regiments. Same thing at Stowe. And they want to be able to say it happened

yesterday. So I'm it. Presto. I'm in."

"Oh no, mate, I don't think so." He said "fink" so. "That's not it," said Harry putting, for the first time, a protective rather than an aggressive arm around Mustafa's shoulders. "It's not like that. You're a swot, aren't you? You were one of the brainy boys. Me? I can never remember what Hanover is. It's a kind of bun, right? Cream-filled?"

"No, it's a place. It's in Germany. It's where George the First came from. Via the Act of Settlement, 1701. The bun with cream is a Bismarck."

"See? Just like I said. I think I might be, what's it called, dyslogic."

"Dyslexic.

Just then one of the British Airways stewardesses appeared in the aisle. She held a large cardboard box in front of her. "Biscuits? Crisps?"

Harry grabbed back his hand and arm from around Mustafa's shoulders. Mustafa thought to himself, that's it. He's my mate when no one's watching. And then he's not. To the stewardess he said glumly "Not for me."

British Airways had told the cabin crew that Harry would be on board and they were under no circumstances to take any special notice of him. She saw some funny business with the hands, but boys playing childish games didn't interest her. She merely paused with a long-suffering expression to see if they really did want something before she moved on.

Harry's experience was that young women always recognized him. Afterwards they usually melted on him like candle wax. Why was she acting any different? She might be the last woman he'd see for a long time. He'd watched her

earlier when she'd given the safety demonstration. Her hair was drawn back in a perky bun. Three buttons at the neck of her blouse were open. He liked all that. "Forgive my friend, here. He meant, 'Not for me, *thank you*.' He's foreign."

"So's he," agreed Mustafa, "German."

"Really?" said the stewardess, dropping her poker face for a moment. She'd never heard of Prince Harry being German before. "So what's he then? Harry von ..."

"*Von und zu*," put in Mustafa, using the aristocratic pronouns that preceded the surnames of the Prussian Junkers. "Through and through."

"No I'm not!"

"Then William is too?" she asked, wide-eyed.

"Of course he is. They call him Vilhelm when they're all alone. Up there on the balcony. Wave to the *volks*, darlings. Wave! You too, Villi."

Here Harry, who was about to hit Mustafa again, was caught by surprise. He paused, listened, and then it struck him. He threw back his head against the seat. He laughed helplessly.

"I never knew," mused the stewardess. She wondered why Harry thought it was so funny. She wanted to go back to the galley to talk it over with the other flight attendants.

Andrew Arbuthnot, who was walking up the aisle to make sure everything was under control, suddenly appeared behind the stewardess. He had a swagger stick under his arm. He was not a swaggerer himself, but as Field Marshal Montgomery had carried one in North Africa, he thought he could too. He liked the look of it, and its historical associations more than anything.

"All well here?"

Harry snapped back up into a rigid sitting position. "Yes, sir!"

The stewardess stepped back. She didn't want to interfere with military authority, but she did want to watch if Harry was going to be rebuked.

"Lieutenant Khan has told you some amusing story, I suppose?"

"Well, no sir. No, it wasn't amusing. It was false. It's a lie."

Andrew looked at Mustafa who was smiling benignly.

"Perhaps you'd like to come with me, lieutenant," Andrew said to Harry, whose cheeks grew a hot red as he stood up. He gestured politely with his swagger stick to the back of the plane and raised his eyebrows.

"Oh?" said the stewardess, pursing her lips, pleased. She watched Harry's camouflaged bottom as it disappeared up the aisle toward the back of the plane.

*

When they reached the rear galley, several of the stewardesses were drinking tea from paper cups and leaning back against the counter tops.

"Pardon us, ladies," said Harry.

Then Andrew came around the corner. All three of them

paused for a moment, and hovered expectantly. When the colonel cleared his throat, they disappeared toward the main cabin with several backward glances.

Harry braced himself. He put his body into a spread-legged stance and stared straight ahead with hands clasped behind his back.

"If you think for one minute that I'm going to let you ruin this mission, I can tell you otherwise," Arbuthnot began. "I don't care who you are, or what strings were pulled to get you here. The moment I catch you impugning Khan again, I will put you on a plane right back to the UK. Do you hear me?

"Yes sir. But he started it, sir."

Andrew became a fraction angrier. "I don't care who started it. He's the only one with us who speaks Dari and Pashto. We're going to have to rely on him to liaise with the Afghans. He's the only one who has firsthand knowledge of local customs and culture. Moreover, he's come up via university and two years with the intelligence services. He is ten times more important than you. You are nothing. Do you understand me?"

"Yes sir. But that's not what he told me, sir."

Andrew glared back at Harry without saying "What did he tell you?"

Harry carried on heedlessly. "He said he was only here to up the diversity numbers."

"Well, that just goes to show that he's had the better of you already. The score is intelligence services one, Sandhurst nil."

Harry looked confused.

"And another thing," said Andrew.

Here the plane hit some turbulence. The aft portion of

the jet twisted and creaked. Both men had to hold on to the bulkhead to steady themselves. Three bells rang and an announcement required all personnel out of their seats, including stewardesses, to return to their seats and fasten their seat belts.

"Sir? Should we go back to our seats?"

"No, just hold up your hand like this." Arbuthnot held his hand up to one of the ceiling panels. "If we hit a pocket it will stop you cracking your head up there." He gestured upward.

Harry held his hand up to the ceiling panel as instructed.

"The other thing is this. The deployment orders have been changed. We're joining a much bigger American unit. And they've members of the press with them who are not part of the agreement with the UK press." Andrew Arbuthnot looked off into the distance to prevent himself from denouncing the army, but it was his impulse nonetheless. It was a typical Whitehall glitch. Enormous effort had been made on this point. The UK press had agreed reluctantly to an embargo on news of Harry's deployment in exchange for photos to be published only after he returned. The army had persuaded the UK press that a general knowledge of his being deployed to Afghanistan would endanger the men with whom he was serving. Then, at the last minute, someone else at the Ministry of Defense had assigned Harry's unit to join forces with the Americans. It hadn't occurred to whoever it was that the embedded US reporter was not part of the agreement with the UK press. That's how it always was. One hand of the army never knew what the other hand was doing.

"An American reporter is on this flight."

Harry's eyes darkened, but he said nothing.

"When I find out which one he is, I will ask that he respect the agreement with the UK media, but there's no guarantee. If he breaks a story that you're there, you go home on the next plane."

Harry looked straight ahead.

"So there are lots of ways for you to get sent back."

The plane hit another wall of air. Those looking down the side of the fuselage could have seen it buckle and bend briefly before resuming its normal shape. Harry and Colonel Arbuthnot were jostled against each other for a moment.

"That's all lieutenant. Return to your seat please."

Harry saluted and walked quickly back to his seat. He kept his face as neutral as possible so as to give nothing away. He knew everyone would have seen him ordered to the back by the colonel. They'd all be wondering about what'd been said to him. They were judging him. He had no chance of explaining and no way of defending himself. He wouldn't have been allowed to anyway. He felt humiliated and powerless. It wasn't the first time.

*

Andrew Arbuthnot went and found his American opposite number. He asked whether the embedded reporter could be sent to the rear galley so Andrew could introduce himself. He returned to the galley and moments later, a young American appeared. He wore sunglasses and what appeared to be a brown ponytail stuffed into his service cap. Andrew understood the necessity of making peace with the media if they were to get fair reporting on the war. It went all the way back to the Crimean War, when a London *Times* reporter's negative reports had interfered with that war effort, even as early as the 1850s. The controversy caused by the newspaper articles then had nearly brought down the military and political heads of the army. Ever since, the army had taken the potential hazards of press reporting seriously.

Nevertheless, Andrew did think embedded reporters should be required to wear the same short hair that was required of the officers and the men. Nor would anyone under his command be allowed to wear sunglasses, and especially not indoors, while addressing him. He swallowed back this irritation and held out his hand, "I'm Colonel Arbuthnot," he said with a smile.

"Sandy Reed," said Cindy. She deepened her voice, but she tried not to overdo it. She was afraid, but she was also determined to carry her plan through. The less she said, the smaller the chances of detection. Being called into an interview with a senior British officer was the first major test of her disguise.

"I gather you work for the Cable Noon Network. Is that a news program at lunchtime?"

"No sir," said Cindy, wondering what planet he lived on

that he'd never heard of CNN before. "It's the Cable News Network. We broadcast twenty-four hours a day." She couldn't stop herself from adding, "Just like the BBC."

"Of course! Much better than the BBC, I have no doubt. Yours is a much bigger, better-funded organization. The old Beeb is quite amateurish really. They still talk to each other via cups attached with string." He laughed.

Cindy was not used to the British method of using self-deprecation to disarm an opponent. Nor was irony her strong point. She didn't understand why he would criticize his own national news media. She decided this time she'd better not answer back. She'd only got on the plane at the last minute. The producer had at first stuck to his guns. However, Cindy and the producer also had a secret history together. She was able to use it to win a concession. He would allow her to replace one of the guys who was already embedded for a few weeks only, while the other guy was back in the States on leave. She agreed that the whole thing was on her own responsibility and she would deny his involvement if she was caught. She knew he was risking a lot to let her go even for a few weeks. She did not intend to get caught. So when Andrew shook his head and made fun of the BBC, she merely said, "Sir."

Here the plane hit a much rougher patch. Several of the galley cabinets popped open. Some cans of Diet Coke rolled out and hit the floor. Andrew hit his shoulder on the opposite bulkhead. Cindy remained upright.

"Gracious," said Andrew.

"Only a little chop, sir. Nothing to worry about."

"Thank you soldier. I mean, thank you, Mr. Reed."

"No problem. What can I do for you sir?"

"Well, the thing is, the British and American units will be together once we leave Kabul. For the next six weeks. And I have in my unit a young man who's a bit awkward."

Cindy gave him a nod, as if she were more than capable of dealing with whatever awkwardness there could possibly be.

"The fact is that he already has a profile with the UK news media, and we'd rather the world not know he's out with us. It could interfere with the mission as a whole. That's why the UK media has agreed to say nothing about his being with us."

"I see, sir," said Cindy, wondering who it could be. Could it be the prime minister's son? Or the son of a media titan? Those could both make for interesting stories. She began to wonder whether this was a lucky break for her.

"The fact is that he's a junior member of the UK royal family."

Cindy couldn't prevent her face from falling. She thought of the British royal family as a topic for celebrity gossip. It was the branch of the media that interested her the least. Moreover, it was the branch of journalism that was always handed to women. Barbara Walters had started out as a serious reporter, but had descended into interviews with Michael Jackson. Cindy wanted nothing to do with that. She aimed to make her mark in hard news. She was ready in advance to assure the colonel that she had no interest in the royal family. Did he really think that a CNN reporter who broadcast in prime time was the same as someone who wrote for *People Magazine*?

"And I would appreciate it," Andrew continued, "if you could help us keep the secret."

"I'm not interested in the royal family, sir."

"You're not?"

"No, sir."

"Your viewers are, though. Your producers must be."

"The war, sir. That's what we're interested in, sir. At CNN."

Andrew was taken aback. He hardly expected it to be this easy. "Well then," he said briefly at a loss, and not sure what to say next.

Cindy saw she'd surprised him and was pleased. She'd wrong-footed a senior officer who'd thought he could manipulate her. She kept her face serious, but internally she smiled. She'd done her job.

"Anything else, sir?"

*

"What was that all about then?" asked Mustafa when Harry came back to his seat.

"Can't tell you. Top secret."

"Oh."

Here Harry turned to Mustafa, made eye contact, and leaned in close to his face. "Like you should already know. Mr. MI5, MI6 and whatever other of the intelligence services you did two whole years with."

Mustafa closed his eyes and leaned back into his seat with

a weary expression.

"Like you could've told me, mate. Instead of letting me make a fool of myself in front of the col."

"I'm not admitting. Or denying."

"And what's this about all the funny languages you speak? Dairy? Pesto? Do you teach me a few words? No. It's like you wanna see me hang. You don't tell me nothing." He said "nuffink." Harry slumped back into his own seat.

Here Mustafa couldn't stop himself from giggling. "All right. All right. I'll teach you a few words. *Salaam aleicum.* Say that when you meet someone."

"What's that?"

"Peace be with you."

"*Salaam aleicum,*" repeated Harry.

"*Wa-aleicum salaam,*" replied Mustafa. He reached up and put his hand on his heart.

"What's that mean?" demanded Harry. "Don't steal my camel and I won't steal yours?"

"I'm amazed at your cultural sensitivity, sheikh. Emir. Caliph. *Seyyed* Harry."

"What's all that?"

"Empty terms of rank. Insincere flattery."

"Now we're getting somewhere," laughed Harry. "Let's take it from the top. *Salaam aleicum,*" he said to Mustafa. He put his hand on his heart.

"Sorry to interrupt," said a smooth-faced American in camouflage fatigues standing in the aisle. "Do you mind if I introduce myself?"

Harry and Mustafa both looked up. It wasn't extraordinary for someone their own age to interrupt them without a prior

introduction, but it was more American than British. Harry was inclined to be friendly the moment he heard the accent. He'd had nothing but an elaborate cold shoulder from fellow Brits so far. They all seemed to be going out of their way to make it hard for him. He was prepared for a bit more easiness and informality from a Yank. "Hey buddy!" he said. "Show me the love." He held up his fist to be punched. "Right on."

Cindy looked down at his fist with dismay. She'd never mastered the intricacies or meanings of fist punches. She was wary of making mistakes. She gave his fist a light touch with the knuckles of her right hand. "Hi. But it's really your friend I want."

Harry's face fell.

"What me?" said Mustafa.

"Yeah. I heard you're going to do some liaising with the Afghans. You know? Down on the ground? When we get there? I want to do a story on you."

"What?"

"Oh sorry, I'm Sandy Reed. CNN." She cleared her throat because that's what she'd heard guys do when they talked to each other. "I'm embedded with the unit from Fort Benning."

"More press," said Harry, the friendliness draining out of his voice.

"I'm not here to talk to you," said Cindy. She'd recognized Harry after the British colonel had given her an idea of whom to look for. She wanted to make something clear to him right away. She'd had experience interviewing well-known people on camera. They generally pretended that they hated media attention, but in her experience they loved it. The more famous they were, the more often they called back to object

to a quote she'd used or a question she'd asked. She expected Harry to be the same. She wanted to let him know right away she wasn't interested in him. "It's Lieutenant Khan I want."

"I'll check with Colonel Arbuthnot," Mustafa said. "And I'll get back to you later, okay?"

She nodded, didn't say goodbye, and moved off down the aisle.

"*Wa-aleicum salaam* to you too mate," said Harry disgustedly.

"He didn't seem that bad," said Mustafa to Harry's jaw.

"Give him half a chance. He'll show you what he's like. It's what they're all like."

Mustafa knew Harry's story too well to ask him what he meant.

"All they want to do is print lies and make people miserable. That's gonna be his story." Harry's chin was down on his neck.

Mustafa tried to josh him out of it. "I bet if we push the call button the flight attendant'll bring us a pack of cards. You must be hopeless at Black Jack."

A glimmer of light passed across Harry's gloomy expression, but he said "Nope."

"Come off it, mate. We'll do ten pence a hand. Dealer takes all ties."

"Watch out. I was taught Black Jack by an expert."

"Who? Some dealer in Vegas? A casino in Monte?"

"Nope."

"Who then? By a jockey? By a master of foxhounds? By Elton fucking John?"

"Wrong, wrong, wrong," smiled Harry, now definitely getting into a better mood. "By my nanny."

"Who?"

"Mudge."

"Oh that's terrific. That's posh, for you. You had a nanny who wore a uniform and wheeled you around in a pram with a hood, and brakes, and springs. And then you grew up and Miss Mudge taught you Black Jack."

"No. It wasn't like that. Her name's Frances. We called her Mudge. I'm not sure why. I think she showed us how to make mud pies in the garden."

"I'll tell you why. Because you were a pair of toffee noses and you lot never call anybody by their right names."

Harry reached over and again locked Mustafa's head in a casual half nelson. "But you called me Whitey, remember? That was your idea, right?"

"Let me go!"

Harry let him go. "And you went to Stowe, which is a school for wankers. But whatever. Just watch who you're callin' toffee nose, mate."

Mustafa slid over to the far corner of his seat where Harry's arm couldn't reach him. "And what happened to poor old Mudge? She's ninety years old, all broken down, lives up in the attic of Buckingham Palace, and you go to visit her every time you're home, right? Just like *Brideshead*. And you call *me* a wanker?"

"Actually no."

"No?"

"Well, when my parents split up, they carried on fighting, right? And Mudge, well, she somehow got in the middle. Collateral damage. Anyway, she moved up north. And I should've kept in touch with her. But I haven't. And that's

bad. Cause she loved me."

Mustafa, having grown up the majority of his life in Britain, was as embarrassed by honest displays of emotion as the average native Briton. At that point one of the flight attendants happened to pass by and Mustafa jumped at the chance to change the subject. "Oh Miss. Pardon me. Have you got any packs of playing cards?"

"I gave out my last pack to 23A and 23B. Maybe they'll share with you." She passed off down the aisle.

"I'll go over and ask them," proposed Mustafa.

"No. Stay here," said Harry, his defiant sincerity dissolving into a resolution. "I wanna go settle something with that Yank. I'm not gonna let him threaten to blow my cover for the next six weeks. I'm gonna fix it with him now. And then I'll get the cards."

Harry unbuckled his seatbelt and went off down the aisle. He passed through one of the galleys down at the far end of the cabin, and came back up the other side looking for the guy from CNN. Harry was surprised to find that the reporter was also one of the card players. The reporter was sitting in 23B with his tray table folded down in front of him. He had a single American quarter sitting on his table. There were also two cards face up, and one card face down on the tray table. "I'll take another card," Harry overheard the reporter say as he approached down the aisle.

The dealer wore a sweatshirt of the 49th Gordon Highlanders as well as a headscarf. On the dealer's tray table was a deck of cards with about two dozen American quarters, arranged in neat stacks of four. "Are you sure?"

"Yeah. Hit me."

The dealer dealt a jack. The American reporter turned up his other card and showed cards worth twenty-four points on the tray table. "Bust," he sighed.

"Too bad," said the dealer, sweeping the American reporter's lone quarter up and placing it on one of the stacks on her fold-down table.

Harry came up behind them.

"Not you?" he said, incredulously.

The dealer turned around and looked up at him. She gave him a warm smile and put an arm around his waist. "Darling! I know you're busy. I know you're working. I didn't like to disturb you earlier. I was hoping you'd come over and say hello."

"But what are you doing here?"

Part II

Low Desires, Lewd Attempts, Barren Pleasures

"Mudge!" Harry repeated. "You can't be!" They were both in the rear galley.

"Well, as I am here," she said, pushing up the sleeves of her oversized sweatshirt, "perhaps you could behave as if you were pleased to see me. That's what I'd like. Please." The flight attendants had disappeared a second time, with one of them casting an annoyed look at Harry and saying "Honestly!"

He leaned over, hands on hips, and said in a low voice, "You're going to get us both into a lot of trouble!"

"We've got at least five minutes. The girls are taking hot lunches up to the cockpit. There's no need to whisper."

"You know what I mean. Being on the plane in the first place." He looked over his shoulder and then came back to her. "Have you been drinking?"

"I haven't had anything for a long time." It had only been

forty-eight hours, but for her that was a long time. What she'd told him was true. She patted her denim pockets to prove nothing was there. She raised her hands in the air, as if he might not believe her.

Harry looked embarrassed. "Stop it. There's no way the army'd put you on a troop carrier to Kabul. We're both in deep shit."

She switched back to being his nanny for a moment. "Language young man!" Then she changed voices. "I'm not going for the army. A charity is sending me. To work in Kabul for a little while." She smiled at him. She was so glad to see him. "The only thing slightly irregular was my coming on board at the last minute."

"Why this plane? When I'm on it?" He felt he suffered enough from fame he'd never sought or enjoyed. Why did he have to put up with it from someone he trusted?

"I'm sorry it's such a hardship. That your poor nanny wanted to say goodbye. Before you went to war. I do actually remember the day you were born."

Harry relented. He gathered her into his arms for a hug. She felt soft and yielding and frail. He remembered her perfume from when he was very little. It smelled like crushed rose petals, with something spiky underneath, an aromatic bark with thorns perhaps.

In a life that had stretched over nearly seven decades, Frances had learned to recognize golden moments. Being hugged by a young man who was taller, stronger, and more capable-looking than she'd seen him before was one of them. Not only had she seen him the day he was born in St. Mary's, Paddington, she'd also seen him falling over on a tricycle and

squalling at the surprise. Here he was a young man flying halfway across the world to fight. She closed her eyes and smelled something acrid, perhaps the starch, in his fatigues.

"It's all right. Nothing's gonna happen to me."

"Of course it won't. They're sending you to the quietest sector they can find."

"What?"

"Don't be silly. They can't risk exposing the reputation of the British army by putting you in real danger. They're going to keep you as safe as possible. They must have squared the media too. Which is why I didn't know you were going until I saw you at London Airport."

Maybe she had talked to Arbuthnot? "How do you know that?"

"Think! Use your head, darling. This is a multi-million pound expenditure of money and materiel. Of course they've squared the media."

Harry looked hurt. "You used to be on my side."

She stepped up to him again and put one arm around his waist. "Of course I'm on your side, darling. But you've got to be realistic about what's going to happen."

"I did the course. I sat the exams. I did the training. With everyone else." He stuck out his lower lip. "I'm as good as them. I didn't ask for any favors."

"Of course you didn't. But the favors have come to you since the moment you were born. And they're not going away."

His eyebrows puckered with his sense of the injustice of it all. "I just want to be treated like everybody else."

"I know you do. But they're not handing you that on a platter. You've got to prove it. You've got to earn it."

"I thought that's what I was doing. Going out there." He nodded in the general direction the plane was flying.

"It's only the start."

"But what've I got to do then?"

"I can't tell you. You've got to find that out for yourself. It's got to be something you do, and not something you are."

They'd reached a stand-off. There was nothing more to say. They stared at each other a moment.

"Sweetheart," she said more softly.

Harry cracked a smile, and put his head at an angle. "What are you going to do when we get to Kabul?"

"I'll cope. I imagine I'll find out when I get there. I've been working for the church group for a while now. Which you'd know, if you ever came to visit me."

"I've tried." He was like any young man found guilty of inattention to an elderly relative. "They don't give us much leave."

"Didn't I see pictures of you in South Africa? With a Miss Someone?"

"Stop."

"Very well. I love you anyway." She went on tiptoe and kissed him on his reddened cheek.

He cleared his throat. "The other thing is. Um. Do you need money, Mudge? Someone told us you were skint."

"If someone told you that, perhaps you ought to have investigated. Rather than waiting to ask me here. And now."

"Are you?"

"None of your business. Anyway, I'm not here for the money. I'm here because they helped me."

"What kind of help? What'd you need? Why didn't you ask

us?"

"I have my pride. I could hardly apply to the private secretary at St. James's for outdoor relief."

"Outdoor relief?" laughed Harry. "What's that?"

"Never mind. The help I've been given wasn't to do with money. Who knows how much time I have left."

Harry looked at Frances skeptically. She looked pretty sturdy to him.

"I need," continued Frances, "to repay the help that's been given me."

Harry reached out and put one hand on either side of her shoulders. He looked her in the eyes. "No one's ashamed of you, Mudge." He thought a moment and then he added, "I'm not. Not me."

"Thank you." She stepped forward and rested her head sideways on his chest, her silver-white hair splaying against the sandy pattern of his tunic. "Thank you, my love."

*

After she'd dispatched Harry back to his seat, Frances took a longer route back to 23A. She wanted to stretch her legs. She scanned row after row of men wearing the same camouflage pattern clothing. Most of them were either asleep or watching

the televisions in the backs of the seats in front of them. She came across one man who was somewhat older than the rest. Why did he look vaguely familiar to her? He was perhaps in his forties. He was reading a thick manuscript loosely bound in a plastic cover. He sighed, closed it up, and put it down on the empty seat next to him. Frances caught sight of the manuscript's cover. *Production and Domination: Afghanistan 1747-1901*, by Ashraf Ghani.

"I'm glad you've brought along some light reading," she said.

He looked up at her over his half glasses. Who was she? What was she doing reading over his shoulder? It might have been a classified document. He was interrupted in this train of thought by the ghost of a recollection.

"Wait a minute."

"Why, it isn't Andrew Arbuthnot, is it?"

His memory was not so quick. "Um."

"It's ages since I've seen you. Twenty years at least. I so miss your parents. Do you know? We used to be in one another's houses for supper at least once a week."

Andrew unbuckled his seatbelt and stood up apologetically. Now he remembered. "Mrs. de Mornay."

"How's your father?"

"He died I'm afraid."

"Oh yes. I did see that. I remember now. He had such a nice obituary in the *Telegraph*, though. Didn't he?"

"He would've disputed the facts. He liked to stay out of the papers."

"He was such an amusing man."

"But yes. It was good."

"And your mother?"

"Living with my sister now. She and her husband have taken my mother in. She lives in the dower house. Only a cottage really. But she's in their house looking after the grandchildren. All the time."

"How heavenly. She'll like that."

"She does. She does." Andrew considered for a moment. He felt like a boy trying to think of something to say to one of the adults at his parents' cocktail parties. "I'm sure she'd love to hear from you."

"Oh," laughed Frances, with a little brittleness. "I think not, young man. How shall I say it? My divorce finished off a lot of those friendships. I never saw your parents again."

This was awkward ground, but as she'd mentioned it, Andrew wasn't going to shy away from it himself. "It seemed so unfair. I remember that. To a sixteen-year-old. I think that's what I was then."

Frances smiled at him. He was being kind.

"But hang on," said Andrew, remembering who he was and why he was there. "What are you doing on this plane?" He had a second thought about whether it was really all right to address someone his mother's age, indeed a friend of his mother's, with such severity. "If you'll forgive me for asking," he added.

"Don't worry," she examined his uniform for some indication of his rank. "Um, what are you now, Andrew? In the army, I mean."

"Lieutenant colonel," he said apologetically.

"Congratulations, dear. Now don't worry. My papers are all in order. I'm accredited to an interfaith group in Kabul."

"Yes. They did having several seats booked on this plane. But they don't ordinarily put their people into Scottish regimental kit."

"Oh this?" she said, and shrugged her shoulders. "It's nothing. We served thirteen gallons of tea to the 49th Highlanders in Glasgow. Yesterday. Before coming down to London. And I personally made a hundred egg salad sandwiches. Wrapped them in cling-film. Would you believe it? What would your mother say?" She laughed easily, as if it were a joke he could share, rather than an evasive answer to his question.

Andrew was uneasy. As she was already on the plane, he didn't see the point of pressing her. Further, he was having a boyhood memory of her walking through the sitting room at home. The other women were in lumpy brown tweeds, but Mrs. de Mornay wore a tight-fitting dress. It was no more than a slim sheath made of turquoise silk. It had small metallic scales sewn on it that shimmered in the light. It was as if she were a long-boned fish swimming lazily through sunlit shallows. The dress fit her so tightly that he remembered his teenaged self wondering whether she was wearing anything underneath it.

"Well, it's all very irregular. I may have to write up a report when we get to Kabul."

"Oh, don't do that colonel."

"Your name should have been submitted to me in advance. I would have recognized it on the roster. Do you realize what my American opposite number would say if he found out that UK security was that lax?"

"I see no need to share everything with the Americans. Do

you?" Then she changed her expression. "Now Andrew," she spoke to him in his mother's voice. "Look here. There's no harm done and you know it. I was selected at the last minute, but all my papers are in order. Somewhere. The church is not the army, after all. I am not here to undermine your mission. I'm here to comfort the troops. Cheer the boys up. I hope to do more of the same in Kabul. That's an aid to your mission rather than otherwise."

He did not look persuaded. "I have been given the responsibility of getting Wales in and out of a warzone. And what I can't do is to let him have any privileges. Like being accompanied to a war by his nanny."

Now Frances put her hand on his shoulder so she could lean in and say quietly, "You mustn't be so exasperated. We mustn't give the others the impression that anything's wrong."

Andrew felt the light pressure of her hand. All of a sudden he was a boy watching her cross the room again. He was a teenager admiring her waist and the angle of her hip. Yes, she was older. Yes, there were now circles under her eyes. Yes, her hair was white. But she still had that determined look. Her bony elegance was intact. Her blue eyes shone.

"That won't do either of us any good," she carried on. "You mentioned your mother looking after your sister's children. You said how much it meant to her. Allow me a little of what your mother has every day, Andrew. Won't you? When we get out there, I will disappear. The interfaith mission is completely above board. Kabul Airport is the last you'll see of me."

He looked at her from under his eyebrows. He still disapproved of whatever she'd done to get on the plane. He

hoped security would be tighter when they arrived. But her head was nearer to his now and he could smell the crushed rose petals of her perfume, just as Harry had. And just as Harry had, Andrew remembered it.

*

Cindy Reed and her producer had been sleeping together for six months. That was their secret. It had been consensual and enjoyable for them both, but she was the one who was beginning to be unhappy with it. He was thirty years older than her. Though she had no moral qualms about that, the difference in their tastes was beginning to cause trouble. He liked different music. He was frustrated that she didn't know more about what she regarded as obscure movies of the 1970s. She could also see he was growing sentimental about her and would have liked a more permanent arrangement. She, on the other hand, wanted to keep her romantic, career, and geographic options open.

Still, she kept a half dozen late-at-night email messages from him saved in her files. She re-read them sometimes. They made her feel loved and appreciated. Perhaps if her father hadn't left them when she was young—so young she couldn't remember him—she wouldn't have had the same

craving for an older man's attention. The producer had taken a warm interest in her when she first arrived at CNN. He listened to her, admired her questions, and gave her time. She hadn't had to sleep with him for him to give her that. He sometimes seemed to recognize in her the kid in ponytail and cheap glasses from a strip mall that she'd used to be. There was something paternal and protective in his attitude toward her career. He put his hands around it as if he were holding away a breeze from a tiny, guttering flame. Of course he was older than her, but she didn't think he was disgusting. She thought he looked all right. Certainly his long experience of broadcasting and his understanding of the way it all worked intrigued and attracted her. She liked his salt and pepper hair.

If discovered, his emails to her would have led to his automatic dismissal from the network. It didn't matter how distinguished his career. It didn't matter that she'd agreed with what was going on. The sexual harassment guidelines, especially those that regulated persons with power over those they supervised, were strict. No matter how busy or important their jobs, they were all repeatedly sent on training courses to be reminded of these rules. She'd teased him about that occasionally. He knew the emails were dynamite, but he was also confident she'd never use them. Their work was too important to both of them to sacrifice what they had.

She had no intention of exposing him, really, until that one evening at Hartsfield when he laughed at her. His laugh was filled with a scorn that made her feel small. That's when she'd retaliated by threatening to use her saved email file against him.

He stood up, refused to look at her, and stalked off down

the hall. He was gone for more than thirty minutes. When he came back, they were already boarding the flight. He didn't speak to her. They sat down together. They opened their laptops and began working. It was only when drinks were served that he'd agreed to her going for several weeks only, to be closely supervised by him. He'd called his Pentagon contact to smooth out the paperwork for her arrival in Afghanistan. They'd been separated at Heathrow, as the Pentagon already had a seat on the British troop transport for her. He was going out to Kabul via a later commercial flight. He'd warned her that both of them would have their careers in broadcast journalism finished if his lies on her behalf were ever exposed. He also told her she was twice as good as the guy she was replacing and if she didn't send in some good material, he'd be god damned.

She didn't take the risk lightly. She knew she was putting herself in danger not only of provoking the military authorities and the network, but also the guys she was hoping to interview. She wanted to experience for herself what it was like for them to be in a war. How would they feel if they found out she was a fraud? She was determined to prove that it wasn't a stunt.

She had several things going for her that other women, placed in the same situation, might not have had. As a toddler and even as an adolescent, she knew only male rough and tumble. She inherited her brothers' hand-me-down clothes. She was always more comfortable in a pair of jeans and flannel shirt than in girls' clothes. She'd had to agree to her hair's being teased for the network. She'd had to wear the designer wardrobe the network chose for her. Those were the

tools of the trade, in her eyes. They were like the hammer her brother, who was a carpenter, hung from a special denim loop of his overalls.

She sometimes wished the job meant less to her. She sometimes wished she had more detachment from it, that she could leave it behind and forget about it when she left the office. She sometimes wished she could dial down her ambition a little, and let things slide. As it was, she couldn't. The closest she could come was to take off her silk shirt when she got home and throw it on a careless heap with her discarded trousers and heels.

The producer's calls to the Pentagon press secretary had made it all happen. She'd been ushered on to the troop carrier without any questions asked. She'd put her hair into her hat and changed into camouflage fatigues in the plane's rear lavatory before she took her seat. A British colonel had taken pains to speak to her on the flight and addressed her as if she were a man. True, he hadn't given her anything she could use. Nevertheless, she liked his respecting her enough to think she was a journalist who could cause him some trouble. Things had been smooth in Kabul too. She'd been assigned a place on one of the buses that would take the combined American and British force to a remote location. She didn't know precisely where they were going. Nor did anyone else. Fine. So far so good. They were all on the same level.

The bus had special armor on the sides and shatterproof glass that was hard to see through. The windows were covered with bars. It was like something that might be used in the States to take convicted men between a courtroom and jail. There were several HUMVEEs and armored trucks

that rolled along in a convoy with them out of the airport. One checkpoint after another slowed their progress. It was hard to make out landmarks and buildings through the thick glass and clouds of dust. None of that bothered Cindy. She was a little upset by the fact that no one wanted to sit with her. The guys all seemed to have buddies from having trained together, or at the very least, having had long waits at the airport together. How was she going to get a story if they wouldn't talk to her?

She did notice that Harry had more energy than the other guys, even after a seven-hour flight. He was on her bus. He knocked several of the guys' caps off, and rolled a soccer ball he'd somehow got out of his pack down the aisle. Judging from the looks on their faces, the UK guys were not that impressed with him. Few of them reacted. Nor did he persist in trying to cultivate them when they turned their backs to him. The American guys, on the other hand, ate him up. One of them kicked the ball back to him. A second told him a joke. A third stood up in the aisle to put his arm around Harry's shoulders. She made mental notes of this, then dozed off. It had been a long flight and she'd been so keyed up by the argument with the producer that she hadn't managed to sleep on the plane.

She was startled and roughly awakened about half an hour later when she felt someone sliding into the empty seat next to hers.

"What's this? Asleep on the job?" whispered a voice near her ear.

Her eyes fluttered open. He was leaning his face into hers.

"Oh no. I. Am. Sorry. Woke you up, didn't I?"

She was still groggy. She couldn't even nod.

"I promise not to. Ever again." He said this with a wink, as if he'd found her weak spot. Liking to sleep. "I know you really wanted to talk to me. Back there. On the plane. But couldn't say so. Thought I'd come over and introduce myself. To an important member of the press party."

She stared at him. Then she remembered. "No, I didn't. It was the guy sitting next to you. Is he on the bus?"

"Can't think where he's got to," grinned Harry, as if the two of them were in some conspiracy together to talk to each other while pretending to want to talk to someone else.

"In that case, I guess I'll go back to sleep."

"Okay. Roger. Wilco. Over and out. I won't bother you anymore." He said it "bovva" you anymore. "It's just to say that we in the UK army are thrilled to bits to have an American reporter along with us. And if there's anything you ever want to know, come to me. Right here!" He slapped himself several times on the chest. "Cause we all believe in the special relationship. If it was good enough for Churchill, it's good enough for us."

She stared back at him.

He got awkwardly to his feet. He looked at her as she remained down in her seat, refusing to respond to him.

"So that's all from me."

She stared up at him.

"Oh, but you know," here he put his head down and lowered his voice. "We forgive you for all that other stuff. You know? That tea party? Not paying your taxes? All that? Forgiven!"

She looked up at him without blinking.

He lowered his voice a little more. "And those laptops we lost? You heard about that, didn't you? Someone from MI6

left them on the train. With all that USA top secret stuff you shared with us still on them? Got picked up in all the newspapers? We're really sorry about that too."

She had heard about that. Here she couldn't help cracking the corner of a smile.

"Right!" he said, standing back up, speaking in his normal voice, and turning to stride back down the aisle. "Mission accomplished. I'm off!"

*

Soon after their arrival at a remote camp in Helmand Province, Andrew Arbuthnot sat down at the spindly table in his tent. He proposed doing the riskiest thing he'd done since arriving in Afghanistan. He was going to expose himself to ridicule and rejection. He was going to write a letter. He didn't have her email address in any case. Women of his parents' generation, he reasoned, liked traditional letters. He uncapped his fountain pen. He looked at the blank page. "Come on, old boy," he whispered to himself.

Dear Mrs. de Mornay,

A free moment has presented itself, and I thought I'd write to see how you are settling in. How are things in town? Have they given you a hard bed, an army blanket, and plenty of

work to do? Are there raisins or rocks in your pulau?

Out here we find ourselves in a quiet posting. It's so remote that nothing remotely ever happens. We are surrounded and out-numbered. Not by the insurgency. It's the Americans. The place is overrun. In the mess we are served pepperoni pizza every other night. There is something called "Monday Night Football" that runs on a continuous loop in the rest and recreation tent. The armored vehicles we take outside the fence for reconnaissance fly the flag not of Uncle Sam, nor of Her Majesty, but of someone called the Pittsburgh Pirate.

The men are understandably bored. The solution proposed by my opposite number commanding the US forces has been more exercise. He wants more baseball games in the sand. I frankly think something more is required, but I haven't come up with anything better to propose. I do not intend, however, to let our side down.

I cannot say whether this highly confidential missive might be intercepted before it reaches its target, so I will not go into detail. Suffice it to say that your former charge is on good form. Some contraband was found in his locker the other day. A can of Tennant's Lager was confiscated, and he was put on five days of extra guard duty.

I'm still annoyed with his father's staff for saddling me with him. I'm sorry. I know you want the best for him. But I feel, somehow, I must tell you the truth. I opened a Henry IV *I brought with me, for of course that has a young man in it not unlike the one we have with us here. Shakespeare's Hal refuses to grow up and threatens to disgrace the throne as well. I wondered whether the play could at least help me*

with an assignment that feels more like a nuisance than a pleasure. So far, nothing.

In my former posting here, we occasionally had visits in our camp from your interfaith charity. The men always benefitted. Is there any reason for giving us hope that this might happen again? It would be so nice to see you.

Andrew re-read what he'd written, nibbling on the end of his pen. How should he end it? *Love, Andrew*? Of course not. *Yours affectionately, Andrew*? No, she'd given him no reason to write that. No, he'd better end as it if he were writing a hundred years ago. That's what his parents' generation liked. He wrote:

With all best wishes,
Very truly yours,
Andrew Arbuthnot

He reread it. Then he crossed out *all best wishes* and wrote in *warm best wishes*. He was folding the letter and putting it into a buff colored army envelope when a voice behind him asked, "Colonel Arbuthnot, sir?"

He slid around on his chair. "Yes, Wales," he said with a sigh.

"It's the Americans, sir. They've got those dogs."

"Bomb sniffer K-9 patrol, Wales."

"I tried to pet one sir, and the Yank who had his lead told me I couldn't." Harry did an accurate impression of an American accent. "Don't touch that dog! That's an attack dog!" He was trying to make Andrew laugh.

"Well, I should listen to him then, lieutenant," said Andrew, not amused.

"The thing is, sir. You know Mustafa Khan, sir? He says it's

not fair we haven't got any UK dogs with us."

"We are out here to secure the population from the insurgency, not to play with dogs, lieutenant."

"No, of course not. You're right, sir. But Khan, sir? He says he can get us an Afghan dog. An Afghan hound. You know, one of the tall ones. They're beauties, sir."

"Wales," Andrew began, sounding as if he wanted to sigh.

Harry interrupted him. "Sorry to cut in, sir. But you know our guys are a bit down. Everything here is controlled by the Yanks. The food, the telly, the sport. Everything." He said it "Evry-fink," in hopes of getting a rise from Andrew.

Andrew took a breath to begin his rejection of this idea.

Harry raced forward. "And if we could have our own dog. It would be a start. It would cheer everyone up. I'm sure of it, sir."

Andrew stared back at him.

"I'd take care of him. Feed him, I mean. Train him. The guys would like a dog, sir."

"There's nothing in our budget for an Afghan hound."

"He'd cost practically nothing at all, sir. Fifty dollars. That's what Khan said."

Andrew sighed again. He was temporarily stymied. Then it occurred to him. "If I were to agree to the dog, Wales ..."

"Yes, sir!"

"Would you be willing to help me with an idea I've had?"

"Of course, sir!"

"It's just that, I've noticed it too. Of course. The Americans. We need to fly the flag a bit ourselves."

"Yes we do, sir!"

"And we may have some visitors before long. From Kabul.

They sometimes send out the British Council. Or, um, embassy staff, now. Maybe even an infrastructure development group from the World Bank. One of the Christian aid groups. That sort of thing. In my experience, there will be visitors. It would be nice if we could show them what our side can do."

"Absolutely, sir."

"And I thought we might do a staged reading of a play."

"What?"

"Yes, why not?"

"Well, what about some skits, sir? Instead. You know Ali G? He interviews real people. And sends them up. And they don't get it. *Da Ali G Show*? He did Boutros Boutros Boutros Boutros Boutros-Ghali? Remember that? It was hysterical."

"You're talking about the former secretary general of the United Nations."

"It's all in good fun, sir."

"No, Wales. Not that."

Harry stood with his shoulders beginning to slope downwards. "What then, sir?"

"I thought Shakespeare."

"Oh sir!" He spoke as if he'd just been given five more days of guard duty. "No. Not that. For fuck's sake."

Andrew gave him ten more days.

*

There was a double wall of chain-link barbed wire fence around the camp. On top of the fences lay scrolled lengths of razor wire. In the center big square tents occupied a grid, with walks and driveways in between. During the day it was hot and each tent had its own air-conditioning unit. The nights were cold and sometimes they even had to blow in some heat. One of the camp's few more solid structures was a fortified guardhouse. It was in the northeastern corner, five minutes' walk from the nearest tents. The officer in charge sat inside at a desk in front of a computer. He was there to oversee three soldiers who took turns outdoors patrolling the fences. Day or night, there was little to see beyond the walls. It was scrub, rock, and unfertile soil. It looked like Arizona. There were cacti, but no coyotes.

That evening, the officer in charge was not sitting indoors. He was sitting outside, on a beach chair, wrapped in a blanket, looking up at the stars. Someone's mother had sent the beach chair when she heard the camp was hot and sunny and there was nothing to do.

A shadowy figure approached in the dark. Harry first heard the crunch of boots and then he saw a human form outlined against the dark. He sat up abruptly.

"Who goes there? Halt!"

"Um, sorry. I didn't know it was you guys on tonight."

"Oh Reed," he yawned. "It's you."

"The duty sheet they showed me definitely has our guys on tonight."

"Well, orders change. Don't they? This is the army, Reed."

"Do they? What happened?"

"My Yankee colleagues have been given some extra bed rest.

For ten nights."

"Oh?"

"Yeah."

"Did you do something wrong?"

"Reed! I need to see your security pass, please. We can't have you interrupting men on active duty at all hours. With silly questions. The enemy's out there." Harry gestured to the fence.

"Really?"

"They're vicious, Reed. Do you know what they'd do to a softie like you? If you're captured, I mean?"

She laughed involuntarily. "Like you know." Then, afraid that her laugh might have been too high, she carried on in a deeper voice. "You've never seen one in your life."

Harry paused a moment. He changed tack. "Have you?"

"Not really. On a satellite feed. Once. I did."

"I don't think that counts."

She heard him say "fink" instead of "think." She laughed in spite of herself.

"You know what, Reed? Are you still going through puberty? Cause your voice changes, you know? Goes up and down. Maybe when you're nervous? Admit it. You can trust me."

"No," she said in a deeper register. "Fuck off."

"All right!" Harry smiled, reassured. "Maybe we can be mates, then."

Harry stood up. His blanket and a book dropped on to the sand.

The book dropped near to Cindy's foot. She stepped forward and picked it up. She looked at the title. *Henry the Fourth, Part One.* "You're not really reading this, are you?"

"Nope."

"Too bad. It's a good book."

"Like you've read it?"

"I did. I liked it. We had to read it in Shakespeare 101. I was like a sophomore or something. It's not hard."

"Well I didn't go to uni, did I?"

"You didn't?" She put in a cynical laugh. "Your parents couldn't afford the tuition?"

"No." He kicked a rock across the sand. "Maybe I'm not clever enough, am I?"

She hadn't paid that much attention to him since she arrived. She was busy trying to get angles on what she regarded as more newsworthy stories. She was more interested in the American guys, anyway. When she had noticed him, he'd usually been goofing around and acting like he was the class clown. He hadn't given her any reason to change what she thought of him the first time she saw him.

"Too bad you don't come from the States. If you're a Bush? Or a Kennedy? It doesn't matter what your test scores are, you get in no matter what."

"Well, that's not the way it works in the UK."

"Yeah, I bet it doesn't. And I bet you don't have satin sheets at the castle, either."

"Why's everyone so interested in the stupid sheets! And where I sleep? They're just sheets." He took a step forward and put his arm around Cindy's waist. "Are you saying you wanna see where I sleep, young man?" He lowered his voice into his notion of what a Parisian lover might sound like. "Eees zat what you want?" He whispered in Cindy's ear. "Do you love, as I do, ze cheeps? Ze, how do you say in Amérique,

ze French fry?"

In the whole two weeks she'd been out in Afghanistan, no one had touched her. She'd been hyper-aware of maintaining her disguise as a guy. It was a touch she wasn't expecting. She jumped at his hand on her hip.

"Oooh darlin'. You like it doncha?"

"Hands off, lieutenant!"

"I guess you've been lonely in that small tent all by yourself."

"I didn't ask for that tent. They put me there. Probably to keep me away from everyone. I'm supposed to be embedded. Isolating me defeats the purpose. I don't want any special favors."

"Well, Reed. You just gotta put up with it. They been giving 'em to me since the day I was born."

Cindy stepped back. "What?"

"Like I said."

Cindy was determined not to waste time with him. It would only yield material for a gossip column. She'd intended to interview some of the American guys on guard duty. Find out where they were from. Why they'd joined up. What they thought of the war. How it felt to be on the front line. Well, no. How it felt to be in a backwater when their buddies were getting shot at elsewhere in Afghanistan. That was the nub of her idea, and it had nothing to do with him. She turned to go.

"Hey, wait a minute," Harry objected. "I've got hours out here. I mean like six still to go. You can't just leave." He sounded pathetic.

She turned back to look at him in the face, and saw by the hint of mischief in his eyebrows that he was probably going to make fun of her again. "You can cope, lieutenant," she said

"No! Wait, wait, wait. Tell me about the play. Maybe if you give me a little, how do Americans say it? Executive summary? Then I can get into it." He sat back down on the long beach chair with its folding leg rest fully extended. He patted the space next to him. "C'mon! Room for two. I'll share me blanket."

The "me" made her laugh again. In spite of her better judgement, which told her to go back to her tent, and make some notes, she sat gingerly down on the beach chair next to him, not touching him.

"That's right, mate." He picked up the blanket and threw it over both their shoulders. "Nice and toasty, ain't we? Life in the fox hole. You can put that on telly, can't you?" Then he elbowed her roughly in the side. "'Cept no foxes!"

It was a dumb joke, the kind one of her brothers would have made. She ignored it.

"So Mr. Shagspeare. Bard of Avon. Whasee all about, then?" He was playing the role of village idiot.

Cindy laughed again, naturally. "Come off it. You should like this play."

Now he changed roles and played an obedient schoolboy. "Why's that then, Mr. Reed, sir?"

"It's about a lazy prince. Nobody thinks he's got a brain. All he does is drink and joke around and hang out with lowlifes in the bar. Even his father thinks he's a zero. Then all of a sudden, he has to go to this war. Nobody thinks he can hack it. He's had all this money and he's never had any responsibility. So they're convinced he's a loser. And you can't rely on him."

"Are you joking?" said Harry in his own voice.

"That's how it starts, anyway."

*

Frances had a room in Kabul recently vacated by an Italian nun. There was a single window. It let in light, but it was high on the wall. She couldn't see out of it. There was a single monastic bed. The nun had set up a makeshift altar, with a worn prayer rug for kneeling on the hard floor, and a small crucifix nailed to the wall. The nun had used the room's one plastic chair and small table to sit at and read devotional literature. Frances sat there to read Andrew Arbuthnot's letter.

It struck her as strange that he should write at all. She remembered him as a bookish teenager, probably not cut out for the army career his father had in mind for him. She hadn't known him well then, though she supposed she'd sought him out and questioned him about his future, as she had with all the adolescent children of her then friends. It encouraged them if an adult took an interest and treated them as if they were older than they were.

Here was a letter that addressed her almost as if she were his chum. She didn't object. It was flattering. She wasn't going to deny that. Not only was he higher in the chain of command than she'd been in touch with for some time, but he was also a young man. He must be forty something. She had to be frank with herself. He couldn't possibly be sending her a letter for any other reason than to be polite. Yet, on the plane, he'd seemed to soften when she put her hand on his shoulder. She

liked that. Did she remind him of his mother? She hoped not.

She supposed he might like an email reply. Or, should she send some other sort of internet message? She was not going to pretend she knew how. When she needed that kind of thing done, one of the young women from the church helped her. Writing a letter required no help.

She took out a sheet of paper headed with the interfaith charity's logo, and scrabbled in the desk drawer. She found the nun's old biro. She hoped that if it wasn't holy, it was at least lucky.

Dear Andrew,

I know that out here you are Colonel Arbuthnot, but I cannot break a habit of more than twenty years.

She looked at that and wondered about it. Would he regard it as patronizing? She tried mollifying it a little.

Though she will never say this to you herself, I know how proud your mother is of you. It's not only your rank, achieved at so young an age, and your service, but the fine man you've grown into. All that will please her every day. Take it from me. As one gets older, one acquires a certain fearlessness. I tell the truth without reserve. So I can tell you what she will not.

Your posting sounds all right. I expect you are understating the tension. Even when things don't happen, one has a way in such situations of bracing for the worst. Many of the men we see here are suffering from that. They haven't any physical wounds, but they experience the side effects of waiting for something to happen. We have no pills to administer. We give them tea and lemon cake. I'm not a priest, but I hear confessions every day. I am holding hands with young men

morning, noon, and night. So the duty's not all bad.

This town is awash in funds from the Foreign Office, the State Department, and who knows where else. I suppose Chevrolet and British Petroleum. The streets are paved. The security is tight. All public places feel reasonably safe. There are several different sorts of restaurant, including one for sushi. There is more choice in Kabul than in Oban.

We have not been told of any upcoming visits of mercy, or of our duty to minister to the hard-working soldiers in the field. You have more experience of the routine out here than I do. Perhaps we will.

In the meantime, Andrew, I can't think that Shakespeare will be a popular choice among the men. In the last war, as I understand it, what the men liked was song and dance. Some off-color lyrics. Girls with short skirts. Film stars on tour. That was the ticket. Not Shakespeare.

Thank you too for news of the young man referred to in your letter. I suppose saying as little as possible is wise from the security standpoint. I haven't been as close to him, or seen as much of him as I would have liked these last few years. Seeing him for just a few minutes on the aeroplane made a world of difference to me.

As did your letter.

I was pleased to have your warm best wishes. I send you an embrace for old time's sake. This is what women of my generation do in a war, Andrew. Accept it as your due. I do hope you will stay safe and sound.

Yours,

Frances

Frances re-read her letter, decided it was okay, and sealed it up in an envelope. It went first in a wicker basket on the hall table and then in a mailbag from the interfaith charity to the coalition forces mailroom. There it was repackaged and put on a truck with other letters and packages. It went into a mailbag destined for the remote camp where Andrew was in command of the British forces.

One of the drivers who'd been assigned to pack the mailbags accepted a bribe to unload several of the mailbags before they reached their destination. They were passed on to an Afghan regional militia, which allied sometimes with the Taliban, sometimes with the coalition forces. It depended on which side paid better, and sometimes on which side promised swifter punishment. The contents of one of the mailbags ended up being dumped on to a fine oriental carpet. This was on the dirt floor of a house built from dried mud mixed with straw. It belonged to a warlord who commanded the militia. It was in a village not far from Andrew's camp.

The warlord was a distant cousin of Mustafa's father. He knew Mustafa was in Andrew's camp as a junior officer serving with the British. He invited Mustafa to come and call on him. After consulting with Andrew, who thought it would be a good idea for Mustafa to acquire some local knowledge, as well as to establish friendly relations with neighbors, Mustafa arrived to pay his visit. He found the warlord sitting cross-legged on the carpet, reading a letter, the contents of the mailbag in a disorderly pile in front of him.

"*Salaam aleicum,*" said Mustafa coming in the room, bowing to the much older man, and holding his hands together.

"*Wa-aleicum salaam,*" said the older man, who was wearing a one-piece woolen robe, and a white turban wound round his head. The turban leaned slightly to one side. The man did not get up, but smiled broadly. He indicated with a sweeping gesture of his hand that Mustafa was welcome, as well as that he should sit opposite him.

They then exchanged a long series of courtesies, demanded by Afghan etiquette. This included hopes that the other's way should never be hard, that the sun should perpetually shine on the other's descendants, and that misfortune should never sting him. A young warrior with dark hair down to his neck, whom Mustafa judged to be four or five years younger than him, brought green tea in glasses as well as unleavened bread. Then he went and folded himself into an athletic crouch next to the steaming samovar. His presence as a fighter in an unusual serving capacity was a tribute to the older man's importance, not unlike young equerries who served a similar position with the queen.

"I hope your father prospers in the land of Western decadence."

"I think he's okay, thanks," said Mustafa, though intending not to take any notice of the political turn of the man's remark. "What a beautiful rug," he said instead, reaching down to run his palm across the tiny silk knots. "From Isfahan? Very old?"

"Seventeenth century," answered the warlord. "If you like historical things, perhaps you will be interested in this too." He made a slight gesture to the young warrior in the corner. He left the room for a moment and returned with a small, elongated oil-burning lamp, about the size of a woman's curved-toe slipper. It had been carved by hand from a smooth

stone. He placed it in Mustafa's hands.

"Can you identify the era of this, young man?"

Mustafa cradled it reverently in both hands. "I believe it must be ancient. It looks like something you might rub to summon a jinn."

"It is from the era of Alexander. He passed through here on his way to conquer India."

"Why then, then," said Mustafa losing his cool for a moment, "it must be more than two thousand years old."

"Very good, my boy. Though raised far away, you still have an appreciation for our history and art."

"My parents have rugs similar to this, though not so fine. My mother used to take me to look at the galleries of Islamic art at the Victoria & Albert Museum when I was little."

"Take the lamp, my son. It is yours."

"I couldn't possibly, sir. It's too valuable."

"I want someone who appreciates it to have it."

"No, really. It's too great a gift. I can't accept it.

"Take it then as homage to your father and his escape from this benighted country."

"No, he wouldn't want that. I don't think it's benighted."

"Thank you, dear boy. We are still here, it's true. After many different invasions. Perhaps you will take the lamp in return for a small service you could do me."

"I am happy to help you without reward."

"Then you could read this letter for me and tell me whether it means what I think it means." He handed over Frances's letter to Andrew.

Mustafa took the letter a little unwillingly. He eyed the pile of other letters sitting in front of him. He could see from

several unopened envelopes that they were addressed to the camp. He suspected that a mailbag had been stolen. He wondered whether, if challenged, the warlord would say it had fallen off the back of a truck. He glanced over the contents of the letter. He could see that it was addressed to his colonel. He looked nervously up at the warlord after he'd finished. He did not speak.

"Is this from the Mrs. de Mornay who was dismissed for being addicted to drink? And does it mean her former charge, Prince Harry, is in your camp?"

"What makes you think that?"

"Come now. Do you think we're stupid?" The warlord's eyes glinted. "We read *The Daily Mail* online. Mrs. de Mornay was in their headlines for weeks."

Mustafa had been trained by the intelligence services not to give away secrets, even when the gist of them had already been discovered by the opposite side. His face assumed an untroubled air. He said nothing to the warlord.

"What a loyal boy you are. You wear their uniform. I am not surprised you do not wish to disclose their secrets. But remember my son, you still belong to us. Your blood is our blood. They will pretend to take you to their hearts, but you will never be one of them."

Mustafa merely nodded and smiled.

"And your father," said the warlord, "has written to say that you have even trained with their intelligence services."

Mustafa was genuinely surprised and thrown off balance. He inhabited the body of a young man, but his mind was still, on occasion, that of a teenager. For a while, all his late adolescent anger had been directed at the boys on the

tube. Then, by degrees, he'd slowly shifted his anger toward his parents, instead. He saw more of them than he did the louts. They infuriated him more. For the most part he did as they wished. He finished school and went on directly to university without a gap year. Nevertheless, resentment of parental control and longing for independence was brewing underneath his outward compliance. The intelligence services recruited him at his university not for his ethnicity but for his languages. In addition to a variety of Afghan languages and dialects, he also knew Arabic. In the post 9/11 world that made him a valuable commodity. They persuaded him that prior service in the army could lead afterwards to a high-level strategic post in Whitehall. That was what had tempted him.

He also knew it would shock his parents if he joined the army after university. They had been quick to assimilate the anti-militarist, liberal views of the London establishment, which, as wealthy immigrants, they wanted desperately to join. He knew they would never want to see a son of theirs in the armed forces. He'd shown them. Over his father's protests, he'd been commissioned as an officer in the Household Cavalry. His mother wailed at the prospect of his deployment to the very land they'd chosen to escape. What this man wearing a lopsided turban had told Mustafa was something he was not prepared for. His father was evidently no longer angry at what he'd done. He was proud of him.

"You could help us bring this war to an end, my son," resumed the warlord.

"What?" replied Mustafa, jolted out of his determination to appear calm and unruffled.

"If young Harry were to be taken, and ransomed, the queen

of the infidels would be sure to withdraw her forces from this conflict. If the British left, the Americans would have to go too."

"What?"

"He wouldn't be hurt. He'd be sent home as soon as they promise to withdraw."

"No. That's absurd. They're not going to let you take him. And even if you did, they wouldn't leave here."

"Ah, thank you. So you confirm for me that he is in the camp."

Mustafa struggled to his feet.

"Whose side are you on, my son? Do you really suppose that His Royal Highness is your friend? Or that it is in your interest to protect him?"

This, if possible, managed to unsettle Mustafa even further. He had dared to think Harry might be his friend. They'd got on well in the short time they'd known each other. Harry enjoyed teasing him, which he knew was a good sign. Not long after they'd arrived in the camp, Mustafa had suggested a night off when they could watch a DVD together. He'd brought along with him in his kit bag a re-mastered version of Peter O'Toole in *Lawrence of Arabia*. When the colonel punished Harry with several extra nights of guard duty, Mustafa had promised to bring out the DVD to the guardroom. They could watch at least fifteen minutes of it on Harry's break. That night he'd also grabbed a bag of popcorn from the mess to take along with the DVD and he'd approached the guardroom in the dark. From twenty yards away, he found that Harry and Sandy Reed, were sitting on a deck chair, a single blanket thrown over both their shoulders, talking and laughing. Mustafa had stopped in his tracks. He'd thought Harry might

be his mate, at least while they were in the camp together. There he was cozying up already with a Yank. Mustafa had turned and trudged back to his tent. It was true what people said. White guys liked to stick together.

*

Two weeks passed and still Andrew had had no reply from Frances. He thought it was odd, but then he had no real reason to expect one. He hoped he hadn't made a fool of himself. He busied himself with routine chores to keep his mind off the disappointment. He met with his American opposite number in the camp. He received reports from the sergeant major. He ordered new rounds of competitive exercise to keep up a sporting rivalry with the Americans and to keep the men fit. He replied to cascades of email from those higher up the chain of command. He examined maps of the local terrain and read intelligence briefs, shared with him by the Americans. On the basis of all this he decided on the areas for reconnaissance missions. He selected places outside the fence that would not put the men at too great a risk, but might also yield some useful information on the state of the local insurgency.

He also put together a small group of his men and began rehearsing *Henry IV*. This included the sergeant major,

Harry, and Mustafa, as well as several men from Harry's and Mustafa's units. He gathered them all together one evening after supper in the mess. The Americans had on a championship match of basketball, which bored most of the men.

"Now," Andrew said, imagining himself to be a director addressing a rehearsal room of seasoned actors at the National Theatre, and raising his voice, "I've knit together two different plays for our text. So I hope it's all right."

"Who's he think he is?" whispered Harry to Mustafa. "Andrew Loud Webber?" He gave Mustafa a broad grin, which Mustafa only half returned. The sergeant major saw them and glowered until they paid solemn attention to the colonel once again.

"I've taken *Henry the Fourth, Part One* and put it together with *Henry the Fourth, Part Two*. Originally, they were of course two different plays."

"Won't that take a long time, sir?" asked Harry.

The sergeant major cleared his throat and stared at him again.

"Well, no, Wales. I've cut out quite a lot. We don't want to bore the audience."

"No, sir," said Harry. "We don't want that. Ha! Ha!" At that everyone laughed together. No stares from the sergeant major could stop them.

"Settle down, men," resumed Andrew. "I think you'll find that it's not irrelevant to your own lives and your own experience. Right here. In this camp."

"Is it a play about wanking then?" asked one of the men.

"Trooper!" roared the sergeant major.

"It's all right sergeant major," said Andrew, who remained calm. "Some young men need a little extra personal time to themselves. We try to accommodate them."

This won Andrew some surprised laughs. The group just about decided the colonel's play might be okay.

"It grows out of a medieval morality play," said Andrew. "It's very black and white. Good versus evil. Vice and virtue fight for the soul of a prince."

"Which side wins, sir?" asked Harry.

"Which side got you ten extra nights of guard duty, Wales?"

The colonel's question produced more general laughter.

"So listen up. This play has a Prince Harry, or Hal. He's heir to the throne."

Harry looked around brightly. "It's not me then."

"No, of course it's not you, Wales. You're acting. Try and remember that. He's got a friend. Poins. Like him, not up to much good."

Here Harry hit Mustafa hard enough on the shoulder to knock him sideways. "That's you, mate."

"Get off," said Mustafa, pretending to be annoyed, though he felt irrationally hopeful and pleased.

"And then there's the king, Hal's father. He's disappointed in his son. He hoped he was raising someone who'd be worthy of the throne. Instead, everyone regards Hal as incorrigible."

Most of the men now began to suspect that the colonel might be willing to cut a big-headed personality down to size. *I'm A Celebrity ... Get Me Out of Here* was one of their favorite reality shows on television. The colonel seemed to have devised a play for them to act that was going to humiliate Harry. They all looked at Harry and sniggered.

Harry looked glum. He felt he was being unfairly treated.

Andrew sensed what the other men thought of Harry. He thought he'd give them a small taste of what they wanted.

"Why don't we try a scene between Harry and his father? Just to warm up. Sergeant major would you mind standing here please and reading these lines of the king's?"

"Yes sir!"

"And Wales. Will you stand next to him and read Hal's lines?"

"Sir, do I have to?"

"If you think you can't do it, Wales, perhaps I can find someone else who has a bit more confidence in front of an audience."

Dragging his feet, Harry came up to stand next to the sergeant major. They both looked at the loose sheets at the place Andrew showed them with his finger.

"Now then. Here's the situation. The king is talking to his son. He's reprimanding him. The king thinks his son's bad behavior is a punishment sent from heaven for his own usurping of the throne."

"Please sir, what's usurping?" said one of the men.

"Harry's father is king. But he's usurped the throne," resumed Andrew, "or taken it away from the legitimate ruler. That's Richard II. And Hal's father thinks that having a bad son is God punishing him for taking the throne from Richard."

"Oof, this is complicated, sir. It's confusing," said Harry, rolling his eyes. "You expect us to remember that?"

Andrew ignored this. "Now then Your Majesty," he said to the sergeant major. "Could you please begin upbraiding your son at *thou dost in thy passages of life*?"

The sergeant major began in a stentorian voice speaking to Harry, who stood opposite him with a drooping script. "*But thou dost in thy passages of life make me believe that thou art only mark'd for the hot vengeance and the rod of heaven, to punish my mistreadings.*"

Harry picked up an imaginary rod and bashed the sergeant major with it.

The men sitting around them on trestle tables were ready to concede this was funny. They smiled at him for the first time.

"*Tell me else,*" the sergeant major continued, "*could such inordinate and low desires, such poor, such bare, such lewd, such mean attempts, such barren pleasures, rude society, as thou art match'd withal, and grafted to, accompany the greatness of thy blood, and hold their level with thy princely heart?*"

"Low desires," repeated one of the men and smirked.

"Barren pleasures," said another, and nodded his head.

"Lewd attempts," said a third and winked at Mustafa.

Mustafa wondered whether that was a sign of disrespect, or not. He decided he'd pretend he hadn't seen it.

Here Cindy walked into the tent. There had been an incident in Kabul. She hoped to get a quote from Andrew about it. She could send it to her producer as a sort of "view from the field of violence taking place in the capital." So far she'd been able to find no stories. She'd sent him almost nothing. She regretted sending him an email mentioning that Harry was in the camp. This was the only thing that had excited him. He'd said it would be a considerable scoop for CNN. If she could be the first to report that he'd been deployed to a war zone, they'd be the first to have a story the rest of the world's

media hadn't discovered. That was not a story she wanted to do, however, so she'd resisted, saying she had better material, when in fact, she didn't. She felt under pressure to come up with something good.

"Ah, Reed," said Andrew. "We're always happy to see members of the USA press corps. But this is a closed meeting."

"Oh, please sir!" said Harry, sensing that an interruption would be more fun than Andrew's play. "Reed actually likes Shakespeare, sir!" He said this as if it were unbelievable, but true. "He told me so himself. Right Reed?"

"I'm afraid not, Reed. This is UK troops only."

Cindy was nonplussed. She turned to go back out, though she was mildly curious about what she was missing.

"Oh, but sir," said Harry, trying to reverse the colonel's ruling. "Look here! Look here. Here's my line." He looked down at his script. "Listen, listen! This is what I say to my dad. Blah, blah, something, something, where is it? Hal defends himself here. Let's see, I just read it. He says his dad has listened to false reports about him. He isn't as bad as everyone says he is. They're spreading rumors, which, um, here it is, which *oft the ear of greatness,"* here Harry smiled and pointed to himself, "That's me!" Then he looked back at his script, "Um, where was I? Which *oft the ear of greatness needs must hear by smiling pickthanks, and base newsmongers."* Harry finished with a look of triumph. "That's Reed, sir. A base newsmonger."

"No, Wales. This is entirely a UK show. Reed is with the Americans."

"No, he's not sir. He's got his own tent. He doesn't even sleep with them. Let him sleep with us. He's not bad looking,

is he, sir?"

Here the men, delighted, sent up a loud cry, "Wo-ah!" followed by laughter. The sergeant major took a step back and frowned. Mustafa looked dismayed. Andrew crossed his arms. Cindy was thrown off balance and taken by surprise.

*

Cindy turned on her heel and was about to walk out of the tent.

Harry saw Reed didn't like it and tried to get him to stop. He held out his arms. "Aw, come back, darlin'. I were only jokin', weren't I?"

This produced more laughs from the men, which Cindy imagined were directed at her. She didn't often worry about her disguise slipping. One-on-one with the other guys, she could count on her innate tom-boyish tendencies to keep her covered. However, she didn't trust herself to trade insult for insult with Harry in front of an audience. Trying to reply with something stinging and funny might make her mask slip. Better to avoid it. Anyway, she couldn't think of anything to say. She reached up her hand to move away the tent flap that stood in the way of her exit.

"Come on, Reed. Everyone thinks you're hot. It's not only me."

"Wo-ah!" cried the men again.

This made Cindy mad enough to wheel around and face them all.

"If any of you guys ever watched the news, you'd know that there was an attack on a British aid group today. In Kabul."

Andrew did follow the news closely, but he hadn't heard this. "What?"

"Two aid workers killed in Kabul and more injured. It was on CNN an hour ago."

"Who?" Andrew looked alarmed. "What aid group?"

"They haven't released names yet. It was at a checkpoint. Meanwhile, look at you. The UK forces are putting on a play. That's what I'll have to tell him when my producer asks for a report from out here."

The men looked back at her wide-eyed for a moment. They felt their commander had exposed them to a justifiable attack from the American reporter. While she had their attention, Cindy decided to continue. She felt humiliated. She hit back hard.

"Oh and another thing. I'd also wire in that the UK press agreed to a demand from the royal family to be muzzled. A curbing of press freedom. And what won't the UK press report? That some rich kid is out in Afghanistan wasting the UK taxpayers' money. Keeping the guys happy with stupid jokes. At the cost of who knows how many thousands a day. Pretending to be an officer, but not doing such a great impersonation."

The men listened to this and didn't know what to think. They partly agreed with what Reed had said. He'd put into words what had been only unspoken dissatisfaction on their

part. They didn't like having to be given special orders about Harry. They didn't like the royal family having more money than them. They didn't want it coming out of their pockets in tax. On the other hand, Reed was a Yank. They were all British. It didn't matter if they were formally allies. They didn't like his being critical of England. It was okay if *they* described the performance of the British army as shambolic. They didn't like it when a foreigner did it. Wordlessly, they felt more knit together by Reed's speech than they'd felt before.

Harry's ears burned too. "Look here, mate," he started in without thinking. "I guess you think you're better than us. You probably are. But don't climb on your high horse just because you're some kind of journalist. You lot are rubbish and you know it. Worse than rubbish. The UK press print lies every day about what I'm up to. If they're taking a break while I'm out here, well, I call that the first time they've told the truth."

Cindy crossed her arms and looked unimpressed.

"And that's not all. You think CNN's so special? You think CNN's all about protecting what? Democracy? You think CNN didn't try to buy those pictures off the guys on the motorbikes? Under the *Pont de l'Alma*? You're wrong, that's what. CNN had round the clock coverage, didn't they? And that brought in millions from advertisers, didn't it? What's that on your hands, Reed?"

After this Harry strode away from the front of the room. He went back to sit with some of the men on the trestle tables at the back. He was red in the face and he wouldn't look anyone in the eye. His rusty hair looked electric and hot to the touch. None of the British guys in the room would look at him either. They were all incredulous. They were shocked

and embarrassed that he should even mention his mother's death. They'd had no idea that Reed was going to push him to go that far. Even Andrew looked at the floor. The man Harry was sitting next to on the table didn't dare touch him with his hand. Instead, he kicked him lightly sideways with his boot. It was a kick of approval. "It's okay, mate," is what the kick meant. Harry did not kick back.

"Well, now," said Andrew, recovering himself and stepping forward with some dignity. "No, I didn't know about the attack in Kabul, Reed. I'd appreciate it if you'd brief me later. In the meantime," he said deepening his voice to suit the occasion, "I think some hasty things have been said just now. On both sides. And it's in all of our best interests to be on good terms with one another. Don't you think so, Reed? Don't you, Wales?"

Neither one replied to him. Both hung their heads and refused to meet any eyes. Cindy had been stung by what Harry had said. She took her job seriously. She had no doubt that what she did was a public service. She believed that a free press was critical to the health of a functioning democracy. She had never in her life thought of what she did as in any way related to those guys on motorbikes chasing Diana. She understood that there was no way she could reply to what he'd said, but she felt at the same time both ashamed and furious.

"If you'll forgive me sir," began Mustafa.

"Yes, Khan, what is it?"

"If I recall correctly, *Henry IV* has in it a young rival of Hal. Hotspur."

"Yes, that's right, Khan. The two of them have a fight at the end of Part One. What about them?"

"Well, perhaps if we rehearsed a scene between Hal and Hotspur, with Reed agreeing to read Hotspur, it might improve everyone's mood." He hoped to play peacemaker. He wanted his friend to feel better, but there was also something self-defeating in his suggestion. He said it with a shade of concealed martyrdom. Mustafa really wanted to be chosen to read a part with Harry himself.

"What an excellent idea, Khan. Yes, why don't we?"

Andrew hurried over to his papers on the table and extracted two pages of script. He came back to where Cindy was standing and said "Now, Reed. Will you humor me a moment?"

Cindy didn't know what to say. She didn't know how to extricate herself from the situation. She couldn't leave the tent now. She was stuck. Reluctantly she looked up at Andrew who was older than her, a high-ranking officer, and addressing her reasonably.

"Yes. That's it," he said taking her look as her agreement. "Thank you. Now, Wales, I wonder whether you'd come up here again and play a scene with Reed?"

Harry stayed seated looking down at the floor. The man next to him kicked him lightly on the boot again. A broad voice on the other side of the room called out, "C'mon 'Arry." Everyone turned around and looked at him. He wouldn't acknowledge them.

"Um," said Cindy in a small voice. "I'm sorry for what I said. Maybe, I mean, I think I went too far."

"Come on, mate," said the man sitting next to Harry. "Did you hear that? Reed apologized. He might even stand us all a pint later. Don't mess it up for us." Here his shyness fell away

and he did put his hand on Harry's shoulder.

Harry shrugged away from the man's hand, but he also slid off the table and on to his feet. A cheer went up and some uneven applause. Harry came to the front of the room and stood next to Reed while still refusing to meet anyone's eyes. He looked resentful and unwilling.

"Now, Reed, you're Hotspur, and your name happens also to be Harry," said the colonel. "There's going to be a fight between you and Hal. This is what you say. Begin right here at *Harry to Harry*."

Cindy took up the script Andrew had given her and read at the place he'd pointed out. "*Harry to Harry shall, hot horse to horse, meet and ne'er part till one drop down a corse.*" She read it in a lifeless monotone, unlike her news-reading voice.

"What's a *corse* then, sir?" called out the man who'd been sitting next to Harry.

"A dead body," answered the colonel. "A corpse. Hotspur's saying that when he meets Hal they'll fight to the death."

"Oooh," said several men together, making light of the situation, but also impressed that Shakespeare should have come up with such a surprisingly high-stakes encounter.

"Now, let's do it again, Reed, shall we?" suggested Andrew. "But put a little life into it this time, all right?"

Cindy looked at Harry standing next to her. His shoulders were slumped. His ears were pink. There was more red than usual in his cheeks. If she reached up with two knuckles to touch him, it looked as if she might burn her fingers. She cleared her throat, and re-read the lines. When she came to "hot," she thought of his cheeks. "*Harry to Harry shall,* hot *horse to horse, meet and ne'er part till one drop down a corse.*"

The men heard the emphasis in the way Reed had said "hot" and roared, once again, "Wo-ah!"

*

That evening, Harry was at his table inside the guardroom filling out paperwork. One of his men had just come inside after patrolling the perimeter of the camp. He felt a bit friendlier to Harry than he had before the rehearsal. Since Harry's outburst, and behind his back, a few of them had started referring to him as "The Loot," or "The Goods," or "His Royal Highnuts."

"Pardon my saying so, sir."

"What is it?"

"It's okay if you're gay, sir."

"What!"

"Cause I think Reed likes you, sir. I mean it was obvious to me."

"For fuck's sake!"

"Ooh, don't let the sergeant major hear you saying that, sir. He'll give us all the what for."

"No. I. Am. Not. Okay? Get that through your pinhead."

"Well, you did go to an all-boys school, didn't you, sir?"

"What's that got to do with it?"

"I did a few months for shoplifting. You know? On the inside. Before I joined the army. It was like that in prison. You know? Everyone was a little that way. It's natural, sir."

"Eton is not a prison."

"Well, there are some certain dissimilarities. If you ask me, sir."

"You mean similarities."

"What, sir?"

Harry was suddenly tired. "You mean Eton and prison are similar, not dissimilar."

"That's what I said, sir."

Harry rolled his eyes and sat back in his chair.

"And another thing, sir ..."

To stop the man from talking, he leaned forward in his chair and tore a piece of scrap paper off a pad. "Look here. There are no more other things. I want you to do me a favor. Could you please run a note for me? Over to Reed?" He scribbled two lines on the scrap paper, folded it and handed it to the man standing next to his desk.

"A favor, sir?"

"It's an order. Take this to Reed in his tent right now, please."

"Is it a love note, sir?"

Harry jumped to his feet as if he were about to hit him. The man rushed out of the guardroom door before Harry could swing.

Twenty minutes later Cindy came through the guardroom door already talking. Her camouflage uniform was immaculate. Her hair was neatly tucked under the service cap. She had her sunglasses on.

"Look. I don't work for you. So in future I don't just show up if you send me some stupid note."

"I'm not gay."

"I never said you were."

"Don't get any ideas. Just back off, okay?"

She stood back and looked at him for a minute. She was at first baffled, and then sly. "Why are you going out of your way to deny it then?"

"I'm not."

"Sure you are. You called me over for a special meeting to deny it."

Harry put his hands on his hips and thrust out his chest. He hoped that he looked intimidating. "Look. No one in my whole life has ever accused me of being gay."

"Accused, huh? Being gay is something you're guilty of?"

"Another thing. There's no way I'm ever going to change what I think. About journalists. That goes back a long way. So don't even try. You and me are never gonna be mates, or anything like that."

"I never said we were."

"And if you want to run with the crap you said about me, just go ahead. You can bust me if you want to. Tell everyone I'm here. Go ahead. They'll send me back to the UK. You can get your big story. Can't you? It'll get you a big promotion. That'll up your pay packet, won't it?"

"Wait a fucking minute."

"Keep it clean, Reed."

"Take your head out of your ass."

Harry relaxed perceptibly. "Oooh."

"I don't report that kind of shit. They may like to read that

in the trashy papers they have in little old England. But it's not serious journalism."

"I think there are respected organs of the press in your great big country too, aren't there Reed? Let's see *Us Magazine, The National Enquirer* ..."

"You may read that stuff, but I don't. I don't know, maybe you even comb through it to see if they printed your name. That probably gives you a thrill, doesn't it? Pathetic."

"What'd you say? Serious journalism? That's a joke. You think what you do is different from the tabloids? You've got to find a story that gives your audience a hard on, don't you? That's how it works. So you twist what you find till it fits, don't you? Till it increases your ratings. And for that you get to wear a shiny badge. Guardian of Freedom. Defender of Free Speech. When actually you guys are all frauds."

"Fine, wise guy. And what are you supposed to be in that uniform? Her Majesty's defender of freedom? A lieutenant because of who he was born instead of merit? Now there's a little irony don't you think? Here we are supposed to be giving Afghanistan alternatives to the Taliban. Showing them about equality between the sexes and merit pay and transparency. When you're just about the opposite of all those things."

The soldier who'd been doing guard duty earlier stepped into the guardroom from outdoors. He overheard the last of what Reed had said and saw the expression on Harry's face.

"Pardon me, sir. Is this what gay guys do when they're not sleeping together? Cause it sounds like a right old catfight to me." Harry took two angry steps toward him. The soldier put up his arms to defend his head. Then he said hurriedly, "Colonel Arbuthnot wants to see you both, sir."

*

Frances had not been in the convoy of aid vehicles that had been attacked at a roadside checkpoint in Kabul. The effect of the incident, however, was to stop all foot traffic to local shops and restaurants. Everyone at the interfaith charity had been permitted before simply to walk out the door. They were all now confined to the group's compound. As this was nothing more than a series of narrow rooms off a dusty courtyard, and as new travel restrictions reduced the number of army personnel who came to visit them, it quickly became boring. To Frances it was intolerable. She liked to be active at all times. Occupation reduced the pains of her rheumatism and the workings of her guilty conscience. With nothing to do, she was thrown back on her own resources. She tried reading a thriller, but she wasn't much of a reader. She tried knitting woolen socks, but she found that her swollen knuckles could no longer manipulate the knitting needles as they once had. She tried cleaning out the chapel they used for services, but the old straw broom she found raised more dust than it swept away. She'd poured out in the sink all the airline-sized bottles of whiskey she'd brought with her. She was wondering whether that wasn't a bit premature. How could she get some more?

That was when she said to herself, "Enough!" She telephoned over to the British Embassy. She decided she'd no longer keep up the pretense of knowing no one and having no

connections. On the basis of her accent and her self-assurance alone, she was put through to the ambassador. She asked him whether he knew that the man who was speaking on behalf of the Foreign Office in the House of Lords was a cousin of her former husband. Funnily enough, he didn't know that. Nevertheless, she was able to use that to be connected to a defense attaché who could tell her where Andrew Arbuthnot was stationed. He refused to divulge the exact location, but he did give her a telephone number. She called from the office of the interfaith charity. She was at first put on to the Americans. They transferred her to several different places where she had to ask for him again. It wasn't until about the fourth try that a voice came on the line and said, "Arbuthnot here." He said it Ar-BUTH-not.

"Ah, Andrew. At last."

"Mrs. de Mornay!" He said it duh-MOR-nee. "What a lovely surprise. But how did you get this number?"

"I was so bored. Your not answering my letter, of course. I decided to pull some strings. You left me no choice."

"No, no, madam. It was you. You didn't answer my letter."

"I did answer your letter."

"Oh really? Well, it never turned up. Perhaps you didn't stick enough postage on."

"I was told just to put it in a basket on the hall table. I didn't think first class postage stamps worked out here."

"No, you're right. They don't." He paused and then came up with an explanation that should have diminished his own distress, had he only thought of it before. "The bags sometimes go astray, you know."

"No, I didn't know."

"What'd this letter say?" asked Andrew. "You've got me curious now. Did I miss something? It sounds rather sensational."

"Oh, rather," she purred, feeling it was a long time since she'd flirted with anyone on the telephone.

Andrew heard her tone of voice and couldn't stop his smile from expanding foolishly across his face. Then he thought he heard someone coming in the tent behind him. He swung around in his chair. He looked at the tent flap. No one.

"Look here Mrs. de Mornay ..."

"Oh, Andrew. Don't you think it's time you started saying Frances? We've known each other such a long time."

Andrew softened. "Frances."

"That's right. Now that wasn't hard. Was it?"

"No, um, it wasn't." Andrew was confused. What had he meant to say? Then he remembered. "Look here, Frances. This isn't a secure line. We mustn't, um, carry on like this. Discuss anything confidential, I mean."

"I haven't divulged any secrets, have I?"

"No, you haven't. But in case you were going to. I just thought it might be as well to warn you."

"Thank you, Andrew."

To him this sounded a bit more cool, as if she didn't like being rebuked. He tried to get things back on friendlier terms. "We were all so worried. When we heard about the aid group's being attacked."

"Oh yes. Frightful."

"I thought you might have been with them, you see?"

"Well, I wasn't. I'm fine. The result's been, though, that we're all confined to base now. And none of our usual, well,

how shall I call them? None of our usual clients can get through. So there's not much for us to do."

"Oh, I see," said Andrew sympathetically. "Not so different from here. I can't go into details. But not a great deal happening. That's all that can be said."

"Well, I'm relieved. I must say. Two of my favorite soldiers in no danger whatsoever. Very glad to hear it."

Andrew smiled again. He could scarcely recall a time when she'd been this warm. He swiveled around in his chair to make sure there was no one there to eavesdrop on the conversation. "We can't go into that Frances. Not on this line. Just to say he's fine."

"Which one?"

"You know which one I mean."

"Do I?"

"The younger one I mean."

"Oh, both of them are considerably younger than me. I'm an old lady."

"Some younger men like that kind of thing, you know?"

"What? What? You're breaking down, Andrew. What'd you say?"

"It's breaking *up*, Frances. When you can't hear what's been said. On the telephone. Not breaking down."

"Now I can hear you perfectly. This is the useful thing about having young friends, you see? They keep you up to date on all the lingo."

A pencil rolled off a desk behind him and hit the floor with a tap. Andrew rolled around in his chair to see where it had fallen. He couldn't see it. As he looked he put in, "Well, he's fine. I mean the other one you're curious about."

"Good."

"Except that he's tangled with that reporter we have here. The American. Embedded with us."

"Oh, he won't like that."

"He doesn't."

"Neither he nor his brother like them. Actually it's too light a word. They hate them."

"Well, naturally, I can understand why."

"Can you, Andrew? He was twelve when she died. You don't recover from that. Superficially, of course, you go on. But down deep ..."

Andrew tried to interrupt her gently. "Frances, I don't think we should say any more ..."

This wasn't a conversational flow she could easily stop. She'd thought and worried about it for a long time. How could she help them? Some maternal feeling in her ached. Perhaps it was a muscle that had never been exercised enough. "The bark of a tree grows around a steel spike, but the spike is still there. You mustn't forget that."

"I won't, Frances, but we really must say no more."

"All right, Andrew, I won't."

In the background she heard, "What in the devil? Who are you? How'd you get in here?" There was a crash, and then the sound of what might have been furniture turning over. She wasn't sure what it was.

"Andrew? Andrew!"

Then a voice came over the phone. It was a foreign voice, but the accent had been acquired from learning British English in school. "I'm sorry. Colonel Arbuthnot is indisposed."

"Who are you!"

"And just to add, there is no reason for confidentiality. We are well aware Prince Hari is in the camp. He is next. Goodbye."

Part III

Reward for the Capture of Harry ibn Windsor al-Wales

As soon as Colonel Arbuthnot's absence was discovered, and the alarm was raised, Harry and Mustafa made straight for the tent of the American commander of the camp. He was now, by default, their senior officer. Harry felt they had to do this right away, though he also felt out of his depth. He'd never been outside the British chain of command. Now he wasn't quite sure what to do. He took along Mustafa for support and they made their way through a thicket of American adjutants who barred their way. No one wanted to deal with him. The camp was going through its first real emergency, an attack that highlighted their vulnerability. The adjutants thought it was more interesting to look at him and share a joke with him when there hadn't been an incident that exposed how close they all were to real danger.

The Texan commander was less put out by what had

happened than his adjutants were. He chewed on a cigar and that helped to keep him calm. He also had a saber in his hand. His grandfather had had it in World War Two. His father had had it in Vietnam. He'd had it himself on an earlier tour of duty in Iraq. The saber had been through much worse than the disappearance of a lone Brit officer, even if he was fairly senior and even if the camp's two fences had both been cut without any of the guards noticing. He sat cantilevered back in his desk chair, saber pointed and propped on the floor as if it were a cane, while chewing his unlit cigar.

"At ease, boys," he said to the two junior officers saluting in front of his desk.

"Sir!" said Harry, searching for the words. Why wouldn't they come? Why was he so stupid? "The thing is. Um. We. Well, Lieutenant Khan and I ..." A bead of sweat fell down his naked side underneath his tunic.

"Spit it out, boy. I'm waiting."

"It's just that. Well. Khan and I. We want to go after him. We need to go find Colonel Arbuthnot, sir." As the American still sat unperturbed in his desk chair, Harry added, "We have to!"

"He might be dead."

"What?"

"The Taliban and the local militias don't put too fine a point on a thing like that. Whoever did it. They'll take a human head off quicker 'n an Abilene slaughterhouse'll put a peg in the head of steer."

"Sir!"

"I'm just sayin' boys. We gotta be realistic."

"We want to go out and find him, sir."

"Go out. Go out where?"

"Follow their tracks, sir. Find where they're holding him."

"Follow their tracks? Are you kiddin' me? They came here in broad daylight. Did a surgical cut of the fence. Didn't touch any stuff in our arms depot. Didn't lay a hand on the choppers. Extracted their man practically with kid gloves so no one noticed. And made a getaway without anyone seeing them. What tracks? They didn't leave any tracks, knucklehead."

Harry had been called a knucklehead, or its equivalent, plenty of times before. His father had said it. Sergeant majors had said it. Teachers in his different schools had all said it. This was the first time an American had said it. He didn't like it. It was the first thing since the colonel's disappearance that steeled his resolve. It suddenly made him angry and serene.

"You propose to do nothing then, sir?"

"I'm gonna do plenty, boy. It's not your job to tell me what. Cause it's my god damned command not yours." Here he picked up the saber with alarming speed, flashed it through the air, and brought it down on the edge of the wooden desk. Bang. A chip of wood flew threw the air and landed on the floor.

Harry and Mustafa both jumped.

"And another thing. Andrew Arbuthnot and I were buddies. I liked that man. The god damned civilians back home gave him a helluva job to do. Here he was a decorated soldier. On his second tour of duty in this hellhole. And they give him you to take care of."

Mustafa looked straight ahead, but Harry couldn't stop himself from wavering a little at this.

"That's right. That's god damned right. You should be

ashamed of yourself."

Harry would not normally have answered back in an encounter with a superior officer, but this man who'd called him a knucklehead had touched a nerve. "Well, it won't be for much longer, sir. Your side is about to send me back to England."

"What the hell you talkin' 'bout, boy?"

"The American reporter. Reed, sir. He's as good as promised to blow my cover. They'll send me back as soon as he does. You won't have me to worry about much longer, sir."

"That's what Nixon said. Later on, he was president."

"What?"

"Get this through your thick head, soldier. CNN is not a department of the Pentagon. Reed don't work for me. He's here on sufferance. Don't you know yet how the god damned media works? They'll kick up a stink and make up stories about how bad the war's goin' if we don't let them put reporters out here with us."

"I know that, sir."

The American commander heard the change in the young man's tone. It was as if he'd finally got through to him. Something else occurred to him that made him pause. It almost made him forget that he was angry with the young lieutenant. "That Reed's a strange one. Don't you think? He's kind of a girlie boy, wouldn't you say?"

Here Mustafa dropped his eyes and blushed. Harry gave him a sidelong glance. They'd both been through long hours of British army training workshops about how to deal with gay soldiers under their command. Harry felt it was incumbent on him to interrupt. "If you'll allow me to say a word, sir? You

shouldn't say girlie boy. That's homophobic. Sir."

"I can say whatever I want, boy!" The American's anger had returned. "Do I have to remind you both that Reed's not a soldier? He may wear the duds, but he isn't under my command. Or yours. And the UK army's god damned political correctness don't apply here!"

Harry and Mustafa looked straight ahead without making eye contact.

"But I'm a tolerant man," resumed the American, softening, and saying the word as if it were spelled "tollrunt." He looked upwards. "It's not my problem if the whole leftwing media's full of homos."

Harry cleared his throat.

"All right. I hear you. You two boys are dismissed. I will keep you informed. Your job now is to go back to the UK side and keep 'em calm. Don't let 'em have any kind of limey meltdown. In the meantime, we'll need you both on extra guard duty while the fence is repaired."

"What good will that do, sir?"

"Dismissed!" The American commander whacked the desktop again with his saber. Another chip flew into the air. Harry and Mustafa saluted hurriedly, wheeled, and left the tent.

They both walked across the camp more slowly than they'd left the American commander's tent.

"What do we do now?" asked Mustafa.

"We go after him."

"What?"

"Like I said."

"He just said not to. What'll happen if he catches us? What'll

Colonel Arbuthnot's higher-ups in Kabul say?"

Harry said nothing for several paces. Then he sighed. The decision came to him as a relief. Doing something felt better than doing nothing. It felt better than hunkering down and waiting for the next thing to hit.

"I don't care what they say. I'm going to look for him. You're coming with me, mate."

*

Harry and Mustafa hadn't quite managed to make it back to their own tent when an American figure in camouflage fatigues came around a corner and joined in step with them.

"You're going after him, aren't you?"

"Reed! This isn't a game. Not anymore. Get the fuck out of here," said Harry.

"You've got to go after him. It's like a point of honor, right?"

Harry stopped and swung around to look at Reed. He planted his feet. "Don't make me laugh."

"I don't expect you to understand what the news is all about."

Harry was stony faced.

Cindy decided to confess. "Look. I'll tell you something true, okay? Being out here is my chance, right? They didn't

want to send me. I had to hold the producer at the end of, well, like the end of a knife. And he gave in. For a limited time. He let me be here. But I've sent back nothing. Worse than nothing. He's even stopped answering my emails. I've pretty much blown it."

Both Harry and Mustafa looked at her, frowning and unmoved.

"And this is a story. No doubt about it. This is a fucking story. Senior British officer kidnapped. This is the story they'll air no matter what. That's why I want you to take me with you."

"Spare me, Reed." Harry wheeled away from her and started walking off. Mustafa skipped around and followed him after a moment's surprised hesitation.

Cindy came running after them. "And it's in your own best interest to let me tell it." Harry and Reed kept walking. "Here's how the media works. You've gotta barter. If you give me an exclusive on this, if you give CNN an exclusive on this, they'll think you're in a relationship with them. They'll guard you from the other media outlets. They won't let anyone near you. You'll be their baby."

Harry stopped again. "You amaze me, Reed. You want CNN to have rights to the rest of my life?"

"No! I'm not asking for that. But if you give me an exclusive on this, the network'll think they can get rights to more. At the very least it'll buy you some time. Out of the glare. That's not nothing. Not in your shoes."

Harry didn't have a reply to that.

"And here's the other thing. They've already got a story for you. You go to Halloween parties and wear Nazi uniforms.

You get drunk and kick out windows. You've got a series of bimbo girlfriends. That's what they decided was your story a long time ago. All you've done so far is play into their hands. You read the lines they wrote for you. Now's your chance to break out of it."

"What do you mean?"

"Now's your chance to do something hard. Now's your chance to man up. And none of the UK media's gonna be there to see it. If they don't see it, it's like a bear shit in the woods. Nobody knows. If I'm there, everybody knows."

"They've already told me and Khan we can't go out after the colonel. If we do go, against orders, we'll be court martialled. CNN will love that, won't they?"

"Really?" said Mustafa, who hadn't imagined it would go all the way to that.

"Well," said Cindy, "that's the risk you take. If you do choke, at least it'll be the truth. At least it'll be a story you made yourself and no one made for you. Everyone'll be disappointed. They might admire you for trying."

Harry and Mustafa turned around more slowly this time and re-commenced striding toward their tent. They didn't object when Cindy fell in step with them. When they all three got inside, Harry sat down and lay back on his unmade bed. After he was flat, he crossed his arms over his chest and stared upward. Mustafa sat down more gingerly on a chair. Cindy wandered tentatively over to the other bed, almost as if she expected they might still chase her out. She looked at the folded army comforter with an elaborately patterned rug placed on top. "Wow. Nice carpet. Where's this from?"

"Tabriz," answered Mustafa without further explanation.

He wasn't happy Reed had followed them into their tent.

"What about these tiles?" Cindy asked of some fragments of brightly-colored architectural ornaments on the bedside table.

"Just some old junk he dragged back from the bazaar," said Harry, still staring at the top of the tent.

"They are from a fourteenth-century minaret. Of a mosque," said Mustafa. "It was destroyed. And the warlord is selling off the remains to European museums. I got a few pieces in the market."

"Cool. And this?" She said pointing to the oil-burning lamp. "It's beautiful. It looks old."

"It is," answered Mustafa. "Hellenistic."

"Wow," she said.

"It's just a load of old rubbish," sighed Harry. "It's not going to get the colonel back."

"You've gotta get one of those patrol vehicles, right? Something with some armor. And some guys for back up?" suggested Cindy.

"The press isn't here to tell us what to do," said Harry, not exactly angry, but not pleased either. "We're not getting any of the guys involved. It'll be bad enough for us if we get caught. It's not our job to make it bad for them too."

Mustafa said nothing to Harry. He was still eyeing Cindy suspiciously.

"I've got it," said Harry brightening. "We ask your Dad's cousin. You know, that guy in the village. The one you went to meet."

"I don't think that's a good idea," said Mustafa.

"Why not?"

"I don't know." Mustafa didn't like exposing a family member. He'd felt obligated to accept the lamp, but he disliked the warlord's exploitation of precious relics. He didn't like telling either of them the whole story. "He's probably being paid by the army on one side. Then he's selling stuff that should be in a proper archaeological dig on the other. And maybe taking some local bribes too. Is that somebody you want to trust? To get back the colonel?"

"Sounds like the right guy to me," said Cindy.

"You just convinced me!" said Harry leaping off his bed and heading for the tent flap.

"What?" asked Mustafa, who realized too late that he should have prevented Harry going anywhere near his father's cousin.

"He's our man," said Harry ducking outside.

*

Frances had managed to borrow some clothes from some of the other aid workers when she arrived. She had on a pair of clean dungarees, a blouse she'd pressed with an iron she found in the nun's cupboard, and a white silk scarf, long and wide enough to wrap around her head and cover her hair if required. She had no wish to offend Afghan sensibilities about

modest dress for women, but she hadn't a skirt to wear. She was alarmed by what she'd heard on the phone and she felt it was urgent to let the authorities know. She'd telephoned and been put through to the ambassador again, but this time he'd refused to give her any information about the whereabouts of Colonel Arbuthnot. He told her he was wrong to have let her be put through to him in the first place. Then he said "Goodbye" curtly, and disengaged the line.

She was not intimidated. She'd have to go to the embassy. She knew something was terribly wrong. She managed a ride to the embassy compound in the car of the director of the interfaith charity. The director of the charity managed to get her through the outer guard post and past the policeman at the door of the embassy, where he had left her. She could not get past the desk of the ambassador's personal assistant.

"I'm afraid, madam, it will be impossible for you to see him," she said and signaled an end to the conversation by returning to her keyboard and consulting her computer screen.

"But he's an old chum." A harmless fib, Frances reflected. "I spoke to him just this morning." That was true.

"Without an appointment, there's nothing I can do."

"I promise not to stay longer than five minutes."

"His diary is booked solidly for the whole day."

It was this moment that the ambassador chose to peek out of his room in order to see if the coast were clear. He wanted to dash out to visit the loo in the corridor. He did find that the cuisine of the embassy's Pathan chef led to these kind of unexpected emergencies.

"Ambassador!" Frances was not sure he was the ambassador, but she guessed that the door behind the assistant led to his

office.

"I'm sorry. Have we met? My memory for names and faces is terrible. I'm sure I'm in the wrong business." He smiled, despite the urgency of his other mission.

"This is Mrs. de Mornay. She doesn't have an appointment," said the assistant.

"Ah, Mrs. de Mornay, of course. We've spoken on the telephone."

"How kind you've been to me. How much kinder than you should have been!" said Frances coming around the desk, taking his arm, and leading him back into his office. She shut the door firmly behind them.

Inside there was a long mahogany table with turned legs. There was a worn Persian rug on the floor. There was a portrait of the queen on the wall. There were two chintz-covered sofas. It looked more like a sitting room on the Surrey-Sussex border than a command post in a war zone. The ambassador crossed his legs while still standing, and leaned on the table with his hand. He knitted together his eyebrows. "Now, Mrs. de Mornay ..." he began.

"I'm worried about Andrew Arbuthnot. It's so unlike him to break off a call in that way."

"As I said earlier, it's not in my power ..."

"There is something I didn't tell you earlier."

"Oh?" He was only mildly curious. If he didn't get away soon, something appalling would happen.

"A strange voice came on the line."

"Telephone communications here are not as they are in England, Mrs. de Mornay. There are party lines. All the lines inside the military installations are monitored. Operators

break in all the time."

"This was not an operator. This was the voice of someone with a BBC accent. But not English."

"Oh?"

"One can tell, of course."

"Can one?"

"Yes. And the voice threatened Harry. It said he would be next."

The ambassador stood up straighter. "There is no official knowledge of his presence here. As far as this UK mission is concerned, he may as well be taking part in training operations on Salisbury Plain."

"Well, I'm telling you he's not. He's right here. He's with Andrew Arbuthnot. And if something has happened to Andrew, something may have happened to him too."

"I can neither confirm nor deny ..."

"I don't need your confirmation. I know it myself."

The ambassador allowed himself to look coolly at the strong-minded, white-haired woman in front of him. He let her see him for a full moment. He wanted to let her know he was no less resolute than she was. "I will confirm this. And only this. His Royal Highness is safe and still well within the perimeter of his encampment. And, now, if you don't mind ..." He looked at the door behind her.

"Thank you, ambassador. But what about Andrew Arbuthnot?"

"As I've told you before, I am not free to share operational details with civilians."

"This is not an operational detail. Andrew Arbuthnot practically grew up in my house. He is a son to me." Another

white lie, Frances reflected, won't hurt. Then she thought of something that would clinch the matter. "He swam in my pool as a boy!"

The only way to get rid of her was to tell her the truth. He had to get rid of her right away. "Andrew Arbuthnot has been captured."

As much as Frances suspected this was the case, she couldn't stop herself from an intake of breath.

"But that fact is not generally known. We are not sharing it with the media. As you might guess, if it were reported that a commander of Arbuthnot's seniority were reported captured, it would be a significant public relations victory for the Taliban. I cannot sanction the news going beyond this office."

"But is he all right? What's happened to him? Has there been a ransom demanded? Who's going out to get him back?"

"That's out of my hands. The Americans are in greater numbers out there. The decision and the tactic will rest with them."

"But he belongs to us! Surely a British force will go out to rescue him."

"Mrs. de Mornay! There is a division between the civilian and the military authorities out here. The UK armed forces keep their own counsel. It's not up to me. I'm only telling you—what I should not—but I have so there we are. Practically speaking, it's up to the Americans."

"Will you lend me a car, please, ambassador? And a driver."

The ambassador couldn't help his amusement at this, even though his situation was critical. He came back up from having bent over double, partly in laughter, partly in pain.

Impending embarrassment overlay both. "No."

"Thank you. That's so kind. I'll have it back to you in no time."

"Mrs. de Mornay, I said no."

"Yes, I quite understand. I'll be careful."

"I really must step away now." A desperate set of creases wrinkled his forehead. "Something rather extraordinary at luncheon."

"Why didn't you say so?" She came over to him with genuine concern and took his arm again. "Come along, I'll help. Slowly! We don't want any accidents. Do we?" She led him back through the door. He hobbled along beside her. He couldn't stand now on his own if he'd wanted to. When they got to the assistant's desk, Frances asked him, "Where to now?"

"Down that corridor," he said in a strangled voice and indicated a hallway to the left. He was holding his breath. "That way."

"I see. Now easy does it." She led him part way around the assistant's desk before saying to the seated young woman. "By the way, the ambassador would like for me to have a car and a driver."

The ambassador by this time was pulling on Frances's arm to indicate they must go forward and there was no time to stop.

Frances stood still and pulled him back. "Isn't that right, ambassador?"

He looked up with an agony that, being British, he was able mainly to hide. "Please," he said. Nevertheless, he was *in extremis*. His forehead was damp with the effort. He used

a breathless voice to his assistant, "Oh god. Whatever she wants."

"Thank you," said Frances. "Now be careful. I can see the door. It's only ten paces. At most. I'm sure you can make it. Come along. Lean on me."

＊

Andrew Arbuthnot was sitting in a guestroom of the Kabul Hilton. Its picture window had a panoramic view of the distant mountains. He happened to have had a pocket-sized book that included both of the *Henry IV* plays in his fatigues when he was taken. So he was sitting contentedly next to the window. He was reading with sunshine coming in on the page. It was an ordinary room, painted a dusty pink. Polyester floral quilts had been imported from a disused Hilton in Indianapolis. There was a big television, but no mini-bar. There was a wooden crate of assault weapons along one of the walls and a hookah sitting on the desk. Prayer rugs were stored under the mattresses of the beds. There were chains on Andrew's ankles.

A key scraped in the outer door's lock for several moments. Then there were thuds and thumps against the door. Suddenly, the door burst open with a bang and hit the adjacent wall. A

young man with a black beard came in, his head covered with a flat wool cap. The young man had a rifle in his hands. He brandished it at Andrew.

"And now your time is up imperialist dog! Murderer of Muslims."

"Goodness me," said Andrew, looking up without alarm from his book, "you needn't kick in the door every time. Have you never seen a lock and key before?"

Andrew's calm irritated the bearded man. "It sticks! And in Helmand the door is opened for me by hosts of my own people, who bow to my every wish."

"Well, if you knocked, I'd be happy to open it for you. But as you see, that's impossible." Andrew lifted up his ankles to show his shackles.

"You cannot move? You don't like that? You are here to suffer. And then die."

"Well, then," said Andrew, laying aside his book. He was cool. "I'd get on with it if I were you."

"Don't you wish to say your prayers? Or are you like everyone else in the West? You have forgotten your god. You worship Apple. You kneel before Barclays Bank. Money is your religion. Immorality is your faith."

"You may have something there."

"What?"

"Apple is far more powerful than Downing Street. They have more resources than the World Bank. More political influence than the UN. I couldn't agree with you more."

"And that is what you're fighting for? Why you come here to oppress us? To pour gold into Mountain View, California?"

"I think they're in Cupertino, actually. That's what my

iPhone weather app is set to. The default setting I mean."

"Really? Mine says Mountain View."

"That's interesting. Yours is probably the later release date."

The bearded man took the phone out of his pocket and brought it over to show to Andrew.

"Oh, yes," said Andrew. "Yours is much slimmer than mine. I haven't replaced mine in ages."

The bearded man looked at his phone with renewed appreciation. Then he remembered. "None of your tricks, dog! You have to die anyway." He pointed his gun at Andrew's chest.

"Oh well, then."

"There is only one hope for your release."

"What's that?"

"Tell me where you are hiding the white queen's son, Hari."

"He's not her son."

"I thought so. Your royal family eats the pig. They wallow in the mud."

"That's as may be, but he's her grandson. Not her son."

He threatened Andrew by holding the gun's muzzle closer to him. "Tell me where he is!"

"I'm afraid you're mistaken. The regiment would never send him out here. He's not one of our best soldiers, I'm afraid. He's probably somewhere in Wiltshire right now. The UK army sends out only our most experienced men to deal with the wily Afghan. We know from long experience how invincible the Afghan fighter is. It goes back more than a century. Before even Rudyard Kipling, of course."

The bearded man thought about this for a minute. He was pleased. Then, changing his mind, he leaned over and

knocked the book out of Andrew's hand on to the floor. "Don't think I will fall for your sorcery! We're not as stupid as you think! Mr. Kipling makes fish fingers!"

"No, that's not the one I meant."

"I don't care what you meant," snarled the bearded man. "Hari arrived via a British Airways triple seven aircraft leased to your army three weeks ago."

Andrew reflected that the opposition did have excellent intelligence.

"We have even," continued the bearded man, "a half-eaten packet of his crisps. He left them in the seat pocket on the plane. Sea salt and vinegar. They are now sacred."

"Oh for goodness sakes no. Not sacred in the least." Andrew chuckled. "We haven't believed in the royal touch for a long time. We used to of course. Do you know I think the last monarch who touched people in that way was Queen Anne? That was in the first quarter of the eighteenth century." Andrew leaned down. He reached over easily to pick up the volume that had been knocked out of his hand. "Now in Shakespeare's time," he said holding up the volume and showing it to his captor. "They did believe in it. They thought if the king touched you it could cure a mortal illness."

"It worked?"

"Well, I suppose it worked if you believed in it. People in those days thought that royalty had magic power. When they executed Charles I? In 1649, you know? They took off his head with an axe. The crowd rushed forward to mop up his blood with their handkerchiefs because they thought it was holy. They thought it would heal them."

"Aha! You see? The hypocrisy of the West? We are accused

of butchery. For beheading our enemies. But you cut off heads too. Just like us!"

"You have a point. Though it was a long time ago," said Andrew, nodding his head in agreement. "There's the world of this play, for example." He held up the book as if he were recommending it to an acquaintance in a bookshop. "I think you'd find it very recognizable. Kings, mullahs, and warlords compete for power. The heroes fight with swords."

The Afghan rubbed his beard. "It sounds good."

"Oh it is," said Andrew, full of renewed enthusiasm. "And another thing ..."

"Enough!" shouted the bearded man, banging the muzzle of his gun on the tabletop that held the television. "I'm not stupid! I know what you're saying. That we in Afghanistan are still lost in the history that England has left behind. I'll show you, dog."

Andrew swallowed. He said nothing.

"Lead me to Hari! Or you die. He will one day be your people's king. He will be a most valuable war prize."

"No, you're wrong about that. He's not going to be king. It's the Prince of Wales after the current sovereign dies. Then after him, Harry's brother William."

The bearded man threw his gun down on the bed. "You lie to try and save his skin! You're coming with me, dog, whether you like it or not. You will show me the way to Hari." He went down on his knees, took a small key out of his pocket, and began trying to unlock the iron rings around Andrew's ankles. "We know better than you what will happen. Hari's father will never be king."

"The Prince of Wales? That's absurd. Of course he will."

"Do you think so? Nine out of ten readers of *The Mail on*

Sunday want Hari to be king. Their opinion poll was posted online. Didn't you see it?" He continued to struggle with the locks and the small key.

"You may well be right. Stranger things have happened to our royal family. But, look here," said Andrew wearily. "Why don't you give me that key? Let me do it."

The bearded man sat back balanced on his knees and toes. He handed over the tiny key. Andrew leaned down and released first the right lock, then the left, with a single twist of his wrist. "There we are." Then he stood up and bent over to give the kneeling man the key. When he reached out to take back the key, Andrew pulled him over with a swift and abrupt clasp of the hand. He fell forward on the floor. Then Andrew vaulted over him and grabbed the gun that was lying on the floral bedspread. He wheeled around and pointed the gun at the bearded man who was still sprawled on the floor.

"And now," said Andrew, "we may *ne'er part till one drop down a corse.*"

*

Mustafa consented to take Harry and Cindy to visit his father's cousin because he couldn't think what else to suggest. He had a pass that gave him leave to go visit the village at a distance

beyond the camp's fences where the warlord lived. His special accreditation with the intelligence services allowed him to take Harry and Cindy with him. The three of them followed a path among dry grasses that bordered a river. They had a thirty-minute hike before they reached the village.

"This could be Scotland now," said Harry cheerfully as they walked. "That purple color in the mountains is just like heather."

"It's not Scotland," said Mustafa, who was in a grim mood. "Stay on the path. There are landmines."

"Cool!" said Harry, who liked the addition of a hazard. He picked up a few rocks and threw them on to the path ahead. "Maybe this will set one off. Boom!" He laughed.

Mustafa stopped. "You idiot. It's not a silly game. It's dangerous."

Harry came up and put his arm around Mustafa's shoulder. "You worry too much, mate."

Physical contact with him pleased Mustafa, but he stepped away and out of Harry's reach. "Look! Listen to me. Will you hold on for one second?"

"What?"

Cindy looked at them curiously. She wondered for the first time what was between them.

"Here's what I didn't tell you before. They're out to get you. They know you're here."

"Really? So what?"

"Don't you see? They must've been coming to get you. In the camp. And they couldn't find you. So they took the colonel instead."

Harry became a shade more serious. Cindy took a small

notebook out of her pocket and made a note with the stub of a pencil.

"So that's why we shouldn't go to the village. That's why I was trying to stop you. My father's cousin is in on it. If I take you to his house, it's like I'll be delivering you to him. I mean he's not Taliban. But he certainly knows where they are. He's in touch with them. He'll hand you over."

Cindy and Harry exchanged a glance.

Mustafa stood in the middle of the path barring their way forward. "Let's turn around and go back now. If they take you in the village, the situation doesn't get better, it gets worse."

"Don't be so wet," said Harry shouldering by Mustafa.

"Yeah," agreed Cindy, "too late now." She was a little anxious herself, but she thought she had to be aggressive and unafraid to keep up her disguise. She was also sure that the material they'd find in the village would be essential to her story. That was what mattered to her. She stepped around Mustafa and followed Harry down the path.

"I'm not a wimp," muttered Mustafa to himself. He turned and walked behind them, shooting angry looks at their backs.

When they arrived in the village, they found a new silvery blue Mercedes sedan outside the mud walls of the warlord's house. "I like this guy already," said Harry.

"This is the other source of his income," said Mustafa.

"What? He's a car dealer?"

"No. Opium."

"Way to go! This guy's a businessman. He's no socialist."

"So are my parents."

"What?"

"That's how my parents got out of here. Money from

opium."

"No kiddin'? And that's what got you to Stowe? And the Household Cavalry?" Harry laughed. "I love it."

Mustafa looked back at him as if to say this is not something to be proud of, but there, I've told you. He said nothing.

"Look, mate. Can you get me some?"

Mustafa went and stood by the open doorway of the house. He gave Harry a challenging look. "You want some? I've got something for you. Follow me."

They all three entered the open door. They found the warlord seated on his carpet with a laptop open on a lacquer chest in front of him. The young warrior still crouched in the corner next to the samovar. Mustafa introduced his companions. Harry went out of his way to use the lengthy and polite greetings that Mustafa had taught him. Then he said, "Sir, I hope you'll forgive me for being direct. But we wonder what you can tell us about the disappearance of our colonel."

"What would I know of this, Your Royal Highness?" said the warlord, calm and determinedly serene.

"Lieutenant Khan has told me of your wisdom. Your power. And, um, your great connections."

Here the warlord gave Mustafa an ambiguous look and blinked slowly. Then he replied, "If the British would quit Afghanistan, I'm sure your colonel would in time be returned to you. Unharmed."

Harry laughed good-humoredly. "Well, sir, you know that's not possible, now, is it? No one stays at home, now, do they? We all live in a global village, right? We're all connected to everybody else. These days London and Helmand Province are not so far apart are they? Worldwide web, 'n all that.

Know what I mean?" Here he leaned forward, snatched the warlord's open laptop off the lacquer chest and handed it to Mustafa. "What's that say then? Read it."

The warlord was surprised, taken off guard, and shocked that he should be treated this way in his own home. He struggled to reach his Kalashnikov. It was just out of his reach leaning against the wall. The young warrior at the samovar got up and was just about to grab the gun when Harry, still sitting down, grabbed the young man's foot, pulled him on to the floor, and dragged him, flailing for a grip, over the carpet. Without much effort, Harry reached over and held the young warrior's neck to his chest in a half nelson using the crook of his left elbow. "Now then," said Harry. "We'll have none of that. Pity if anything should happen to this pretty boy. How old are you, mate?"

Mustafa translated Harry's question. "Eighteen," said the young man, angry and still struggling.

"Nice eighteen-year-old boy, and, what's this? Look at 'im! Wearing some black eyeliner too?"

"Don't hurt him," said Mustafa to Harry. "That's normal. It's the custom here." Then he glanced back at the laptop.

Harry loosened his grip, so the young man was a little more comfortable, but still pinioned and unable to get away. The warlord resumed his cross-legged position with an expression that silently wished unpleasant deaths upon them all.

Mustafa began reading and translating from the email on the warlord's laptop. "*The reward for the capture of Harry ibn Windsor al-Wales has been increased to $100,000.*"

"Is that all?" said Harry smiling. "A hundred grand?" Harry turned to Cindy and said quietly. "Be a love and hand me that

weapon, would you?"

Cindy handed him the Kalashnikov and then removed a small camera from her pocket. She turned on the video function. A red light came on. She brought it to her eye and filmed Harry, the rifle in his right hand, the Afghan warrior in his left, seated on the carpet. She panned slowly over to Mustafa reading from the laptop and the warlord glaring at them all.

"Who's it from, Lieutenant Khan?" asked Harry.

"I can't tell exactly, but the email server is one used by al Qaeda in Saudi Arabia."

"See what I mean?" said Harry to the warlord. "We're all inter-connected, aren't we? Helmand and Saudi. Taliban and Qaeda. London and Kabul. German cars and Russian guns. One little world, hmm?"

The warlord said nothing.

"Well, sir, I guess we came to the right place, didn't we?" resumed Harry. He tightened his grip on the young warrior and lowered the rifle so it was pointing directly at the warlord's chest.

"Let him go," said Mustafa to Harry.

"Hang on a second, whose side are you on? He's in league with the enemy."

"Let him go." Mustafa exchanged several words with the young man in Pashto. Then he turned back to Harry. "He's not dangerous."

Harry held out his left arm and released his grip. The young warrior slid away and rubbed his neck. Then he went to sit on the carpet behind Mustafa.

"I think our friend here should take us for a little ride, don't

you, Khan?"

Mustafa looked at the warlord.

"I think he should take us all for a spin in his beautiful car. And show us where they're keeping the colonel. Don't you think so, Reed?"

Cindy nodded.

"I did not take the colonel," protested the warlord.

"Well you may not have taken him yourself, sir. But you gave what's called some material assistance, didn't you? Else why would they be sending you the email? What do you say we all stand up? Very slowly. And approach the vehicular transport?"

*

An hour later the five of them were barreling across a plain, kicking up a cloud of dust, on a gravel road. The warlord in his leaning turban was at the wheel. Mustafa was in the front passenger seat with the eighteen-year-old squeezed in next to him. The young man had refused to get in the back, where Harry and Cindy were sitting. It was difficult to communicate between the front seats and the back. The gravel on the road created a loud rumble, even inside the car with the windows up and the air conditioner on.

Cindy took the small digital camera she'd used earlier out of her pocket. It also had a video function. She took a brief film of the warlord's profile as he faced forward in the car. "Do you think he knows where your colonel is?" she asked Harry sitting next to her, and loud enough only for him to hear.

"Nope."

"Do you trust him?"

"Negative."

"Where do you think he's taking us?"

"Don't know. But it'll lead to something."

Cindy looked at him. He looked unconcerned. He looked as if he were enjoying himself. He looked as if danger weirdly excited him in some way, rather than making him nervous. He looked in command of the situation, even though he'd just admitted to not knowing exactly what that was.

"There's something you should see," she said. "Came up on my live feed several minutes ago."

"What's that?"

"It's unedited footage. CNN is considering putting it on the air. It hasn't been broadcast yet, but they're reviewing it for the news program."

"What's on it?"

She showed him her cellphone. On it was a short video, purportedly filmed by the Taliban and communicated to Al Jazeera, the media network based in Qatar. It showed Andrew Arbuthnot in a pink club chair, in front of a background of what looked like closed picture window curtains. His feet were in chains. There was a laminated card reading "Tasty Room Service" on the table next to him. A bearded man gesticulated at Andrew with an assault weapon and then said something

in a foreign language that had not yet been translated into subtitles. The bearded man looked angry. Andrew looked unruffled.

With the phone still in his hand, Harry called out to the front seat in a raised voice. "So where do you think he is then, sir? Our colonel? Where we gonna try first?"

"He will be in one of their mountain hideaways," shouted the warlord over the noise from the road. "The road begins to climb from here. Into a rocky region. The first inhabited cave is up there. We try there first."

Harry said in a low voice to Cindy, indicating the video screen still on her phone, "Does that look like a cave to you?"

She gave him a serious look. She shook her head.

"Sir, listen! Change of plan," called out Harry from the back seat to the front.

At this the warlord turned briefly around in his seat and did not conceal his look of annoyance before turning back to the road. "What?"

"Yeah," said Harry, not bothered in the least by the look. "What about Kabul? Let's try there."

"What are you talking about? They won't have taken him there. He'll be in one of their caves. I'm sure of it."

Cindy stopped Harry before he could answer. She called out to the front seat, "Would you be willing to go on the record to say that?"

"What?"

"Yeah," said Harry, beginning to get Cindy's drift. "Reed here is gonna send back a little report on the progress we're making. You know? To get back the colonel. So it's not all bad news, right? Keep the folks back at home happy."

"I am paid a small retainer by the Americans in your camp. In return for local help. They won't let me go on camera to say that."

"Sure they will," said Harry. "No problem. I'll take care of that. We also gotta keep the media happy." He said "meeja." It was for Reed's benefit. He was having fun with it. "Don't you worry. Reed here will interview you and I'll film it. Stop the car!"

Five minutes later, Cindy and warlord were posed in the middle of the desert, with some distant rocky outcrops of mountain behind them. Cindy had a little microphone that plugged into her phone. She held this out to the warlord, after introducing him as a senior Afghan warrior who was working in coordination with the American army. Harry was several steps away from them and filming them with Cindy's camera. Mustafa was standing next to him. The young warrior watched, half hiding himself from the warlord by standing behind Mustafa.

"And so Seyyed Khan," Cindy was asking, using the pan-Islamic term of respect that was the rough equivalent of mister, but which also denoted someone who'd made the pilgrimage to Mecca, "you believe Colonel Arbuthnot is being held in a cave somewhere in that mountain range behind us?"

The warlord's eyes darted first left and then right. "Yes, I think so."

"And can you tell us why you think so?"

"Oh no, I cannot reveal my sources. But the caves are usually safe from detection. Usama ibn Laden has probably been hiding in those caves for several years."

"If you know the caves where Osama bin Laden has been

hiding," asked Cindy, "why haven't you led the American special forces to him?"

Harry, who was still holding the camera, raised his eyebrows. His expression said "Not bad." Then he let out a little whoop.

The warlord was as discomfited by Harry's whoop as he was by Cindy's question. "Well, I have not always been in as close contact with my American brothers as I am now. And ..."

"And what?" called out Harry laughing, though he was still aiming the camera at the pair in front of him and filming them.

"Why do you think Colonel Arbuthnot was abducted?" persisted Cindy.

"I am not sure. I do know the Taliban is ruthless. They will be giving him a rough time."

Cindy just stared at him, as if that were an inadequate reply.

"And there may have been a bounty on him."

Harry whooped again. "Now we're talking."

"How would that work?" pursued Cindy. "How would you know about it?"

"The enemy sometimes offers financial incentives for the capture of high profile persons in the coalition."

"Do they really?" called out Harry.

Cindy ignored him. "Incentives?" she repeated. "Like how much?"

"That I could not say," said the warlord. He stepped out of the frame and said to Cindy "That is all! That is enough. There is nothing more to add. You are making me look foolish."

Harry put down the camera and came genially up to the warlord. "Don't worry, sir. Reed's just doing his job. He's got

to send in a report every once in a while. I think we should try Kabul. Humor me, okay? Can I drive the Merc now? Please?"

*

As they approached Kabul, the roads became better. Asphalt and tar replaced loose gravel. Make-shift vehicle checkpoints were also more frequent. Oil barrels and wooden crates were set up to block the middle of the road. The young men at the checkpoints were sometimes only teenagers who pointed wobbling semi-automatic weapons at them. Nor did the young men often speak English. Mustafa could speak to most of them, but they sometimes spoke languages and dialects he didn't know. There was room for misunderstanding. All of them seemed hostile.

With each new checkpoint, Cindy's nervousness grew. Harry on the other hand, grew calmer. He'd cruise slowly up to the young men, lower the driver's side window, and say "How's it going boys?" He'd smile broadly, and pretend he was the youngest uncle arriving at someone's wedding. He'd found a Palestinian scarf in the trunk and draped it around his head against the dust. He also put on a big pair of sunglasses he always carried with him to reduce the possibility of recognition, but they recognized his friendliness right away.

"Is the bride ready?" he'd say. "Which way to the sweets table?" His mimed silliness and anticipation of pleasure disarmed them faster than Mustafa's spoken explanations of who they were and where they were going.

It was the same when they got to Kabul. He drove straight to the Hilton and into its semicircular driveway. The young men at the rural checkpoints hadn't recognized him. Now he took off his scarf and removed his sunglasses so that the doormen at the Hilton did see immediately who he was. The women at the front desk did too. The manager appeared from his office and shook Harry's hand with both of his. They were all delighted to see him. He put this to use. From the doormen he won the right to keep the car out front in case they needed to make a quick getaway. From the women at the front desk he extracted a room, free of charge, to serve as their base while they collected intelligence and assessed the possibilities in town. The manager agreed at once to give him a printout of who was staying in every guest room. When they got to their room, he fell backwards on to one of the double beds with a satisfied "Oof."

The warlord stood and looked at him disapprovingly. Just then there were recorded calls to prayer broadcast from a nearby mosque. The warlord said he and the young warrior would have to excuse themselves. Mustafa went with them to keep an eye on them. After the three of them had gone, Cindy sat on the other bed watching Harry. He was lying back, looking at the ceiling. His tunic rode up and exposed the skin above the waistline of his trousers. She noticed that there was a ridge of abdominal muscle, probably from push-ups in the gym. He also had the fleshy beginnings of a belly.

"So did you send our film to your producer?" he asked her.

"Yes."

"What did he think of the camera work? Ace, hmm?"

"It's the interview that counts."

"Sure, but you have to admit. I got both you and him in the frame, plus the mountain behind. You know? The caves might be up there? It was great."

"Whatever."

"So is he gonna go with it?"

"It's just the first part of our story. It's too early to air it. All it says now is that the army's in bed with some sketchy warlord from an Afghan village. We need more."

"That guy's all right, Reed. Don't be too hard on him. He's just a petty criminal."

"Just a petty criminal? Not a bounty hunter?"

"Yeah. That was interesting."

She watched him as he gave the pale white of his belly an absent-minded scratch. A reddish trail of curling hair led down under his canvas belt, beyond his curving fingers.

Suddenly Harry sat up and looked at Cindy. "Were you looking at me funny, mate? I already told you, I'm not . . ."

Before she could reply, he was up and jumping over from his bed on to hers. He crouched down and bent her over backward from her sitting position on to the bed. He pinned her hands behind her head. "Not gay." He punctuated the two words by bouncing her against the mattress.

"I never said you were."

"No, but you gave me the look, didn't you? You were admiring my abs of steel, weren't you?"

"I wasn't!" She struggled against his hands holding her

back on the bed. "They could use some work."

"Oh, Reed, mate. They don't make you do strength training at CNN, do they? Your upper body is pathetic. You've gotta get to the gym sometimes."

"Stop it. Get off me!"

"I'll let you go in a minute. But before I do, I'm gonna teach you a lesson. So you don't cruise me ever again, see? I'm gonna give your nuts a little squeeze. Won't hurt you too bad, just a little."

Cindy tossed her head from one side to the next. She kicked up her feet in order to try and free herself.

"Oh no you don't. I've got enough here to hold you down with one hand." Harry pulled her hands up above her head on the bed. Then he leaned up and held them down with his right forearm. With his left hand he reached down between her legs. But it didn't feel quite right. He wrinkled his eyebrows. Making eye contact the whole time, he investigated slowly, but he couldn't find anything to squeeze. He searched around holding different handfuls of the fabric of her camo pants for a few seconds each. "Hang on Reed. Where're your balls? I can't find 'em. Are you wearing spandex, or something? Compression shorts?"

In the midst of Cindy's struggling against him harder, she knocked off her cap against Harry's arm. Her long dark hair fell down around her ears and neck. It pooled on the bed in a shiny, textured heap that reflected the light.

"What's this?" said Harry, surprised.

"I said get off me."

"Hang on, hang on. I'll let you go in a second. Do you know what, Reed? I never knew you had hair like that before.

Always tucked up in your cap, it was. I never suspected." He was puzzled. "And another thing. I've never seen you out of those Ray Bans. You're always wearing 'em. Even on the plane out here. And never been out of 'em."

"Eye condition. I'm light sensitive."

"Eye condition, is it? I don't think so." Harry reached up with his free left hand and took off Cindy's sunglasses.

Her mask was off. With her hair down around her neck, her long eyelashes, and the soft fullness of her cheeks, rouged from the effort of resisting him, all was revealed. She stopped struggling and just glared at Harry.

"Reed! That's why I couldn't find your nuts, mate. Cause you don't have any."

"Yes, I do," she growled, unsure of what to do now that she'd been exposed. She didn't have a fallback plan.

"Prove it, mate. You gotta show 'em to me then."

"I don't have to prove anything to you. I don't have to show you anything."

"You know, Reed. Now that we haven't got any secrets from each other? I've got something to confess too. Shouldn't have hid it from you, mate. Actually, I might be a little bit gay. Cause you're turning me on, mate, and I wouldn't mind kissing you right now."

"Don't come near me, asshole."

"Oh, sweetheart. That's love poetry to me. You must want it a little bit. Maybe not as much as me. But a little bit. Or you wouldn't talk to me that way."

"I do not!" Here she began to try and slide away from him on the bed.

"Oh no you don't, Reed." Harry grabbed her hands again

and pinned her back against the bed. "One little kiss, just between mates." He leaned down and rubbed Cindy's nose once back and forth with his. He was about to kiss her when the outer door burst open. Another bearded fighter, different from the one who'd held Andrew, came rushing through. He stood above them on the bed and pointed his gun at them.

*

Andrew knew that his first duty was to the regiment and that he must let them know that he was safe. However, he couldn't help feeling that, while in Kabul, it would be a pity not to go and call in on Frances de Mornay at the interfaith charity. She might be more worried than the army in any case. After all, he'd never had time to finish their telephone call properly. He walked straight out of the Hilton's lobby still carrying the bearded soldier's gun. He guided his footsteps from his dim recollection of where he thought the interfaith charity was based. It was only twenty minutes' walk away. He thought of himself as having disarmed his captor, not having stolen his gun. One thing he would admit to having stolen. He was wearing the soldier's flat woolen Afghan cap. He regarded that as justifiable war booty.

He walked down a road that would carry him by the front

gates of the British Embassy. Here he began to have second thoughts. Perhaps he had better put a call in quickly to the brigadier to say he was all right before making his way to the interfaith charity. He was just about to speak to the sentry when the sentry got a call and asked him to wait. The sentry then moved to unlock the big iron gate in front of the driveway. A vintage Range Rover, covered in dust, dented and dinged from long service in outposts with unpaved roads, came racing though the forecourt and out through the front gates. A woman in a white scarf was at the wheel. The end of her long scarf flapped out of the open window. A frightened-looking man was in the passenger seat.

"What an appalling driver," said Andrew to the sentry as he showed him his military identification. "You'd think they were on their way to the accident and emergency of Kabul Hospital."

"I couldn't say, sir."

"Late for tiffin at the club, I expect."

"Tiffin, sir?"

"Never mind. May I just put my head through the door over there and make a quick telephone call?"

"As you like, sir, but I have to take that gun off you, I'm afraid."

Andrew handed over the machine gun. "It's all yours."

"I'll hold it for you in here, sir," said the man gesturing at his sentry box. "If you hang on a minute, I'll give you a claim ticket."

"Thank you," said Andrew, feeling that the sentry was remarkably like the young man who ran the cloakroom at the Naval and Military in St. James's Square.

Andrew came in through the front door off the courtyard,

flashing his identification once again, and asked to see the ambassador's personal assistant. He knew her from his previous posting. She'd give him a room and let him put a call through, he had no doubt. She came forward from her office in the back and met him in the marbled foyer.

"Ah, Colonel Arbuthnot." She offered her cool hand. "So pleased to see you again. I'm afraid you've just missed the ambassador."

"I didn't come to see him."

"Oh, no?"

"No. I wondered if you'd let me use one of your secure lines, please. I just have to put several quick calls through."

"Of course."

"I've just been released from captivity, you see."

"Ah." She was unsurprised. "Are you all right?"

"As you see," he said smiling, if a little wanly. He brushed his hands down the front of his tunic. "Nothing that a cup of tea won't repair."

"Well, I think we can just about manage that. If you'll come with me then?"

She turned and began walking through a long corridor of framed artwork on loan from the Foreign Office art stores. There were original oils by major figures of British twentieth-century art, Duncan Grant, John Piper, and Graham Sutherland. Andrew joined her at her side and took a quick look at the art they were passing. He thought the Foreign Office was being typically careless about sending valuable paintings into a war zone.

"The ambassador's on an unscheduled mission. Rather urgent. Not in his diary, at any rate. He left just now. With

Mrs. de Mornay."

Andrew only paused in their walk down the corridor a moment, but caught himself. He resumed walking after only a slight hesitation. "Mrs. de Mornay?" he asked with feigned indifference.

"Yes, she persuaded him to give her a car. Well, he wouldn't let her go without him. So the two of them went off together. Just now."

"Together, were they?"

"Yes, it was curious. He had a bit of a tummy upset. I wouldn't have thought he was in the mood for an adventure. As it were."

"Perhaps they were going to see a doctor then?"

"I don't think so." She stopped next to an empty office and pointed him in to a desk that had a phone sitting on it. "That's a secure line, colonel. Would you like to use it?"

"Oh thank you. That's very kind."

"I'll see what I can do about that cup of tea."

"I should be forever grateful."

She turned to leave him and carry on down the corridor.

Ten minutes later Andrew had a Spode teacup and saucer in front of him on the desk. It was in a floral pattern from the Cotswold garden series. He'd telephoned the brigadier and told him what'd happened. He'd agreed to a meeting on improving security at the camp, and to reviewing the available intelligence on his capture. He'd declined a medical examination. He'd telephoned his American opposite number at the camp. He'd learned of Wales, Khan and Reed disappearing using Khan's special pass. The American colonel suspected Wales of disobeying his command not to go out

looking for Andrew.

"If he was in one of my units, I'd court martial his ass."

Andrew could hear the man's wet cigar in the corner of his mouth as he said this. "Well, that's understandable. Let me see if I can't clear things up from my side. Sorry to have troubled you."

Andrew replaced the receiver and was drumming his fingers on the desktop, when, somewhat to his surprise, the ambassador appeared in the doorway. He was wearing a pinstriped Jermyn Street suit over lightweight hiking boots. He had a Union Jack pin in his lapel. He looked a little pale.

"Colonel Arbuthnot. Are you well?"

"As you can see," replied Andrew standing up and shaking the ambassador's hand.

At that moment, Frances appeared in the doorway too. Her silk scarf was flying off in the corridor behind her. Her sapphire eyes were moist. Her white hair was shining. She was out of breath. "Andrew!"

"Frances?" he said, more warmly than he'd greeted the ambassador. He nevertheless used a question mark because it was the first time he'd used her Christian name with her in person. He looked her in the eyes, happy to see her.

"But we thought you'd been abducted. You disappeared. You've no idea how worried I was. We drove out to find you, but the traffic was impossible. We couldn't get more than fifty yards away."

"I am sorry. It was a minor difficulty. Really nothing more than that. And now I'm back."

"I would like to hear the whole story, but I'm afraid I must excuse myself for just a moment."

"Oh dear," said Frances to him, concerned. "Ambassador, I want you to try two fingers. It will bring everything up. Instant relief." She turned to Andrew and said "The poor man hasn't been well."

The ambassador hurried off down the hall.

"But Andrew," she said, turning back to him. "Are you all right? Did they hurt you?"

"No, no, I'm fine."

"I don't believe you. Stop minimizing things. Where'd you get that hat?" She reached up impulsively and pulled the cap off his head. She ran a hand through his hair. Before he knew what was happening she leaned forward and kissed him on the mouth. "There! I'm sorry. I couldn't stop myself. I'm so glad you're all right."

Initially taken by surprise, Andrew now smiled broadly. "I'm better than all right."

"Don't get any ideas. It was a maternal kiss. I'm standing in for her, of course."

"But nothing like my mother's kiss."

"Stop it, Andrew. I'm very old. Let's not pretend. Tell me what happened."

"I'm not pretending. Well. It's very simple. One moment I was on the telephone talking to you. The next I had a sack over my head and I was bundled into the back of a car. A lengthy ride in the car. Then, when the sack came off, I was in the Kabul Hilton. My ankles locked to an armchair."

"How awful. Did they threaten you?"

"Oh the usual. They pointed a gun in my direction. They shouted. They promised to beat me. They didn't."

"Never mind. The verbal assault alone is enough to give

you the old PTSD. You must have a thorough examination, Andrew." She took both his hands in hers. "Promise me you will."

"I will if you will."

"What?"

At this moment, the ambassador re-appeared. He looked relieved, as if he were feeling better. He looked surprised to find the two of them holding hands. "I'm sorry."

"Oh, hello ambassador," said Andrew, looking up, less cool and more embarrassed than he'd been a moment before.

*

At that moment, the secure phone on the desk behind them rang twice. There was a pause and then it rang twice again. They all looked at each other for several seconds. The phone rang again.

"Are you expecting a call, Colonel Arbuthnot?" asked the ambassador.

"No. Are you?"

"No. How strange. That's a secure line. My assistant wouldn't have put it through unless you'd requested it."

"Well, I didn't."

The phone rang twice more.

"Oh for heaven's sake," said Frances. "We may as well answer it." She picked up the receiver and said tentatively, curiously "Hel-lo?"

"Mrs. de Mornay, I believe," said a cultivated voice.

"As a matter of fact it is," she turned and held her hand on her chest as she exchanged glances with Andrew and the ambassador. Then, while re-arranging her white scarf she turned back to the desk and said, "I hope you'll forgive me, but I don't recognize your voice."

"We've never met."

"I see."

"But it is a very great honor to speak to you."

"Look here. I really must ask for you to identify yourself."

"Oh, we will meet before long."

"Who are you!"

"I am no one. Like you, a subject of Her Majesty, though in Afghanistan we fight on different sides."

"What are you talking about?"

"Could you pass a message to the ambassador and Colonel Arbuthnot for me? Perhaps they are in the room with you?"

Frances whipped around to look at Andrew and the ambassador, her eyes wide.

"But how did you know?"

"I hope you'll excuse me. We've hacked into the embassy security system. The three of you make such a pretty picture via the security cam."

"What do you want?" said Frances, suddenly stern. She looked around the room for possible cameras. She settled on what might be a camera lens that was disguised inside an ugly wall clock. It had round glass balls for numerals.

"If you wouldn't mind telling the colonel that we have Lieutenant Wales with us, I would be grateful."

"You what?"

"Unharmed I can assure you. And the American reporter, Mr. Reed. Well, Miss Reed actually, but that is another issue."

"What are you talking about?"

"Only that we are holding him unharmed, but I'm afraid he certainly will be killed unless the UK government is willing to meet our demand."

"What do you want? Money, I suppose?" said Frances, her lips curling in distaste.

"Oh no. Our funds are more than sufficient. We would like the UK forces," the voice on the phone continued, "to withdraw from the coalition, to cease hostilities, and to return to Britain."

"Surely you see that's not likely to happen anytime soon."

"Please put this to Colonel Arbuthnot and the ambassador, then. If our demands are not met, we will release a video of Prince Harry as our prisoner."

"I see."

"It would show the world our power and our intention. Perhaps, in Britain, it could even lead to the fall of the government itself. I leave you to judge for yourself. The newspapers will, after all, ask why the government dared to dangle such a valuable prize before insurgents and terrorists. Forgive me for employing your words. And then our Muslim brothers in Birmingham, Tower Hamlets, Luton, and Bradford will rise to support us."

"That is a fantasy," said Frances, ready to give him a piece of her mind.

"Well, it is your choice. You have forty-eight hours. Goodbye." There was a click and the line went dead.

Frances replaced the receiver. The three of them were silent for a moment and said nothing as they looked from one to the other.

At length, the ambassador broke the spell. "I expect that whatever that was, it wasn't good."

"They have Harry. They want the UK out of Afghanistan. They threaten to release a video of him," replied Frances. "They threaten to kill him."

"What a nuisance," sighed Andrew. "I think I'd better nip this one in the bud. If you'll excuse me, I've got to go."

"I'm coming with you," said Frances.

"No, you're not."

"Yes, I am."

"It would be better if we divided up the tasks," said Andrew to Frances with gentleness and reasonableness in his voice. "I'm no good at dealing with St. James's. Why don't you telephone them for me and tell them what's happened. You'd be doing me a favor."

"Oh, Andrew," said Frances with an exasperated laugh. "They don't take calls from me at St. James's. Not anymore. I'd much rather come with you."

Andrew shrugged his shoulders. He'd preferred to have ladies left out of this, but he couldn't say he wouldn't enjoy her company.

"I could call St. James's," said the ambassador, remaining poker faced, but raising his eyebrows slightly at the prospect of placing a call to the Prince of Wales's private secretary. He'd rather liked it the last time he'd been invited to a drinks party

there. He thought the Duchess of Cornwall was charming.

"There you are," said Frances accompanying Andrew out of the room after quick farewell nods to the ambassador. They were both out in the corridor before Frances remembered to call back to the ambassador, taking two steps backward. "Do you mind if I keep the Range Rover for a little while longer?"

"Please do, Mrs. de Mornay," he said, relieved that she now became Colonel Arbuthnot's responsibility and not his.

Then she was by Andrew's side, striding down the hall.

"Do you have the keys?" he asked.

She rooted in her denim pocket. She found the keys and held them up in the air.

"I'll take those, please," said Andrew.

"Oh no you don't. I'm driving."

"You haven't any idea where to go."

"Neither do you."

"I have an idea, actually."

"Good. You direct me."

"Frances, really. It's bad enough to have you involved in the first place. I cannot let you drive as well."

"Look here. Stop speaking down to me."

"I wasn't."

"You were!"

"But it's dangerous. And you're unarmed. You're lovely, but on this mission, I'm afraid you're going to be a liability."

As they continued walking she dug in her other pocket. She brought out a pearl-handled revolver. She showed it to him.

"My god. Where'd you get that? It's preposterous."

"Nancy Reagan had one. I bought one for myself."

By this time they were out the front door of the embassy

and climbing into the battered Range Rover in the embassy forecourt. Andrew climbed into the passenger seat. Frances turned over the engine, reversed abruptly, and then accelerated toward the black gate that barred their way on to the street. She pulled up suddenly in a cloud of dust. The sentry came out of his box waving the cloud of dust out of the way with his hands. Andrew rolled down the passenger side window to speak to him. "Oh, hello. It's me again. Do you suppose I could have my gun back, please?" He handed over the claim check.

*

After they entered the roadway in front of the embassy, Frances and Andrew found their way slowed down by one detour after another. The authorities in Kabul had shut down a number of thoroughfares precisely to make quick navigation impossible. Before long they were stuck in traffic too. Large 12-wheeled tractor-trailers mixed with up-to-the-minute black armored SUVs, which cost more than six figures, and were used by coalition administrators. There were also antique Soviet cars from the 1980s, people on foot, and wagons drawn by animals.

"And so," finished Andrew, "they held me at the Hilton

until I managed to get free. I think it'd be best if we tried the hotel first."

"Fancy them holding you there."

"I know. It's brilliant, actually."

"Well. I wouldn't go that far." She looked over at him, raised her eyebrows, and held out her hand to take one of his. She squeezed it for a moment. "I'm so glad you're all right."

The traffic began to move ahead of them. She put both hands back on the steering wheel and drove ahead slowly. Andrew coughed and held out his hand to her again. He raised his eyebrows.

"Andrew I can't hold your hand. I'm driving."

"It's going at a snail's pace. You can drive with one hand."

"Andrew!"

"I'm walking wounded. I may be psychologically damaged. I need care and attention. I might be about to have a flashback."

She laughed and continued driving with one hand. With her other, she reached out and held Andrew's hand again. "You seem all right to me."

He stared straight ahead out the windshield. "Actually, I am feeling a bit better now."

"Oh Andrew. Don't make me laugh."

"I didn't intend to make you laugh."

"I can't take you seriously, young man."

"Maybe you should," he said, increasing slightly his pressure on her hand, and compelling her to take her eyes briefly off the road to look at him.

"Now, look here," she said in a voice that was more brisk than friendly. "It's all very well for us to flirt with one another. While we're out here. But it won't work when we're at home."

"Why not?"

She laughed at him. "Well, I won't review the obvious reasons."

"Maybe the obvious reasons why not are the reasons why we should."

"What?"

"Never mind. We'll come back to that. Say your piece, darling."

That light diminutive used at the end of what he'd said, so often used in joking, or exaggeration, caught Frances by surprise. She felt a little catch in her throat that prevented her from saying what she'd been intending to say.

"Go on." He encouraged her.

She cleared her throat. "Well, I live in Scotland for one and I live on the charity of the parish."

"Surely de Mornay pays you some alimony."

"He did. Lump sum. It's gone."

"What?"

"It wasn't a lot. I agreed to a pitifully small sum in the pre-nuptial agreement. I was young and naïve and I never thought it'd come to that. There we are."

Andrew didn't know what to say. He dropped her hand.

Well, it didn't surprise her. Men were like that. They changed their minds. She imagined Andrew was in the process of changing his mind too.

"I have a flat in London," he said. "In Knightsbridge. Pretty hideous. You know what army-commissioned architecture is like. But it has a view of the park. We could live there."

"Living together now, are we?"

"Well, staying together, perhaps. From time to time?"

Frances laughed to cover her surprise. "Oh, the army'll adore that. Living together or staying together won't make the slightest difference to them. It won't help your career. That's certain." She imitated a general's voice with plummy vowels and a weary habit of command. "There's old Frances. She likes her drop of the bottle. How does Andrew stand it?"

"Do you? I hadn't noticed."

"Do I what?"

"Like a drop of the bottle?"

"I do."

"And?"

"And what?" she said, a little more shrilly than she'd been speaking before. "It all got away from me. The divorce. Then being separated from the boys. Living on my own. You know? I am trying, Andrew. I haven't had anything since London Airport. That's three weeks ago. It's the longest I've ever gone."

He reached out and took her hand again. "My poor darling."

There it was again. She could scarcely believe it. She held him at bay. "I don't want pity."

"Sympathy, Frances. That's not the same as pity."

She took her eyes off the slow-moving traffic for an instant. She looked over at him again, imagining, no matter what he'd said, that disapproval and condemnation must be lurking there instead.

*

Meanwhile, in one of the Hilton guest rooms, Cindy and Harry were seated in front of the picture window. Their ankles were locked to the legs of their pink armchairs.

The new bearded Afghan soldier was seated on the bed watching a soccer game. His automatic weapon lay beside him on the bed. Harry made eye contact with Cindy. Then, without moving anything other than his eyes he indicated the gun to her on the bed. She followed his eyes and blinked slowly.

"So!" she called out to the bearded man. "I don't really get the rules to soccer. Who's winning?"

"Football," he corrected her.

"He's right," said Harry. "Football. Arsenal's winning! Arsenal always wins. Right mate?"

"I am not your mate," replied the bearded man. "Tell your girlfriend to cover her head. She shouldn't hang her long hair in front of me. She is a harlot."

"Are you trying to seduce my Afghan mate over here, Reed?"

"Shut up," she said.

Then the fans in the stadium in London sent up a wild, inarticulate, tribal roar. The voiceover announcers also lost their cool. The bearded man and Harry both leaped to their feet. They looked at one another with delight, raised their hands in the air, and did a victory dance. They punched one fist in the air, then the other. All the while they hopped up and down, first on one foot, then the other. "Ar-se-nal, Ar-se-nal!" Harry's dance was more constrained because he couldn't move more than twelve inches beyond the chair to which he was chained. At the very height of the dance, Harry lunged for the gun on the bed. If he'd been three seconds quicker, he would have got to it in time. Instead, the bearded man saw

what he was doing and grabbed away the gun before Harry could get to it. He then raised the gun in the air and clipped Harry against the ear with the barrel.

Harry fell back into the pink chair. "Ow! Will you watch it with that thing! You could kill someone with it." He held his hand up to his injured ear.

"It is not your gun!"

Harry crumpled further into the back of the chair without straightening up. He still held his ear. When he took the hand away to look at it, he found blood.

"Now look what you've done!" said Cindy, angry for the first time that afternoon. "He's bleeding."

The bearded man looked abashed. "I am sorry, sir. But the gun was not yours to take. The same could be said of my country as a whole."

"We're not here to take your stinking country," said Harry, in a smaller voice than usual. "We're here to stop your crazed jihad against innocent people going to work on the Piccadilly Line."

"Sir," said the Afghan taking a colored rag out of his pocket. "Perhaps I could help you."

"Get away from me with that! I don't want your germs."

"Come here," said Cindy to him. "Stand up. I've got some Wet Ones here in my pocket. I can clean you up."

They both had enough extra in their chains for them to approach one another standing in between the chairs. Cindy tore open the foil packet and took out a moisturized paper towel. She dabbed at Harry's bleeding ear.

"Ow!"

"Don't be such a baby. It's just got a little rubbing alcohol

on it. Helps disinfect the wound."

"Ow!" he cried out more loudly than before. The bearded man looked on at them helplessly and apologetically.

Then the door to the corridor burst open. Frances walked in with the white scarf around her head. Andrew was behind her. She held both arms outstretched with one hand steadying the other on the barrel of her pearl-handled revival. She raised it high and fired it twice into the foam-lined panels dropped from the ceiling. Little pellets of microfiber drifted down on to the room like snow. Her voice was icy. "Hands in the air!"

Part IV

Could You Get
Me St. James's
Palace, Please?

The four of them were in four pink club chairs. All their ankles were chained to the chair legs. The chairs were arranged in a circle. The chairs were from the hotel, but they were no longer in the hotel. They were inside a cave, with a rough rocky ceiling and a feeling of damp. Frances was warming her feet in front of a three-ring electric burner that was sitting in the center of their circle and plugged into an extension cord. The cord ran out the opening to their chamber of the cave and was plugged into a generator that hummed in the distance. This time their hands were all chained to one another too, though the chains were loose. They could maneuver a little, but not much. They were unsupervised.

"Isn't it my turn, Mudge?" said Harry. "My feet are perishing."

"Your turn is last," said Andrew.

"Colonel, didn't the whole ladies first thing go down with the *Titanic*? I mean, we're all equal now."

"Who said?" murmured Cindy.

"Children," said Frances clapping her hands and speaking to them all. "I will not have unkind words. Not in our situation." As she spoke she moved the heater with her toe so it faced mid-way between Harry and Cindy.

Then she cleared her throat and said not unkindly to Cindy, "My dear, I was under the impression on the flight out here that the American reporter we had with us was a man." Then with a hint of mischief: "Are you in fact an actress? Do you perform with Danny LaRue?"

"Danny LaRue's Blue Review, of course," said Andrew chuckling.

"Mudge," said Harry reaching up to scratch under the plaster the Afghans had put on his injured ear, "you've got to leave Reed alone. She's been through a lot."

"Who's Danny LaRue?" asked Cindy, surprised that she should be expected to identify what sounded like some pop culture reference from a long time ago.

"A very entertaining cabaret entertainer. In Soho. Man dressed as a woman," answered Andrew. "The club was still open when I was a boy."

"What? You mean like Boy George? Karma Chameleon? Mudge, you can't really expect us to know where you went clubbing in, I don't know, the last world war."

"I'm not an actress," said Cindy, keeping her temper. "I'm a reporter. The army wouldn't let me report from the front line if I was a woman."

"Well, that's quite wrong of them," said Frances, deciding

to ignore the young woman's hostile tone. She felt that young people did rather lack tact and kindness sometimes, but you had to rise above that, and ignore it, if you were going to encourage them, bring them forward. "But how did you keep it up so long?"

"I grew up with boys in the house. I had to know how to fight back." She said this last in a deeper, fiercer register, the voice she'd been using when she was Sandy Reed.

"Brilliant, wasn't it?" said Harry, brightening up. "I totally fell for it. Didn't you colonel?"

"Well."

"Oh, c'mon. Admit it colonel."

"And you unmasked her, I take it," said Frances raising her eyebrow.

"Well, sort of," agreed Harry. "But before that we did some work together. She was on to the warlord before I was. You know? The one Khan's related to. She made him look all dodgy on camera. With the questions she asked him. I helped her send the video to her producer." He looked over at Frances for approval.

"Ordinarily, Wales, a second lieutenant requires permission before he speaks to a member of the press."

"I wasn't speaking to her, sir. I was holding the camera!"

"What camera?" asked Andrew.

"Well, I've got a Nikon mini," said Cindy. "It'll hook up to a cellphone and you can attach stuff to email and send video footage like that."

"That's that, then," sighed Andrew. "They took away all our mobiles."

"Isn't that a computer over in the corner, sir? If we could

get over to that ..."

"Yeah," Cindy, taking up Harry's idea, "I could do a little video footage of all of us sitting here and send it to my producer. Maybe through a USB port."

"Except that we have no idea where we are," objected Frances.

"No, but it would show that we're all okay. And someone looking at it might be able to identify some of the interior." Cindy shrugged. "I don't know. Couldn't hurt."

"But surely they took your camera too," Andrew said to Cindy.

"Nope. Got it right here. In my sports bra." She jangled her wrist chains and reached down into the top of her camouflage tunic. She rooted around for a minute. Then she came up with a small black camera, about four inches square. "I hated having these in high school." She referred vaguely to her chest. "But there's one advantage. You can hide stuff in there."

"Can you?" observed Harry, more wide-eyed than he'd been a moment before.

"What are you planning to say?" asked Andrew.

"Well, I'm going to identify myself. Say that we're being held by insurgents in an undisclosed location. A cave. Identify us all. And say we're all safe."

"I don't see any harm in that, Andrew," pointed out Frances, "do you?"

"Well let's do it quickly, then, before they find us doing it," replied Andrew. I don't know how much longer they'll leave us alone in here."

"Give me the camera. I know what to do," said Harry reaching out his hand to take the black box from Cindy. As

she handed it to him, he held it briefly to his nose, locked eyes with her, and smelled it. Then he gave the little device a kiss.

"Don't be gross!"

"Get on with it, Reed. You heard the colonel," said Harry bringing the camera up to his eye and pressing the button. A red light came on. Clinking the chains on his wrists, Harry aimed the camera at Cindy.

"This is Cindy Reed, reporting for CNN, from a remote location in Afghanistan. Ten hours ago I was taken in captivity by a group of Afghan insurgents. Two British nationals attempted to rescue us. They were overwhelmed by a superior Afghan force. Now all four of us are captive. We are inside what appears to be a cave, though I do not know for certain, nor do I know where it is. It was about a six-hour drive from Kabul. We all had burlap bags placed over our heads. We were brought here in the back seat of a car from the Hilton Hotel."

"The Hilton's where these dreadful armchairs come from of course," interjected Frances off camera. She tapped the arms of her chair lightly.

A look of annoyance at the interruption crossed Cindy's face. Nevertheless, she continued, "The Afghan warlord with whom we were traveling, who is in the pay of the US Army, may well have been involved in our capture."

Harry panned away from Cindy, put a wobbly focus on one of the club chairs, and then jerked back to Cindy. Andrew looked nervously at the door, then down at his watch. He made a circular gesture in the air. He wanted her to wrap it up.

"In order to escape detection," Cindy continued, "I'm going to have to curtail this report. The others being held with me are Ms. Frances de Mornay, aid worker in Kabul."

Harry turned the camera to show Frances with fierce blue eyes, and silvery hair covered in her white scarf. "Colonel Andrew Arbuthnot, with the UK armed forces acting as part of the coalition in Afghanistan." Harry took a shot of Andrew looking back angrily into the camera. "And ..."

"Reed," interrupted Andrew. "Perhaps you'd better not mention ..." He cleared his throat. "My colleague. Shall we keep that quiet for now?"

Harry briefly held the camera in front of himself, took a video selfie, and gave the camera a broad, silent wink before turning it back toward Cindy.

Before Andrew could remonstrate with him, there was a crash outside.

"This is Cindy Reed reporting from captivity. Over."

Harry pressed the off button and dropped the camera into the neck of his tunic.

All four of them cast an anxious look toward the door.

Nothing happened.

After several moments of no one coming, Andrew turned to Harry and said. "Look here, Wales, that was an act of insubordination. I asked Reed not to bring you into it."

"Quite right, sir," said Harry, giving his colonel a friendly, soft salute. "I think CNN will cut that bit out if we ask them to, sir. But I just thought. You know. It's just this. It might get Reed's report a bit more airtime, if you see what I mean. It might get the message out a bit further. That is, if they have a little glimpse of yours truly. Such as I am." He made a little comic squint to suggest that that wasn't much.

"He's right, colonel," put in Cindy. "With him thrown in, it'll get higher ratings." She regretted it was true.

Andrew didn't look satisfied with either one of them. "I don't agree. But for the time being, let's just see if we can download it on the computer, and send it off, before they find out we've got a camera."

"How're we going to do that, Andrew," asked Frances, "when we're all chained together over here?"

"Everyone picks up and drag his own chair. We've got to do this together."

All four of them got to their feet, and began stamping with small steps across the carpet, dragging their four pink chairs behind them. Harry picked up one of the chains of Frances's chair and helped her drag it. Andrew put his hand around Cindy's waist. It looked like an awkward elephant walk, all of them rattling their chains and pulling their chairs.

When they got to the computer, Cindy found a USB cable stuffed in loosely behind the display monitor. "Whatever next?" said Frances, with a mild hint of disapproval. Harry attached it to the camera. Cindy leaned over, found that the internet was up, and signed into her Gmail account. Harry attached the cable to the computer. She wrote a quick email to her producer, attached the video, and pressed send. Then she signed out. "Okay!"

"Back!" ordered Andrew.

They all four dragged their chairs back to their original locations with the same stamping dance. Then they fell back into their chairs and assumed nonchalant expressions.

Frances noticed what might have been a mouse, or some furry creature with a long tail, along the rocky wall of the cave. As if nothing had just happened, she proposed, "I spy with my little eye something in this very room. Six letters. Guess. The

clue is 'I smell a rat.'"

"Does it have an 'a' in it, Mudge?"

"No, it doesn't."

"What about an 'o'?" proposed Cindy.

"Yes. Very good, my dear. You may have another turn."

"How about an 'e'?"

"Right again!"

The warlord in the white turban came through the door with an automatic weapon slung over his shoulder. Two bearded men carrying copper serving dishes followed him. "Ladies and gentlemen. Pashtuns know how to treat their guests. The evening banquet begins."

Then a guilty-looking Mustafa Khan came into the room with an automatic rifle over his shoulder. He was hanging his head. The other four sat back in their chairs, stupefied to see him. He appeared to be there in support of their captor.

"Mustafa! No. This is crazy. How could you?"

Mustafa was unwilling to meet Harry's eyes, or anyone else's. The warlord's eyes glittered with a kind of revenge.

After an awkward pause, Andrew, who had been thinking with his eyebrows furrowed, suddenly brightened. "Rodent. R-o-d-e-n-t!"

*

Cindy's producer, who'd been based this whole time in Kabul, had gotten used to hearing nothing from her. After she'd refused to permit the Harry scoop, she'd gone silent. He wouldn't air the Harry news without her cooperation. He had that much respect for her, but he'd also begun to hope she'd recognized that what she was doing wasn't going to work. In a couple of weeks they could fly back to the States without the army's ever finding out how they'd both broken the rules. That's what he hoped. That's when he'd received her first videotape of an interview with a suspicious looking warlord. Then he got the video from the cave. He took it straight to the British Embassy. That's how he came to be sitting at the ambassador's mahogany table. The ambassador was sitting on the other side looking worried.

"What do you think we should do?" asked the producer.

"I can't think that St. James's Palace," here he clasped his hands over his belly, to stop himself from twitching, "would agree to the prince's captivity being announced in a videotape on an American news program."

"Why're you worried about what a god damned palace will say?"

"The Prince of Wales's son is popular. His capture will embarrass the government. It will have an effect on the conduct of the war. There will be some sort of outcry. A demand for revenge. I don't know for certain. But that sort of thing anyway."

"So you don't want me releasing these videotapes?"

"If you'd be so kind."

"But I'm not going to just sit here when one of my people is in danger," said the CNN producer with heat. "God knows

what they're doing to her."

The ambassador thought he detected something unusual in the heat of the producer's remarks. He made a mental note of it for later. Instead, he said smoothly, "I quite understand. I think we begin by consulting with military intelligence. Why don't we see if there's anything someone used to looking at these sorts of tapes can identify? Maybe they could help us narrow down a list of locations."

"That could take days. Even weeks!"

The ambassador sighed. "What do you propose then?"

"Why don't we at least air the first tape?"

"Do you think the American armed forces will like that? To suggest that a warlord they've relied upon is untrustworthy? Nor will the Afghan authorities like it if we embarrass a prominent local chieftain. Our relations with the Afghan administration are delicate. We need their cooperation."

"We've got to do something, buddy. We can't worry about being diplomatic. That's your job not mine. My job is to get the story out. This is news god damn it."

The ambassador jumped involuntarily at the producer's calling him "buddy."

"Could you not simply say that one of your reporters has been taken into captivity together with some others and leave it at that? That the story is, um, developing? Isn't that the way you usually put it? Air it without the video."

"All right. And what else?"

"Well, we show the tapes to military intelligence. We alert armed units—quietly—to what's happened. As well as to our suspicions about the warlord's involvement. And leave the means of rescue for them to decide."

"No!" The producer leaned forward suddenly and banged the shining table with his fist. "That's not enough!"

The ambassador jumped again. "What do you want then?"

"I want a car, with diplomatic plates, and access to all areas. I want a local guide. Someone who knows where there are inhabited caves."

The ambassador looked helplessly at the ceiling. "Why does everyone want an embassy car?" He looked back at the producer. "Mrs. de Mornay and Colonel Arbuthnot already took one of my cars. I don't know where it is. There's only one more. And its brakes are a bit ropey."

"That'll do," said the producer jumping to his feet. "Let's go!"

"I must just place several telephone calls before we go."

"Go ahead. I'll wait."

"In privacy." The ambassador cleared his throat. "I cannot discuss UK business in front of a representative of the American press."

The producer heard, or thought he heard, a hint of distaste in the ambassador's use of the word "American." Did he mean to imply that the American press was likely to be worse than the press in general?

"Look here you limey bastard," growled the producer. "You can have one call. I ain't goin' nowhere. The rest you make from the car." The producer gave the ambassador a menacing look over the table. "Or, I put out a report saying that UK diplomats refuse to cooperate with the stars and stripes."

The ambassador sighed. He picked up the telephone as the producer stood up to glower at him. "Could you get me St. James's Palace, please?"

"Oh hell!"

"Yes, that's right. I'd like to speak to His Royal Highness's private secretary, if you can find him. Yes, I'll wait."

"You have got to be kidding me."

The ambassador stared back at the producer as he waited. He held his ground.

"Ah, Sir Mortimer," he said after several seconds. "Yes, yes. That's right. From Kabul." He paused and listened. "Why it's sunny here. Quite warm. And London?"

The ambassador chuckled. He held his hand over the mouthpiece and smiled. "Raining there," he told the producer.

"Will you get to the god damned point? We don't have all day."

"Sir Mortimer, I *am* sorry to trouble you. But a little something has come up."

*

"Do you really think they're going to kill us?" Cindy asked. She was lying with Harry on a rug in a locked inner chamber of the cave.

"Don' know, mate. That's what 'e said." Harry stared into the darkness with eyes open. "I don't think they would've let us be together if they weren't planning something pretty

drastic for dawn."

"How? How'll they do it?"

He reached over with his arms and pulled her head and shoulders up against his chest. She did not resist. "Don't think about it. Anyway, I'm gonna get us out of here. So why don't you get some sleep?"

"How? How're you going to get us out of here?"

"Don't know yet."

"I thought Mustafa was your friend."

"I thought so too."

"Then how could he all of a sudden go over to the other side?"

"I don't know." Harry paused and thought. "Don't be too hard on him."

"What. You saw him. Carrying that gun. He even seemed to know that guy who came in afterwards, the one in the black turban."

"Yeah, he was the worst."

"Taliban."

"How do you know that? I didn't think the warlord chappie was."

"No, he's probably not. But the Taliban often wear black turbans. He was the one who promised to kill us. He was the one who said we'd be more valuable dead than alive."

"Yeah the one in the white turban just wanted to make some money off us." Here Harry leaned down and kissed the hair on top of Cindy's head. "I went to school with blokes like him. What you call hunter preneurs."

"Entrepreneurs."

"That's what I said."

"But Mustafa ..."

"It ain't easy bein' brown, sweetheart. Not in Blighty. If you're Muslim, it's worse. If you're gay on top of that, well, it's like the trifecta of stuff you're not supposed to be."

"I watched the two of you together. I wondered if there wasn't something going on between you guys."

"Ooh, baby. You were watching us, were you? Did that turn you on?" He was amused for the first time. It had so far been a sleepless night for them both. He squeezed her shoulders and gave her a little shake. "A little man-on-man action. Girls like that, don't they?"

"No, they don't." She pulled away from him.

"Just a little?"

"Look. There's something I have to tell you."

"You've got a little lesbian side to you? That's okay, baby. I'm cool with it."

"No!" She pulled away from him on the rug and leaned her back up against the wall with a wide space in between them.

"Oh come back, Reed. I were only jokin,' weren't I?"

"Why do you joke around and use goofy accents all time? Like right now? I mean that's half your problem. You're never serious. You're always like let's-have-a good-time, let's-have-a-party boy."

Harry was silent.

A more intense mood began to creep over them both.

"I don't believe it," she resumed.

Still, Harry said nothing.

"It's some kind of an act. It's not who you really are."

"Who am I then?" said Harry in a smaller voice than usual. It was neither entirely plaintive, nor skeptical, but contained

elements of both.

"I don't know. Sometimes you're a different guy. Sometimes you're a better guy, a smarter guy. Like back in the camp. When you decided to go out after the colonel even though they told you not to. Or back in the Hilton. When you started getting everyone organized."

Harry didn't say anything to that.

"And then you just sort of fall back into this douche bag, stupid frat guy personality."

For a while Harry said nothing. Then he said, "I'm not."

"Yes you are. I don't know what it is. Something you don't want people to see. Something you're ashamed of, maybe."

"I'm not ashamed."

"Okay, then. Maybe it's something else. But I've seen it. Being a goofus is not totally who you are."

"Maybe I just wanna little privacy, okay. Maybe I wanna little time off. Maybe I don't want everything in my life to be public, okay?"

"Then why do you play the fool all the time? Keep doing what you're doing and the camera's always going to be swinging right to you. They're going to want to see what dumb trick you'll try to pull off next. That's not going to get you a whole lot of privacy. It's more like you're trying to prove something."

"Prove what?"

"You tell me, buster."

He was then silent for a long time, so silent that she looked over at him after a while to see whether he'd fallen asleep. His eyes were closed, but his breath wasn't the even, thoughtless breathing of a sleeping person. It was conscious and fully

awake breathing.

She waited. She breathed. She began to fall asleep herself.

Then, after a long time, maybe a half hour, she didn't know because she was feeling submerged herself, she heard him say, in a whisper. "It was a long time ago."

Then his voice broke and there was an intake of breath.

"And?" she said, looking over at him across the distance on the carpet between them.

His breath became more jagged.

She scooted across the space and put an arm around his shoulders. She pulled him toward her. Instead of merely accepting the embrace, the whole of his body sagged and collapsed into hers. His head fell on her chest. He threw a leg over her leg. He put an arm around her waist. He was shuddering. His voice was suddenly choked with phlegm and saliva and snot. He breathed in to try and clear his nose. "I didn't want anyone to see. The way I felt. I didn't want them to. Feel sorry. For me. I didn't want them to. Know."

She tightened her hold on him. "C'mon. It's okay. Everyone knew how bad it was."

"That's what I didn't want."

"But it was obvious."

"Not if I didn't let them see it."

Cindy didn't know what to say to that. It seemed irrational to her. It seemed to go against the facts. Everyone on TV could see how terrible it was, and what he'd had to go through. She didn't want to argue with a crying man.

"Not if I showed them, like, it never happened to me. I'm not sad or anything. And I never was."

It was nuts. How could he possibly think that? He's crazy,

thought Cindy.

Then she felt his hand at her waist. He was working his hand from on top of her camouflage tunic and trying to find a way underneath. All of a sudden, there it was, his warm hand on the skin of her soft side. He didn't stop there. He started working the hand upwards. She almost laughed. He was like a child, as if by some blind animal instinct, seeking a nipple to suckle.

Then, quickly, he was on top of her in the dark and his lips lightly crossed her cheek as he looked for her mouth.

That's when the scene changed.

He didn't kiss like a boy. He didn't kiss like the marauding teens she remembered who'd kiss her hard while twisting and turning and grinding on top of her. Crushing her. His lips were feathery. They might have even been female lips. He kissed her gently, enquiringly. His face was wet, but he was no longer urgent or upset. He was exploring. He was not the male avenger she'd encountered among some of the other guys she'd slept with. He was carrying on a conversation with her via a different, non-verbal means. It was as if he said, without saying, "Oh. Hi. Is that you? Did you mean that? Me here. How're we doing?"

And then, when he got her out of her clothes, which she allowed because he'd made her curious, because he seemed genuinely forgetful of himself, because she was in awe of his fascinated, tactile investigation of her body, he stroked her with his flattened fingers. He didn't rub. He didn't poke. He smoothed and he brushed. He tapped more than he thrust. Instead of groaning or gritting his teeth, he made nonsense remarks into her neck and prodded her with gentle touches

of his nose. All this was even before he was undressed. When they were both naked and pressed into one another from ankle to ear, she had a vague memory of some class she'd taken at Emory. Had they read about some ancient part-male, part-female human being? Had a jealous god cut this androgyne into two? Had the two parts spent the rest of their wounded lives searching? Trying to reclaim what was missing? She couldn't remember. She didn't care. It didn't matter anymore. She matched her breathing to his, and fell asleep.

*

In the next cell over, Frances was awake and leaning her back against the wall. Andrew was on his side in a fetal position, his hands held between his legs for warmth, his head on Frances's lap for comfort. He was asleep. She watched the unconscious movement of his shoulders and the occasional, involuntary vibrations of his feet. How many generations of women had watched over their lovers sleeping? She didn't know, but she liked being one of an infinite number. Did she dare to call herself his lover? They hadn't actually become lovers yet, but he felt comfortable enough with her to lay his head in her lap. His losing himself in sleep as she watched was a form of intimacy that was new to them both. It was almost better

than being made love to. It kept her wide-awake. It was the reverse of alcohol, which numbed and deadened. It felt as if he'd administered an elixir with life-giving properties. How had she gone so long without this? How had she let herself forget what this was like?

Nor had she felt anything before that was quite like this combination of the maternal and the erotic. She kept her hand lightly in his hair, just enough to give herself contact with him, but not enough to wake him up. At length, though, he woke up anyway. He straightened out his arms, as if he were a cat with outstretched paws, made fists of his hands, and smiled up at her with the languorous look of an animal that had only comfort to think of.

"How long was I asleep?"

"Not long."

"Did I say anything?"

"Nothing very revealing. You slobbered a little." She reached down with a handkerchief she had in her hand and wiped the corners of his mouth.

He allowed this. "That's lucky."

"We mayn't have long now," she sighed. "You may as well tell me all your secrets."

"Don't worry. I'm going to get us out of here."

"I don't see how," she said, rattling her shackles gently. "But if it can be done, you're the one who'll know how."

"Thank you," he said. He sounded like he meant it.

Reassured by his tone of voice, she couldn't stop herself from carrying on. "One might wonder why a resourceful man like you never married. Loving parents. Handsome face. Rapid rise through the ranks of the army. I'd have thought

that made you a very eligible young man."

"That's not for me to say."

"You must have had girlfriends, though."

"Well, ye-es," he allowed.

"You did?"

He said nothing.

"Or you do?" she added.

"Did." He swallowed before saying, "and do."

"Well that's that," she said lightly, laughingly, secretly a little hurt. She pretended as if it meant nothing to her. "I'm not going to be the old witch who stole you away from Annabel or Arabella or Harriet. Or whoever she is." She pushed him off her lap.

"Whoever they are," he said sitting up with a groan.

"*They* are! You scoundrel. Typical man. Two women at home in Britain. I see it now. Pining for you. Miles apart. Neither one knows about the other."

"Actually," he tried to interrupt.

She continued in her mock fantasy, which was an overlay for her hidden disappointment. "One young miss in Shropshire, and the other in, I don't know, the Scottish Borders. I'm glad I found out what you're really like."

"If you must know, they're across the square from each other. Bernice and Marie. And they each know the other."

"How very modern and sensible of you all."

"And they're not young misses."

Frances said nothing.

"Bernice is sixty-one. She's at retiring age, but she's staying on because she doesn't really know what else she'd like to do. She's a waitress at the club. Marie is younger, it's true. She's

fifty-five. She looks after membership at the London Library."

Still, Frances said nothing. She was thinking of the repercussions of this. How did it affect her?

"I believe they have coffee every once in a while. In the *Prêt* around the corner. They talk about my bad habits. They share my emails with each other."

"You've quite a harem, then? Polygamy. I knew some Afghans practiced it, but I had no idea it went on in St. James's Square."

"I'm not actually married to either one of them."

"How convenient for you. Gives you a free hand, doesn't it?"

Now for the first time, Andrew was not exactly angry, but he was exercised. "Look here. D'you think it's easy? Liking women who're older than me? I had to keep it a secret in school. At that age boys say cruel things that tend to stick. Nor can you exactly share it with fellows in the army."

"A terrible burden for you," Frances observed, a bit crisply.

"It's fine for you to say that. But what about when you try and tell the lady in question? She laughs in your face, most of the time. It's humiliating, Frances. And I'm surprised that you don't understand it."

"Oh Andrew," she softened.

"And then, if people find out, they blame your mother. As if I were abused in the cradle."

"Andrew," she repeated.

"It wasn't like that. I just enjoyed her company. Especially when I was in my twenties. We'd have lunch. She'd come and meet me in town. We'd go someplace special, someplace smart. Bibendum, or Sheekey, or Leith's. And you ought to

have seen her. She took trouble with what she wore. She glowed. I so loved being with her. She'd tell me things about herself I never knew. She became my friend. Not my mother. She wasn't embarrassed. She treated me as her beau, not her son."

Frances reached out now to take his hand. "That's lovely Andrew. Nothing wrong with it. Nothing in the least."

He wasn't ready to forgive her earlier coldness, not yet. "And you didn't notice me, either."

"What do you mean?"

"When you were at my parents' house. For drinks. For supper. I'd watch you. I'd see what you were wearing. I'd go up to my room and think about it. I'd try to remember it. You never took the least notice."

"Andrew. Flirting with the teenaged son of close friends is not a thing that ladies in Norfolk then did. I don't think it's encouraged, even now. In our forward times."

"You had a green dress. With sequins. That flashed in the light. Very form fitting."

"Oh, that old thing."

"So form fitting, that I could see your breasts. On a cold night I could even sometimes see the outline of a nipple."

Here she couldn't take his recollection seriously any longer. She laughed. She was delighted. A teenaged boy had observed her when she wasn't aware that he'd even been looking.

It wasn't absurd to him. He refused to laugh. He looked straight ahead and remembered what it felt like to be invisible, unattractive, and sexually insignificant.

Frances glanced over and saw the look. "Oh for heaven's sake, Andrew. It's all right. I'm only sorry that there's not

more left." She reached over gently and took his hand in hers. She brought it over slowly and guided it to her left breast. She pressed his hand to it. She looked at him with all the tenderness she could muster. "They're both a good deal more, well," here she laughed again, "more deflated than they once were."

"It's lovely. They're ..." he began. "You're lovely. Believe me please. When I say that."

She leaned over and kissed him on the lips. Both their mouths were open. She breathed in and felt grateful.

When they leaned back, he reached out and held both of his hands in hers. They looked at one another. Unafraid. Giddy smiles began to play at the corners of both of their mouths.

"I don't know what you're grinning at," she told him. "The situation is still pretty grim."

"Right. Now we set to work. I'm sorry about this. But we've both got to stand up now. There's not enough slack in the chains."

She didn't question him about what he proposed to do. She followed his lead.

They both struggled to their feet. Andrew led the way as they shuffled over to the door, which was a locked grill. The cave had been used as a prison before. In a surprisingly loud voice he called out into the corridor. "Oi! Hello! You there! You call this hospitality? You in the black turban! I'll bring the Geneva Convention down on your ears. Bring me the key to these shackles!"

*

In another chamber of the cave, the warlord was speaking harshly to Harry. Mustafa stood behind the warlord's back with a gun trained on Harry. "Listen to me! The cruel one— the one in the black turban—he will kill you in the morning if you don't tell me. He is Taliban. They show no mercy."

"I believe you," said Harry, laughing at the thought that he might have to be convinced of that.

"Only I can save you."

"You and my old mate, Mustafa, there."

"Quiet!" roared the warlord.

Harry was not afraid. "Or he used to be my mate. Before he joined up on the other side."

"He is family. He is the son of my cousin. He is my brother forever. He is Pashtun. Our families hold together. A prince of the infidel blood must understand that."

"Yeah. I get that. It's being a traitor I don't get."

"Silence!"

"Look. I'm not gonna give you Granny's phone number, whatever you say. It's on my speed dial anyway. I don't think I can remember it."

"A money order from the infidel queen is the only thing that can save you. A telephone call to her is the only way to get the money here before the cock crows. That is the hour when he has promised to kill you. If a wire of $250,000 from her arrives before then, I can get you all out of here before he

awakes."

"Look, it used to be $100,000. When did it go up?"

"I have had certain expenses since then."

"Right. I bet you have. I personally think I'm worth a lot more than that."

"If the sum is, as you yourself say, insignificant, then it will be all the easier for her to send it."

"I doubt she keeps that much in dollars hanging about. She likes sterling. Her picture's on it, and all."

"I would accept £170,000."

"Nah. No deal. We're not bringing her into it. Just forget it. I'd rather face Darth Turban than haggle with you."

They glared at one another.

Mustafa cleared his throat. "Um, maybe he'd tell us if we gave him the Lawrence of Arabia treatment."

"What's that?" asked the warlord.

Harry stared silently at Mustafa, but the look in his eyes said, "I don't know what that is, but, whatever it is, I don't forgive you."

"T. E. Lawrence. An English officer captured in Saudi Arabia during the First World War. They stripped him. Whipped him. And ravished him." Mustafa spoke this to the warlord, while staring at Harry the whole time.

The warlord rubbed his hands together. "Yes. Excellent. Subjected to that, he will certainly give us the telephone number. He will make the call himself. She will wave her scepter and I will be rich."

"You have got to be kidding me," said Harry with a disbelieving laugh. He didn't look at the warlord. He continued looking at Mustafa.

Mustafa, still standing behind the warlord's back, where he couldn't see him, kept his eyes locked on Harry's. Then silently, he gave Harry a broad wink with his left eye. He shifted the gun to one hand and with the other, raised an index finger to his lips. "Go on," he said. "If you won't give us that phone number, maybe you'd better start taking off your clothes. Mate."

"You heard him," said the warlord said to Harry.

Harry had seen the wink, and the finger to the lips, but he wasn't entirely sure what they meant. He pulled off his camouflage tunic. Underneath he had on a green army tee shirt.

"Now the boots," said the warlord. "I can sell those."

Harry started to pull off one boot, and hopped off balance for a moment, as he struggled to get it off. "Are you sure? I haven't changed these socks in weeks." He pulled off the other boot.

The warlord stepped forward and with a thrust of his hand, whisked the desert boots away. He turned around and set them down in the corner.

"And the socks," said Mustafa with the beginnings of a smile.

"You are weird, mate," said Harry, removing first one sock, then the other. He finished by throwing them across the room and hitting Mustafa in the chest with them. "You want to have that head looked at. By a good shrink."

"What whiteness of alabaster. What long toes," said the warlord. He was not ashamed of appreciating the look of a young man's slender feet.

"Tee shirt and trousers, Wales," said Mustafa.

"I was right the first time. Messed up. That's what you are. Messed-up-a, Mustafa."

Harry pulled off the tee shirt. His chest was white and his nipples pink. There were light patches of reddish fuzz on his lower belly. He was still wearing the pendant that Mustafa had made fun of earlier.

The warlord beamed. He'd almost forgotten the purpose of the exercise. Then it occurred to him. This young man came from a family that had a fortune beyond imagining. That made him angry. "Are you ready to give us that phone number yet? I will tell her she may save your life. The money will be transferred. And you will be free."

Harry undid his canvas belt. The waist of the trousers hung down low on his hips. Then he unzipped his trousers and stepped out of them on to the floor. He was wearing a pair of black, nylon boxer briefs, with red stitches outlining the seams and elastic waistband. His underwear clung to him like the skin of an aquatic mammal.

"Nope," he said to the warlord.

"What now?" said the warlord turning to Mustafa, whose eyes were still on Harry's, his gun still pointed at Harry's chest. "We whip him? What with?"

"Do whatever you want," said Harry, "but I've gotta warn you." Here he put his thumbs down and snapped the waistband of his underwear. "Haven't had a shower for days!"

"No, we don't need a whip," said Mustafa to the warlord. He suddenly sounded tired. "Leave him to me. I'll get the number out of him."

"What do you mean leave him to you?" asked the warlord.

"Leave us alone. What I'm gonna do next you can't watch."

"But I am in charge here!"

"Do you want the number or don't you? Do you want the money or don't you?"

The warlord was torn. He looked back and forth between Mustafa and Harry. Then he thought of the money appearing as if by magic in his account at the New Kabul Bank.

"All right. I will give you ten minutes, but no more. And I will lock you in the room with him." He went to the door, opened the metal grill, which was similar to the one on the door of Andrew and Frances's room. He went through, and pulled the gate shut until the lock clicked. He disappeared somewhere into the inner reaches of the cave.

Now Mustafa and Harry were alone in the room. One stood and held the gun pointed at the other. One stood there in his underpants.

"Right, mate," said Harry using a different, more confidential voice. "What's this all about then?"

"You were going to be my friend."

"I am your friend."

"No. My real friend. We were going to go into battle together. We were going to be in the trenches. We were going to be mates. For life."

"We did. We are," said Harry, snorting with his nose as if he couldn't believe Mustafa didn't see it the same way he did. "We will."

"No, we're not. You're with Reed."

"That's different. She's a girl."

"You liked her even before she was a girl. Everyone could see it. Not just me." Mustafa threw his gun down on the pounded dirt floor. It made a metallic thud. He went and sat

down with his knees up and his arms across his knees. He put his face in his arms as if he were going to sleep.

Harry was surprised at this turn of events. He walked around the gun on the floor and went to sit down next to Mustafa. He put his arm around him. "Come on, mate. You're not in competition. Not with her. You're separate."

Mustafa ignored him. He would not be consoled. "And I had you right where I wanted you. I could've made you pay."

"Pay? Pay how? We're not talking about the 250K, are we?"

"No."

"Oh," Harry snickered. "You wanted to see me naked, didn't you, mate? You were lookin' forward to ravishin' me, you devil." He laughed more, so that his belly jiggled. "It's okay. I'll show you. I'll let you cop a feel. Is that what you want?" Harry put out his hand to try and take Mustafa's hand. He was about to pull the hand over to his lap, but Mustafa jerked his hand away.

"Get off!"

"Look, mate. It's okay." Harry tightened his grip on Mustafa's shoulders. He shook him. "I've got an idea. When we get back, I'll get you into the senior XV at the rugby union."

"I'm not interested."

"No mate. You don't get it."

"I don't do sports."

"Here's the thing. Rugger's totally gay. You'll love it. The guys are always getting wasted and naked and grabbing each other's nuts."

"They do?"

"Straight up. It's your sport, mate. Totally."

Mustafa raised his head from his arms, still not looking at

Harry, but looking less ashamed, and less defeated.

"That's it, mate," said Harry, encouraging what he took to be the improvement in Mustafa's mood. "Life's not so tragic, is it?"

Just then they heard their colonel's voice shouting somewhere outside the door. "Oi. Hello." It was loud enough to bring back the warlord, and wake up the man in the black turban, wherever he was, if he was asleep.

"Go, go, go!" said Mustafa jumping to his feet.

Harry jumped up too. "Go? How? Where? The door's locked."

"Grab the gun. Shoot the lock," Mustafa pointed at the gun on the cave floor.

Harry did as he was told. He shot three shots at the door until the metal grill swung part way open with a rusty creak. Mustafa pulled the door the rest of the way open. Harry looked back indecisively. There was his pile of clothes on the floor.

"There isn't time for that. We have to go. Come on!" He ran out the door in the direction of the colonel's voice and Harry, wearing only his underpants, and carrying the gun, ran after him.

✳

Mustafa and Harry raced down a dark hall. At the first lit room they came to, Mustafa went forward and waved at Harry to stay behind him outside the room. Mustafa encountered the man in the black turban together with the warlord. On a table were several stone figures of human beings. Each of them was about a yard long. They dated from when northern Afghanistan had been in active contact with the Roman Empire, between the first and fourth centuries. Twentieth-century archaeologists had excavated the sculpture near Bagram. The statues had vivid, lifelike expression. Their bare arms and legs were the smooth tributes of an ancient sculptor to the beauty of the human body. The man in the black turban was raising a sledgehammer to destroy them. The warlord in the white turban was looking on in dismay.

"You madman!" said Mustafa with raised voice as he interrupted them. "What are you doing?"

The two men in turbans looked up in surprise.

"These are idolatrous."

"This is pre-Islamic art, you thug. It comes from before the sixth century. Before the prophet. You don't even understand what idolatry is!" With that, Mustafa knocked the man in the black turban over on to the ground. Harry took this as his invitation to enter. He rushed in and over-powered the warlord. The two men's turbans, having become dislodged in the scuffle, unwound into long narrow strips of cloth. Harry and Mustafa used these strips to bind the men's wrists and their ankles so they couldn't move from sitting positions on the floor. They took their keys. Then they raced back out to free Frances and Cindy and Andrew.

Once released from their chains, all five of them passed

through several empty rooms, barren except for carpets on the dirt floors, as they headed further inside the mountain. Mustafa, who was leading, stopped them on the verge of entering another chamber of the cave.

"We can't go any further," he said over his shoulder.

"Why not?" asked Harry.

"This is the women's part of the cave. Men not allowed. This part of Afghanistan is strictly sex-segregated."

"So! We've got to get out of here. That room's the only way forward."

"Perhaps if you were to speak to them in their language," suggested Andrew to Mustafa. "Then maybe they'd tell us how to get out."

"The last time I saw him, he wasn't even on our side," objected Frances.

"Brilliant bait and switch, Mudge. He fooled the chappie in the white turban into thinking he'd switched sides," said Harry. "But Khan's with us. He got me out."

"But where are your clothes, darling?"

"Oh that. Long story. Cut to the chase. Khan here clobbered the Taliban as he was about to smash the Elgin Marbles."

"They weren't Greek," said Mustafa, annoyed. "They were ..."

Andrew interrupted him. "Lieutenant Khan! Proceed."

Mustafa entered the room making friendly bows and salaams as the other four held back outside the doorway. The four Afghan women in the room were alarmed. They put their headscarves up around their hair and held the ends of the scarves up to cover their faces. Mustafa addressed them in Pashto. Calmed by his language, his manner, and his

explanations, they seemed to grow less shy and less upset. Now he beckoned to the four who remained outside. In came Cindy, Frances, and Andrew. Mustafa introduced them. Harry came in last.

"And this," said Mustafa, "is Hari."

He needed no introduction. They knew who he was. They giggled more animatedly than before and held their headscarves firmly from ear to ear. They watched him, fascinated.

"No need to hide, ladies!" said Harry. "We're not here to hurt you."

"The scarves are for modesty!" said one of the women, who apparently had no problem understanding or speaking perfect English, though she'd led Mustafa to believe otherwise. "Hari could learn something about modesty too." She nodded down to his naked navel.

"Hey! This wasn't my idea."

"Ladies," interrupted Mustafa. "We need your help. We have to get Hari out of here. Or they'll kill him."

The four young women looked at each other. "No!"

"Can you help us find the way out?" asked Mustafa. "And loan us something for him to wear?"

The four women looked at each other again. One said something to the others that not even Mustafa could understand. They all four covered their noses again and bent over double, their laughing voices sounding like silk rubbing on silk. Then two disappeared to the back of the room and re-appeared a minute later carrying highly-colored folded fabrics. All four of them surrounded Harry. He disappeared beneath a flurry of long gowns being thrown in the air and

placed over his head. One of the four women uttered high-pitched ululations, as if they were at an Egyptian wedding. They all giggled. A long headscarf whipped out from their female scrum in a ballet-like gesture as it was tied, re-tied, and re-arranged.

When they stepped away, Harry stood in the middle of the room wearing a long pink gown that went from his neck to the ground. He had a diaphanous floral headscarf around his head and jeweled slippers that were slightly too small for him on his big, pale feet. All he could do was spread his arms and allow the others to laugh at him.

Cindy now stepped forward and took the initiative. She went over and selected the one of the four women who'd spoken earlier. She put her arm around the woman and led her over to a computer screen in the corner. Cindy brought up a map of Afghanistan via Google Maps. "Where are we?" The woman showed her by pointing to a spot on the map on the screen.

Then Cindy took out the small black video camera she'd retrieved from Harry earlier. She handed the camera to Frances and went to sit on a rug where the women had made Harry sit down also, cross-legged, wearing his pink gown. The women, one after the other, were bringing him little books and scraps of paper. He understood what they wanted and he was less embarrassed. He recovered his sense of what he was supposed to do.

He switched into his friendliest voice. "You want my autograph, love? Isn't that sweet?" He bent over and signed one of the women's little books with an offered pen. "What's your name then? Aeisha? Shall I make it out to Aeisha from

Harry?" She nodded vigorously. "You know, I'm no one. Right? Bet you wish it was me brother, hmm?" He said it bruvva.

She shook her head "No!"

Cindy spoke to Frances. "Use that as the establishing shot." She nodded toward Harry. "Behind me." Then when Frances had turned the camera on, and the red light was illuminated, Cindy, all business, said "This is Cindy Reed reporting for CNN. I am in a cave approximately four miles to the west of Mazar e Sharif. I am still being held together with three UK nationals. One of them, behind me," she indicated Harry in his dress with the women, "has been using our captivity to win the hearts and minds of the local population."

*

After Cindy had finished her report, she had a hurried conference with the woman who'd helped her. They sent off Cindy's video from the computer in the corner. Then with her hand raised, this same woman led the way out of the room. The other three women stayed behind and watched them go. They went via a labyrinth of passages, different from the way they'd come in, back out to the front of the cave. They encountered no one. After twenty minutes of following the woman in her long dress, sometimes crouched over so as not

to hit their heads on the rocky roof of the cave, they came suddenly upon harsh outdoor sunlight shining on a dirt floor. They were at the lip of the cave. The Afghan woman pointed their way forward. They must go out and downwards. Then she turned and stole silently back into the cave's interior. The five of them stumbled outside into the blinding light. They were confused and didn't know which way to turn. In front of them was a slope littered with enormous stones and a steeply descending dirt path. Cindy was the first out. The others began to follow her down the path, when two fighter jets came shrieking across the sky. They all looked up. Something fell upon the lower reaches of the path in front of them and exploded. Cindy and Frances and Mustafa jumped instinctively to the left. They sheltered in the lee of a big boulder that had an overhang under which they could crouch. Harry and Andrew jumped right, but in the shuddering of the ground from the explosion, they both lost their step. They rolled head over heels, Harry's long gown making him look like a pastel tumbleweed, until they both came to rest in a rocky ditch twenty yards further down the path.

Harry quickly got up on his haunches and dusted himself off. "That was quick, colonel!" He was more excited than frightened. "They must have got Cindy's report already. They know where we are. The Americans flew out some fire power."

Andrew remained curled in a fetal position.

"It's all right, sir. I think we've got the all clear. I don't hear any more planes."

Andrew winced.

Harry interpreted Andrew's grimace as a verdict on Cindy's reporting. "It's good having someone from CNN along, isn't

it, sir? I mean she's done quite a lot for us so far."

Andrew winced again.

"Are you all right, sir?"

"I don't think I am, actually."

Harry leaned over and tried to pull Andrew up into a sitting position.

"Ow!"

"Sorry, sir!"

Andrew made a pained face and slowly righted himself so that he was sitting cross-legged at the bottom of the ditch. "It's just a cracked rib probably. Not your fault, Wales. Don't apologize."

"It *is* my fault. I got us all captured, back at the Hilton, didn't I? That was my mistake. It was a trap. They knew I'd come out looking for you. I walked right into it."

Andrew looked over and, even in the midst of his own pain, saw the younger man's being hard on himself. "We don't know that for certain," he said.

"There was an emergency medical module. At Sandhurst. I sat through it twice. Couldn't do it. Failed it both times. They gave me a commission anyway. So I don't even know what to do with someone who needs urgent care."

"Don't exaggerate, Wales. It's not urgent. Broken ribs heal on their own."

"I don't deserve to be out here. I thought I could prove I was up to it. That I could be good." He looked into his lap and shook his head.

"Don't feel sorry for yourself, Wales. It's unattractive." The young man looked so sad at that, Andrew thought he probably needed some more tactile help. Despite the pain in his side,

he reached out with his right hand. He put a hand on Harry's shoulder. "It's natural to feel a bit overcome. Don't dwell on it. It doesn't help."

Here two more planes came overhead with little warning. Ordinance began falling on the slope of green scrub and white rock. Andrew and Harry had to lean over and cover their heads with their arms.

"Damn!" said Harry, straightening back up to a sitting position, covered in white dust. "That was close!"

"Just doing their job."

Harry shook his head again. "I'm the only one not doing his job."

"You sound like Eeyore." Andrew reached out his hand to brush some of the white dust off Harry's shoulders.

"Who?"

Andrew showed some exasperation. "You don't know Shakespeare. You've never heard of *Winnie the Pooh*. They're not in the Sandhurst curriculum, it's true. But you should have learned a few of these things before now."

"School, sir, was never . . ."

"Never mind. You are doing your job, Wales."

"How am I?"

"By getting those women back there in the cave on our side."

"That's not work. That's not being a soldier."

"It's what comes naturally to you."

"That back there is a total zero, sir, if you'll pardon my saying so. It's what people've always done to me. Since I was a kid. I thought in the army I could get away from all that. But even in a cave in the back of beyond, they want my bloody picture."

"Wales."

"Sorry, sir."

"Hotspur."

"Tottenham Hotspur? You wanna talk about football? You like the Spurs?"

"No, Hotspur, Hal's rival."

"What's he got to do with anything?"

"Hotspur and Hal are both young men. They have to fight to see who'll get the throne."

"Why'd anyone want it?"

"Because the throne is their chance. To bring glory to their families. To bring honor to themselves. To bring peace and good government to Britain."

"You'll forgive my asking, sir, wasn't that a long time ago? Like aeons? Like those were the days they were still doing animal sacrifice, right? And Stonehenge was their Westminster Abbey? I saw it all on *Dr. Who* once."

"Yes, it was a long time ago. Several centuries. But the principle's the same."

"What principle?"

"Both Hotspur and Hal are prominent young men. Everyone knows them. One's the son of the Earl of Northumberland. The other's the son of King Henry IV. Each of them learns to use that fame and that recognition. They have to. In order to inspire and to motivate the men."

"I don't get it."

"When the two eventually do fight, and Hotspur is struck down, Shakespeare says all the energy goes out of Hotspur's men. When they can't see their young man fighting, they don't feel like fighting themselves. *For from his metal was his party steel'd.*"

"Yeah, well, the guys don't like me that much. They're not gonna fight because of me."

"If they don't, it's because they're hanging back. They're watching you."

"Why? There's nothing to see."

"They want you to be more like a prince."

"What?"

"I don't know. How should a prince be? It's up to you. You show them."

"I'm sorry, sir. I'm not sure that's right."

"What if you treated the men more like you treated those women in the cave? They might go with you. That's a place to start."

"I don't think I can, sir."

*

Cindy heard a shout from somewhere below them. "Hey!" She and Frances both got up on their knees to see further down the slope. There, beneath them, struggling against the rocky terrain, Harry had his arm around Andrew's waist. Andrew had his arm around Harry's shoulder. Harry was part pulling and part supporting Andrew as they struggled to climb up the hill. Andrew was frowning.

Frances was the first to stick her head out from underneath the ledge of the rock where she and Cindy were sitting.

Harry saw her. "Mudge! I need you. Come help me. Quickly."

As soon as they got Andrew under the ledge of the boulder, Frances pulled off his camouflage tunic to expose his bare chest. She soon discovered the trouble. A small bit of cracked bone had pushed up and pierced the skin. A trickle of blood ran down his chest from where the bone had broken the skin.

Harry and Cindy leaned over Frances's shoulder as she inspected him. Andrew turned his head away and gritted his teeth.

"What do we do now?"

"Well, we bind him up. Try and do as good a re-setting of the bone as we can."

"Bind him up with what?" asked Harry. "We haven't got anything. No bandages, no plasters."

"This scarf'll do," said Frances, taking the flowered scarf away from Harry's neck. She was practical. "But you'll both need to hold his hands. When I run it around his chest, and tie it up, it's going to pinch. Just a bit." She bent over and whispered in Andrew's ear. "Is that all right, my darling? I'll do it quickly. Over before you know it."

Andrew shut his eyes and nodded his head. Cindy held Andrew's right hand. Harry held his left. Frances reached under Andrew, lifted him up slightly, and ran the scarf under him. Then, because it was long enough, she ran it around him again. She tied it tightly over the wound, pressing down on the bone with her fingertips until it felt as if it might be threading back together. During this, the only sound was a

sharp intake of Andrew's breath between gritted teeth. He clamped the two hands holding his.

Harry reached down and stroked Andrew's hair. "That wasn't so bad, was it, sir?"

Andrew didn't reply. His eyes were still closed.

"That'll hold him for a while," said Frances. "But I'm afraid you and Cindy are going to have to go for help. He'll need a scan to see if the bone's in place. And to make sure it hasn't punctured anything vital."

"But where do we go?" asked Harry, a little helplessly. "And what about him?" Harry noticed Mustafa for the first time. He was lying down with one knee up and the other flat on the ground.

"Broken ankle," said Frances.

Harry went over and knelt on the ground next to him. "Oi. Don't just lie there. Get up."

"Oi, Whitey." He gave Harry a friendly wink.

"You useless camel bollocks."

"Harry!" reproved Frances. "Language."

"He likes it, Mudge." He put his hand lightly on Mustafa's chest. "Don't you, mate?"

"No way," said Mustafa, though his tone of voice said otherwise.

"Break it up you two," said Frances. "You've got to bring back proper medical attention. And transport. Soon."

Harry sat back on his haunches, unsure of what to do next.

"C'mon, let's go," said Cindy grabbing him by the arm. "Down the path. Before they send over more planes."

She pulled him out from under the stone ledge and on to the downward path before he could think. He pulled up his

gown around his calves. They went hopping and skidding down the path, dislodging small rocks, occasionally slipping on gravel when they lost their footing. Several times they both nearly fell. They went down, down, down, with no more sign of aircraft overhead, and meeting no one as they went. The terrain was mainly rocks, short grasses, and coniferous shrubs. They were high enough on the mountain still to be above the line of deciduous trees.

After an hour of steep descent, a village came into view beneath them. It was no more than a dozen primitive houses, built of the same white and chalky stone they'd encountered all the way down the mountain. Smoke floated up into the air from a single chimney. In a big dry space between the houses, where the earth had been beaten down flat, a dozen bare-footed children were kicking a soccer ball back and forth.

Cindy had been leading the way down the path, but she sensed Harry was no longer behind her. She turned to see him five yards further up the path, stalled, an uncertain look on his face. "Come on," she urged him.

"Hang on a minute. What's the plan here?"

"We go in and tell them we need help."

"Dressed like this?" protested Harry and indicating his dress. "What if they're Taliban in there?"

"What do you want to do then?"

"I don't know."

Cindy turned to look at the village again from their vantage point. "Look at that. They've got electricity." She pointed to a single cable looped across several barren tree trunks that served as electric poles.

"So?"

"If they've got electricity, I bet they've got a computer and maybe DSL internet too. We can maybe Skype the base. Or send them an email? Tell them where the others are. Get them to send in a helicopter. I can send in another report. Tell them we're free."

"Oh great. But if they're Taliban, we're not gonna be free for long."

"All right." She put her hands on her hips. "What do you think we should do then?"

"I don't know." Having admitted that, Harry came down the path and stepped around Cindy who stood in his way. He did not touch her. Then he led the way the remainder of the way into the village, more cautiously and more slowly than she'd led the way down the mountainside. The first people they encountered were the children playing with the ball. They were of different ages, between about eight and fourteen. They stopped and stared at the two strangers approaching them.

"All right, you lot!" said Harry, his caution evaporating. "You call that football?" He kicked off his jeweled slippers, ran up to one of the boys, and with a deft movement of his right ankle, stole the ball that was standing on the ground in front of him. Then he ran off down the ground, holding up his skirt, knocking the ball back and forth between his feet. The kids needed no further invitation. They tore off after him in a pack. Two grabbed fistfuls of his skirt. Another darted in to try and steal back the ball. Another picked up a stick and came running after Harry threatening to hit him with it.

"Hold on you ragamuffin, you," said Harry, turning serious a moment. He stopped kicking the ball. He addressed the

little boy with the stick. "Sticks are not allowed, mate. Throw it away." He made a tossing gesture.

The boy, abashed, threw his stick on to a rock pile next to one of the houses.

"That's it," said Harry. "Here you go, mate." He kicked the ball in the direction of the little boy who'd just thrown away his stick. The boy received Harry's soft pass with delight. Then he kicked the ball back to him. Harry ran off down the ground again and the boy followed. They passed the ball back and forth between them as the other children tried ineffectually to get the ball for themselves. All of them shouted and laughed.

"No! Oi! Over this way! Okay! Mine! Yes!"

Harry's shouts were the only ones Cindy understood. She stood aside. The children were no longer interested in her. While they played, she took out her camera and filmed them. She had ten minutes' good footage of their game. Harry ran back and forth as if he were exactly their age. He forgot about the dress. He lost self-consciousness. He was not faking it. It was the most natural, unaffected thing she'd seen him do. Then, through the viewfinder, she noticed something different. There were several women beginning to congregate in the doorways of the houses. She took the camera away from her eye, and was about to warn Harry, when two of the smaller kids, a boy and a girl wearing thin cotton smocks, who hadn't managed to get the ball back, tackled him in their frustration. Harry swooped the girl up into one armful. He held the boy upside down by his bare ankle. The boy yelled a loud, indignant protest. "All right, all right," he said to the screaming boy. He put him down on the ground. Then he bent over, looked around, and spoke to the boy on the ground.

"What you doing down there, then?" He squatted slightly and looked over his shoulder, and encouraged him. "Up you go then. Piggyback."

The boy needed no translation and no instructions. He jumped up, took a flying leap on to Harry's back, and threw his hands around Harry's neck to hold on. Harry walked a few steps forward, the little girl still in the curve of his arm, the boy on his back, ten others trailing behind him with the ball, when one of the women from the doorway assailed him. Perhaps she was the mother of one of the children. She approached Harry speaking angrily in a language he didn't understand. She waved with her arms to indicate he should put down the children.

Harry turned to speak to the woman. He put his hand on one of the bare feet of the girl cradled in his arm. "Right. I'll give her back to you in a minute. But look here. These kids need trainers. You can't kick right with a bare foot." He manipulated the girl's bare leg to indicate a kicking motion. "Shoes, love. That's what they need. "

Cindy had turned the camera back on.

The woman looked at him. She was still angry, but at a loss how to answer him.

Harry continued. "You can have mine. Too small for me. I kicked 'em off back there." With a nod of his head, he indicated where he'd kicked off his slippers before running on to the playing ground in front of the houses. "And they need some jerseys too. With long sleeves. It's too cold out for this." He pulled on the hem of the little girl's smock.

She didn't know how to react to this either. Before she could reply, however, several other women came running across the

beaten earth. "Hari! Hari! Hari!"

"Oh god," said Harry sighing, but he also turned to Cindy. He gave her a resigned and crooked smile.

Then one of the bigger boys came up and gave Harry a light, parallel kick on the bottom before running away, grinning, hoping for Harry to chase him. Harry turned and ran after him with the village women in hot pursuit.

*

A half hour later Cindy and Harry were sitting cross-legged on the carpet inside one of the village houses. In front of them was an iron teapot and several baskets of unleavened bread. The bread had just come out of a stone fireplace. Also in the circle were the children of different ages, and half a dozen women. They all held small earthenware cups in their two hands, partly for the warmth. Many of them were chewing the crusty bread. One young woman spoke English. She was translating questions for Harry from the other women in the circle.

"She wants to know," said the young woman, "what the old lady of the reflecting spectacles is like."

"Well, you know what grannies are like. Pretty cross-cultural that one, I expect," answered Harry. "She's got a

pocket full of sweeties. She'd slip me one on the down low when I was little." He demonstrated with a covert gesture of his hand opened behind his back.

This met with a murmur of approval after it had been translated.

"Except that," Harry continued, "they were made of sugar and barley. And she gave the same ones to the horses." The women and children chuckled. "And the ponies in Scotland for trekking." One or two women laughed and pulled their scarves over their mouths. "And the dogs."

Here the amusement was general and less restrained. Cindy sat back and marveled. Why was he so much more at ease than she was? He seemed unafraid of who would come in the door. She couldn't help interrupting. "But where are the men of the village?"

The woman explained that they were out on a patrol that would last several days.

"Are they fighters?" asked Cindy.

"Most assuredly," replied the woman.

"Who do they fight for?"

"For Allah. Also they fight to protect us, their women and children."

"Ooh," said Harry in a comic voice. "The great white gran won't like that. Not if they're Taliban." He reached over and pulled one of the soccer-playing boys into his lap. "There'll be no horse sweeties for you, kid. Not if you join up."

The woman replied with gravity. "The Taliban hold courts. They send us judges. They decide our disputes fairly. When we relied on the government in Kabul the judges never came. Or, if they did come, they had to be bribed."

"That's a pity," replied Harry. "But isn't it true they stone a woman to death if she happens to look at a guy the wrong way? That they cut off a guy's hand if he steals something?"

"We have no adultery. We have no stealing. Those are lies of the Western media."

"Over to you, love," said Harry looking at Cindy with an encouraging wink. "That one's got your name on it."

Cindy cleared her throat. "But in the States we hear that the Taliban doesn't allow women to go to school. That they're punished if they do. Is that true?"

"We have no school here. So there is no punishment."

Cindy wasn't sure how to respond to that. Harry had an idea. "Um, if you have no school, how'd you come to speak such great English? I mean, like, you're fluent. You could order a chai latte on the Fulham Road, no problem."

The woman blushed with pride, but behind her it became apparent that several of the other women who'd pretended to speak no English, had also understood what Harry had said. They spoke into the blushing woman's ear.

"We have a very intermittent internet," she said. "And an old computer. I have learned English that way. So have the others. We have no school. The internet has been our school."

"Right. I think school's overrated. But sports kit I can do. Computers I can do. Someone to hook you up with wifi I can do. Loads of all that back where I come from," said Harry. "And loads of people falling all over themselves to give it to me. For free. So. It's not much, but there I've got you covered. I can set you up."

Not all the women understood everything he said, but they grasped the emphasis. There were several calls to the English-

speaker for translation. She gave a Pashto version. Then a gust of pleased laughter whooshed through the room. Several of the women shut their eyes as they laughed. The children took it up and added their higher voices. One of the women at the back jumped up and produced an old-fashioned, battery-operated cassette player from a basket. This seemed to her cause for celebration. She pushed a button and began playing a song that sounded like disco music written for a souk or a bazaar. There were high wind instruments, perhaps Turkish clarinets. There was also an insistent, up-tempo, mood-improving beat that might have been recorded in a gay club. There was tambourine percussion. The music filled the room. The women jumped up one by one and began moving to the music. The English speaker got up and pulled up Cindy with her hands. The two of them danced together. Harry stood up and began dancing with several of the soccer-playing children. All twenty of them danced in a circle around the bread and the teapot.

The music was so loud and they were all so engaged in the dance that they didn't hear the two British protected mobility vehicles, called Foxhounds, grinding up the narrow dirt road into the village. Nor did they see the dozen men with helmets, bulletproof vests under their uniforms, and their weapons at the ready as they climbed out. Nor did they see them nosing around the ground outside the house. It wasn't until a British sergeant and two men came to the door, blocking the light, that anyone knew anything was happening. A cry went up from the Afghan women. They all fled to crouch in the corner, pulling their children into a huddle with them. Harry and Cindy were left dancing

with one another. He had his eyes closed and a hand on her waist. She had both hands raised in the air. She was waving her arms in time to the beat. When the music from the old cassette player came to an abrupt halt, Harry looked up. Cindy lowered her arms.

The sergeant in the doorway spoke. "Look what we have here."

One of the men standing behind said. "Yeah. A deployment's work for some, but here he is dancing with some bird."

"They sent us out to look for you, mate," said a third. "Said it'd be dangerous. Said we might have to storm a cave full of Taliban."

"Some guys have all the luck," said the sergeant.

"He dances," said one of the two men. "We sweat."

Harry looked at the three. He kicked open his legs so his stance was wide on the ground even though he was still bare-footed and wearing a dress. Then he used a voice with them he'd never used in the regiment before. It was the same voice that Andrew Arbuthnot usually used with him. He didn't explain the dance. He put his hands on his hips.

"Look here, sergeant! Very glad to see you. What took you so long?"

"What?"

"Reed here sent in her report to CNN ages ago. The Americans have already strafed the entrance to the cave where we were being held. But it's taken you lot hours to get this far. The cave's further up. What's your explanation?"

Although the sergeant shared the general skepticism of Harry's fitness for his commission, they were in different units. They'd never encountered each other before. The tone

of Harry's voice indicated dismay. Harry outranked him. His army training kicked in before he had time to think about it. He began to apologize. "Well, we're sorry, sir, but ..."

"Sorry won't do in this situation, sergeant! There are two officers up above, both ours, both injured, outside the cave. A civilian's looking after them. They're all vulnerable. The longer we take to get them help, the more likely it is they'll be taken back into captivity."

"Well, sir, don't we get back in the Foxhounds, then? And try to find a way to drive up there?"

"Your first sensible decision so far, sergeant."

The three men turned to go back out of the house. Harry followed them and Cindy tagged along behind him. The sergeant objected. "Hang on a minute. Who's she? She can't come. It's UK army only."

"She's got a press pass. She's embedded with the Yanks. We're in a coalition with them. Remember?"

The sergeant looked at her and nodded his head unwillingly. Harry put his arm around the sergeant's shoulder. "She's also my bird. So hands off."

"Your what?" said Cindy.

As the two men walked ahead of her to the Foxhounds Harry said to the sergeant, "Oh, and you can help me send an email to the Football Association."

This made the sergeant half a shade more cheerful and willing than a moment before. "Right you are, sir."

"We're gonna get them to send a load of kit up here to these kids, aren't we?"

One of the little girls came running and protesting over to Harry as he was about to climb up into the Foxhound. Harry

picked her up, kissed her on the forehead, shook her up and down until she laughed, and then said "Aren't we, mate?" He then showed her off proudly to the other soldiers in the Foxhound. "Our hope for the World Cup, right here. We have to show her Arsenal, don't we? You're gonna play at Emirates Stadium, aren't you, darling?" After that, Harry set her down and promised he'd be back. He hopped up into the Foxhound, and both vehicles began groaning up a dirt track that ran upwards from the other side of the village.

*

Andrew and Frances were both sitting in a hospital room in Kabul. Andrew was in a big hospital armchair next to the window. The chair was a cheerful aqua color and intended to suggest leather, although it was made of plastic. Sunshine flowed into the room. Andrew was wearing striped pajamas. The pajama jacket was open to reveal lengths of broad surgical tape that had been wrapped several times around his chest. Frances was sitting up on the sheets of his unmade hospital bed, with the back of the bed raised to support her. She had on a blue Liberty print shirt and pressed cotton trousers that ended in the middle of her calf. Although nearing seventy, her legs were still slim and sha

was barefoot. Her flat shoes were kicked off on the floor. They were both watching CNN on a television fixed high on a cinder block wall.

Under the headline "Special Report," could be heard Cindy's voiceover narration. It joined together several different sequences of film, obviously shot at different times. There was the warlord in his white turban with darting eyes. There was a sequence filmed in the cave with the Hilton club chairs. There was a bit of Harry playing soccer with the children, followed by the village women, and Harry dancing to Afghan pop music. The most dramatic sequence came last. It was taken from the back of a Foxhound. Filmed from the rear, it showed Harry dismounting from the vehicle, and leading the way forward with a wave of his hand.

"Oi, you lot!"

A group of Afghan fighters was standing at a distance before the mouth of the cave. There was the snap of bullets in the air. Soldiers in British camouflage uniforms ran forward behind Harry. The camera looked several different directions and was held with a shaking hand. It became steadier as it followed Harry, in his pastel gown, as he crept up to the entrance of the cave. The camera showed two Afghan fighters struggling with equipment. They were trying to set up a tripod to support a rapid-firing gun. Harry leapt on to the back of one of the men, wrestled with him, and pinned him down. Then the camera was dropped on the ground. The last sequence was of Andrew and Mustafa being carried on stretchers down the hillside and Frances picking her footholds behind them as they came down the path.

"Hooray!" cheered Frances with an ironic note from the bed.

"Well, you look all right, at least," said Andrew from his armchair.

The last filmed bit was from a conventional angle. It was Cindy interviewing Harry. They were now both in camouflage fatigues. His were slightly browner and less green than the American version she was wearing. She was holding a CNN microphone. He was wearing a beret with a regimental badge on the front.

"And so," she began, looking a little unlike her on-camera persona. She might even have lost her way.

Harry looked at her, not the camera. He nodded to encourage her.

"And so, Your Royal ... um, no. I mean lieutenant ..."

"Harry?" he said with a raising of his eyebrows.

"And so, now that you've seen action, Harry, do you think the war in Afghanistan has more of a point than you thought it did before? Or, is it a hopeless debacle?"

He squinted at her. "Um?"

She pressed forward. "I mean a lot of people in the States, in the UK too, don't approve of this war. It's just like Iraq. A lot of money. A lot of blood. A few elections. And then chaos all over again. Why is the UK in Afghanistan?"

"Well, it's about what you call, um, ..." He stumbled and looked for the word.

"Infrastructure?" she offered.

"Yeah. Roads, bridges. Helping people out. That sort of thing."

"Is that worth it for the UK taxpayer?"

"I think in the UK they'd like people out here to lead a decent life. Just like most people have in the UK and a lot of

people here don't. Why shouldn't they?"

"So you think Afghanistan ought to bring back its monarchy? Just like in Britain? Would that make for a better future here?"

"No," said Harry laughing good-humoredly. "It's not a great job description. Luckily, it's not up to me."

"Is it realistic to think that the US and UK are going to get rid of the Taliban?"

"I don't know. I've only been out here for a few weeks. Terry's nasty, no doubt. But everyone here knows them. The Taliban works for some people. Can we get rid of them? Maybe we bring the Afghan security force to London to help root out some of our gangs. You know? We could use the help."

"What is it realistic for the coalition to aim for, then?"

"I think we can do something for the kids." For the first time in the interview, he seemed to mean it, and not to be faintly making fun of what he was saying. "Let's get the kids shoes. Let's get them balls. Let's get them warm clothes." At this he turned his head to look straight into the camera. "It's not right for kids to suffer."

"What about schools?"

"Oh right. And schools. A Taliban-free zone where kids can go to school. Yeah. And where the kids who're no good at school, can be taught something else. Some work. Something useful."

Here Cindy turned to the person out of the shot holding the camera and said "Okay, let's cut it there." She made a cutting gesture with her finger across her neck. She turned to Harry and lowered her hand holding the microphone. Her voice, though fainter, was still audible. "All right that's enough.

We're done."

Harry stepped closer to Cindy and put his arm around her waist. "Nope. Not done. Just getting started."

"Hey, wait," she said, before he leaned in and kissed her squarely on the lips. She waved him away several times swinging the microphone in her right hand. After a few moments she gave in. The hand with the microphone then came up around Harry's waist as she kissed him back. The microphone rubbed along the fabric of his tunic making a "Shussh" sound. Here the film of the special report came to an end. There was an image of a CNN female anchor in Atlanta. "That was Cindy Reed reporting from Afghanistan. With additional reporting from Sandy Reed in the early part of the film," she said, with one eyebrow raised.

Frances and Andrew gave one another a lopsided grin. She pressed the remote in her hand and turned off the television. "He's been called to a meeting at the embassy. Do you suppose he'll be decorated?" she asked.

"Possibly," allowed Andrew. "Usually it would be the army that would do something like that. Not the diplomatic service."

"Well, I hope it's to be something good. I know I'm not impartial. But I do think the way he led those men up the mountain was terrific." She emphasized the word with maternal pride.

Andrew was more muted. "He did all right."

"And what's to become of us all now?"

"Those decisions will be made over our heads. London always decides."

"You must concentrate on getting well. It's back in the bed

with you now. You've been down there in that chair for half an hour. That's enough strain on the old rib cage."

Before she could climb out of the bed, Andrew had nimbly jumped up out of his chair. He hopped over the space between chair and bed. Then he slid in alongside her on the bed.

"Andrew! Stop it. One of the staff might walk in at any minute." She coughed lightly because he'd surprised her.

"Oh? What's that cough all about?" said Andrew, putting one arm protectively around Frances's shoulders.

"It's nothing. The dust out here doesn't agree with me."

"We'll have to examine you, patient." Andrew reached over with his other hand and began unbuttoning the Liberty blouse.

"Andrew, stop!" she said laughing.

"Doctor knows best. We'll just have a little listen to the breathing."

"Andrew really! Stop messing about."

Here Andrew had unbuttoned enough of the blouse to reveal her brown, sun-freckled neck, two prominent collarbones, and a champagne-colored camisole. He ran his hand gently over her neck and upper chest. He ran his index finger over the rolled neckline of the camisole. "Now, will the patient breathe in deeply, several times, for me please?" He put his head down on her chest to listen to the breathing in her lungs. "Mmm, Floris. Lavender," he said.

"Andrew," she laughed. She lifted her right hand to run it down the cotton flannel of his pajama arm. Then she bent her head and chin to put her nose into his hair.

"Oh, patient," he said after several moments of listening with his head in a luxuriant position, ear down, on top of her

breasts. "I'm afraid this is not good at all. It's going to call for a more thorough examination."

She crossed her ankles with contentment. "Well then, please lock the door, Andrew."

*

Harry appeared in his dress uniform across the desk from the ambassador. He did not salute, but his posture and bearing suggested a salute. He stood up straight, thrust out his chest, and folded his beret under his arm. "You sent for me, sir?"

"I did." The ambassador was in his pin-striped suit, with a little UK flag in his lapel. When he was a junior officer in the foreign service, no one ever wore flag pins. He did it now to imitate the US flag lapel pin the American president wore to please his most rabidly patriotic followers. The ambassador didn't like excesses of patriotism, but he thought he ought to model himself on what the Americans were doing. Just to be safe.

"I gather you and Cindy Reed's producer came out to look for us."

"We did," said the ambassador drily.

"Well, I'm sorry we didn't meet up, but I did just want to say thank you, sir. Much appreciated."

The ambassador was still angry about being led on a two-day wild goose chase through the desert. It had landed them nowhere near the cave where the Afghan fighters had held the captives. Moreover, his superiors at the Foreign Office in London had hinted that he was somehow responsible for having allowed Harry to be captured in the first place. It had happened on his watch, they said. Even though Harry had escaped, and helped the other captives to safety, the ambassador was already feeling the chill blast of Whitehall's disapproval. He felt it was most unfair and unreasonable. "Well, you're welcome, is I suppose the thing to say. It wasn't easy, I'll admit."

"No, sir, I'm sure it wasn't."

"That American was mad. And drove like it too. He nearly killed us both. Several times. All because he's in the midst of an affair with that reporter."

"What?"

"That's what I understood. And the reporter works for him. It wouldn't do at the BBC. But perhaps these things are tolerated in America."

"They're not."

"Well, that's what I understood, certainly. It's why he was so insistent we go out looking for you ourselves, rather than waiting for the army to do it."

"They just work together. They're not a couple."

"That's not what he told me. Sitting round the campfire. As it were."

Harry was silent. He struggled to keep his face impassive, but the color rose into his cheeks.

"Anyway. That's not the reason you're here." He looked up

to see the redness in Harry's cheeks. He thought the young man probably had already imagined the purpose of the meeting. It gave the ambassador courage to tell him more straightforwardly than he would have done otherwise. "You're being recalled to the UK. This afternoon, in fact. There's a seat on a flight for you leaving at fourteen hundred hours."

Harry had not guessed. "What!"

"Not my decision of course. Not even the Foreign Office's decision. It was taken even above the Ministry of Defense, as I understand. St. James's asked me to let you know that much." He sighed. "Having you out here is too great a risk to the coalition effort. They've seen that now. So you get a reprieve. You're going home."

"No!"

"I'm afraid so." The telephone on the ambassador's desk began to ring. "Now that'll be the real reason you're here. They wanted you to speak on the secure line."

Harry looked at the ringing phone. He was angry and confused.

The ambassador picked up the receiver. "Kabul embassy," he said assuming the voice of a trusted servant. "Ah, Your Royal Highness. Yes, he's right here." He handed the receiver to Harry standing across the desk from him and said, changing his tone to something more stern, "Your father."

Harry took the phone. "Hello?"

"Dear boy," said the Prince of Wales's voice down the other end of the line. "We're all so proud of you."

"For what?"

"For the way you behaved in captivity, son. For the rescue of Colonel Arbuthnot and Mrs. de Mornay." The Prince of

Wales had a velvety voice. He sounded the way Alec Guinness and Peggy Ashcroft had once spoken on stage in the 1950s, but mixed together with self-mockery and self-deprecation. "It was MAR-vel-lous. It's been on telly. Camillar and I have watched it again and again. You gave the old Tally-ban a little what-ho, didn't you, darling?"

"Dad! They want to send me home."

"I know, petal."

"They can't. I just got here!"

"I do know what you mean. But what the government asks, we must do."

"There are these kids in a village. I played football with them. They don't have any shoes."

"I don't doubt it for a second."

"I sent an email. To the FA. And Beckham's going to send some kit. And they need computers too."

"How's his wife? Isn't she called Victoria? Such a lovely name. Why does she go by Posh?"

"Dad! We didn't talk about that."

"Well, your mother did quite a lot for Oxfam, you know? They might be persuaded to help. Or, Save the Children, maybe?"

"Right! Good idea. That's why I've got to stay out here. I can help coordinate. I can make sure the stuff gets there. So one of the warlords doesn't sell it off."

"But the government has called you home, Harry. You're still only a second lieutenant. You've got to follow orders."

"Not when the orders are wrong."

"Yes, dear. Even when the orders are wrong. If the Foreign Office says the Duchess of Cornwall and I must go and meet

the good people of Alberta or Azerbaijan, well, we must just go. There's no choice."

"Well, I'm not going."

"Harry. Listen to me. If you disobey orders, it'll kick up a tremendous fuss. Do you know what Number Ten will say then? And your grandmother's been through a lot. It's time for her to put her feet up. *The Guardian*'ll have a field day, of course. They'll declare a republic within forty-eight hours. No, you can't do that, my dear."

"Dad, I don't care. I'm staying here. Where I can do some good. It's the first time in my life I can. I know I can."

There was silence down the line. Even the Prince of Wales could hear the faint ring of truth, from many thousands of miles away, in what Harry had just said. "Um, Harry?" Prince Charles said at last.

"Yes, Dad."

"Has this something to do with that reporter from the Central News Nonsense?"

"*Cable* News *Network*, Dad."

"Of course, but has it?"

"Her name is Cindy Reed, Dad."

"Yes, that's the one," said Harry's father with a warm chuckle. "We could see at the end of her report that you, um, ..."

"What Dad?"

"Liked one another. I don't blame you, of course. She's stunning. Absolutely."

"But Dad," Harry protested.

"Invite her on holiday with us. The end of August. We'll take her fishing."

"I don't think she likes to fish."

"Oh come now. Stop pulling my leg. Do you know any decent girls who don't like to fish?"

"Dad, I'm not talking about this. I'm not even sure she likes me."

"Don't be silly. That's where you're wrong. Everyone could see it. Just be a good boy, come back home now."

"Dad, for the last time: I am not coming home." Having said that, Harry handed the telephone to the ambassador. Then he turned and walked through the door.

"Now look here, Harry. You mustn't do this."

The ambassador put his finger in his collar as if it had suddenly become tighter. "Um, Your Royal Highness," he began. "I'm afraid that His Royal Highness has just left the room."

Part V

Go Not to
These Wars

Harry walked across the dusty forecourt of the British Embassy. He walked by the pair of beat-up ambassadorial cars. He made straight for the iron gate and the sentry's box on the right. Each of his angry footsteps ground the gravel with a crunch. As he grew closer to the gate, he could see a crowd of shouting people. Was it an anti-British demonstration? He could see pushing and shoving. Were people trying to get in to apply for asylum? Or a visa waiver program? It was only as he got closer that he saw that several people had microphones in their hands and almost everyone had a camera. The sentry was speaking to them through the gate and refusing them entry. When Harry came up behind him, everyone lost interest in the sentry. Harry could now see that several of the microphones in people's hands had the logos of global media organizations: RAI, Sky, and MSNBC. They all began

shouting at him at once.

"Harry!" "Over here, Harry." "Hey, Prince!"

Dozens of flashes went off in his eyes, even though it was broad daylight and the sunlight shone down on him so that everyone could recognize him. He skidded to a stop and held up his hands to shield himself. He looked to the left and to the right. Then he looked around the direction he'd just come out of the building. He was looking for a way to retreat. That's when he heard a voice different from the others. It was a "Harry!" that was loud, but there was also a pleading note in it. It was a woman's voice. He looked to the left hand side of the crowd and saw Cindy's mane of brown hair. She didn't have a microphone or a camera. She was out of camouflage fatigues and wearing a blue blazer and white shirt. It looked as if she might be preparing to go on camera. "Over here!" she said, making eye contact with him for the first time.

He walked over to her. He put down his head and whispered to her through the gate. He used his friendly *East Enders* accent, though there was also a faint element of hurt in his voice. "What're you doin' 'ere?"

The others saw that he'd spoken private words to her and howled their questions in protest.

"Are you giving CNN another exclusive?" "Is it true you've been ordered back to Britain?" "Did you get yourself captured on purpose?"

"I'm a reporter, remember? I'm supposed to report." She said this to him in a low but urgent voice. It was loud enough so he could hear over the others.

"I thought you were my mate, like?" He leaned down and said this through the gate and into her ear.

"Let me in. I'll explain."

"You and your producer? And you didn't even tell me, love? That's what you wanna explain?"

"No! Let me in and I'll tell you."

Harry stood back and puzzled over what his response to that should be. Meanwhile, the other reporters and cameramen shouted after watching his whispered conference with Cindy. They had strained to listen, but found it impossible to hear what had been said between them.

"Is she your girlfriend?" "Did you guys get Stockholm Syndrome? Sympathize with your captors? Like Patty Hearst?" "If you go back, is your career in the army over?"

Harry looked at the sentry and told him to let in Cindy, but only Cindy. When the sentry opened the gate a crack, however, and pointed to Cindy, all the reporters streamed through, like rushing water through a canal lock. Harry was quickly surrounded by the shouting press pack. He held up his hands again. It was only when he glimpsed Cindy, on the outer edge of the circle, beckoning to him, that he understood what she wanted him to do. She pointed to one of the cars parked in the forecourt. She motioned with her hands. He should climb up on the hood and talk to them all. That was the only way of getting them to go away.

He retreated back to where the cars were parked. Then he climbed up on the hood of a dusty Range Rover, the metal making drumming noises. Because it was an old and sturdy model, it did not dent with his weight. He leaned on to the car's windshield for support. Cindy pushed and shoved her way to the front of the pack. She climbed up on the step to the driver's seat. She was near enough to Harry for him to hear

when she spoke without raising her voice.

"What am I supposed to say?" he hissed, bending over and speaking to her.

"Just tell them what's happened."

"Why were you at the embassy, Harry?" shouted one reporter.

"Call from my father."

"What'd he say!" called out one or two of the others. "Was he angry?" asked a third.

Harry laughed and looked more at ease. "Bad news. The army wants me to go home this afternoon. And so does my dad."

"Why!" called out someone in protest. Someone in London wanted to kill their story just as it was getting going.

"Risk to the other guys," quoted Harry. "Too many people want me." He laughed good humoredly at that. "You lot more than the insurgency, I reckon."

"What are you gonna do?" "Lead a strike force?" "Re-take the mountains?" "Go after the Taliban in Mazar e Sharif?"

Harry wasn't sure what to say. He looked down at Cindy. She shook her head silently.

"No," Harry answered the reporters. He wasn't sure what to say next. Then it struck him. He blurted it out on impulse. "Reed here and I wanna go back up there and try to help those kids."

"What does the army think of that?"

"I don't know. I didn't ask."

"Won't you get into trouble if you don't go back to London? Or are they giving you a special pass because you're royal?"

"I don't know. I don't care. I'm not good at much. I think I

can make a little difference. That's all I know."

"Are you and Cindy Reed getting married Harry?"

Here Harry looked down at Cindy. She held his eyes for an instant.

"Too early to tell," said Harry laughing. Cindy's unflinching look had suddenly made him irrationally cheerful again. "And now ladies and gentlemen, I think that's all. I need a little one-on-one with my, um, press adviser."

The pack of reporters dispersed quickly in the direction of the gate. They all wanted to be the first to transmit their stories and video footage. The film of Harry on top of a Range Rover would head the evening news in Boston, Bangkok, and Delhi. Only in London would they put the story at number two or number three on the roster, out of a sense of self-respect, embarrassment, and the fitness of things. Harry slid off the hood of the car, opened the door, and climbed into the driver's seat. "C'mon," he called out to Cindy. "Climb in. It's too hot out. We can sit inside. More private. I'll switch on the air con."

She looked at him for a moment with her hands on her hips. Then she went chin down and semi-unwillingly around to the passenger side, pulled open the door, climbed up to the seat, and sat down. She pulled the door shut with what might have been an angry slam. Harry ignored this. He looked into the glove compartment, found the key, and turned on the ignition. He set the air conditioning on high. He found a CD of London Jazz FM's greatest hits. He slid it into the car's player and turned the volume down low. A saxophone played its invitation. Then he looked over at Cindy. She was sitting in the passenger seat, not looking at

him, and staring straight ahead.

"Now, then." He said it sweetly, coaxingly, non-judgmentally.

She said nothing at first. She crossed her arms over her chest. She scowled.

"You don't have to tell me if you don't want to."

Then something broke. She threw herself on top of his chest and put one arm around his neck, another around his waist. She started crying. "I know I should've said something. I tried to. Once."

He raised his eyebrows and lay his chin on top of her head. He squeezed her in toward him with one hand stroking her hair and the other around her waist. "It's all right, darlin'. We're all human. We all need it, don't we? Don't blub."

*

Within an hour of Harry's impromptu press conference, what he'd said had begun to make waves in London. The press offices at the Ministry of Defense, Downing Street, and Buckingham Palace all received enquiries. "When was the last time a member of the royal family refused to follow orders?" "Given her special connection to the armed forces, did the sovereign herself now feel free to ignore advice from

the prime minister on military affairs?" "Who was Harry's immediate superior in his regiment and would this officer be disciplined?"

Some of these questions had been forwarded to Andrew Arbuthnot for comment. He was still in his hospital bed in Kabul. He was sitting up in the armchair by the window. His pajama jacket was buttoned closed. He looked sterner than before. Harry was sitting cross-legged, Indian-style on the unmade bed. Frances was standing behind Andrew in her blue print shirt, her hand on the back of the armchair.

"I didn't think, sir, ..." began Harry.

"You didn't think. Yes. Very good. That's the problem, Wales."

"But I didn't mean to get you into trouble, colonel. I want to help the kids."

"Will you please try to see the bigger picture? The war is bigger than you've seen so far. The insurgency in Afghanistan has connections to fundamentalist Islam all over the world."

"I don't care about that."

"It's not just a handful of children on a mountainside. It's millions of people. Not only here. In Africa. In Indonesia. In the capitals of Western Europe. All of them are threatened."

"I can't deal with millions. I can help those kids."

"A single village near Mazar e Sharif is not part of the broader coalition strategy, surely you can *deal with* that. Where'd you get that expression anyway?"

Harry wouldn't make eye contact. "Cind says it."

"Sinned? No one's speaking of sin here."

Frances leaned over and said gently, "No, Andrew. Cindy Reed."

"What has she got to do with anything?" said Andrew. His injury, the disobedience of his charge, being confined to a hospital when he didn't feel he needed it, all these contributed to his frustration.

"That's just it, sir. You don't get the global side either. Her report. The one of us. It's got ratings through the roof on CNN. It's got hundreds of thousands of hits on YouTube. It's not just 'The War in Afghanistan—Boring!' It's an 'Escape Story with Real People Getting out of Trouble—Interesting!'"

"What?" said Andrew.

"Doesn't that help the coalition too, sir?"

"Look, I can appreciate that those children are vulnerable ..." Andrew started.

"Not just vulnerable," said Harry in a burst of passion. "Wounded. Just like you, sir. But worse than you. Because they're at the beginning of their lives. At the time they should be safe and secure. With a real mum and dad. And no fighting. No shouting. No making them feel worried about what's gonna happen next."

Frances moved her hand to Andrew's shoulder. He glanced up at her.

"It's the least that we can do. To make sure they're not damaged. For life. Give them a little love. Which they need. So they don't feel abandoned."

"Your parents, Harry." Andrew cleared his throat. "It wasn't your fault. It was nobody's fault. They were both such graceful people. Especially when they were together. Both of them. They looked so well together. They represented us all. They made us feel better about ourselves. For a time. While it lasted."

Harry looked at Andrew for a moment. Then, he hung his head. Frances stepped across the small space between the armchair and the bed. She bent over and put her arm around Harry's shoulders. At that moment an Afghan doctor in a white coat, about sixty years old, wearing rimless spectacles, and a stethoscope around his neck walked in the room. He had on a shirt and tie. He also wore low, embroidered slippers made from a kilim, but with hard, stacked heels. He held up his arms as if he were a conductor before an orchestra. "Who is the patient here?"

Andrew silently raised his hand.

The doctor went over to Harry on the bed, instead. "But this one is the most troubled." Frances stood back. The doctor put his stethoscope into his ears and placed the metal piece on Harry's back. "Will you remove your jacket, unbutton your shirt, and breathe in, sir?"

Harry did as he'd been instructed. "Please don't call me sir."

The doctor spoke sharply to Andrew and Frances. "Carry on please. Pretend I am not here."

Frances started a little tentatively. "Perhaps it would be better, dear, if you got on that plane this afternoon. It might save a lot of trouble."

"It would," agreed Andrew. "Work through the normal channels. Nobody says you can't raise funds for the children. Of Mazar e Sharif. When you get home."

"Of course you could," said Frances. "Ask people to sponsor an event. Get donations of the sports kit. Collect the technology. Send it out to them."

"Pardon me," broke in the doctor, moving his instrument around inside Harry's unbuttoned shirt, the instrument on

his naked chest. He was continuing to listen, though clearly following the conversation too. "That will not work."

"What won't?" asked Frances.

"Raising money for the children of Mazar e Sharif in Britain. Sending it to them here. I watched Ms. Reed's report on CNN."

"Why not?" asked Andrew.

"Because the money will be stolen. The Taliban here will take their cut. Some charities in Britain will skim off a bit. The tax authorities in both countries will have their slice. Barclays and the New Kabul Bank will have their percentages too, which they will claim for the conversion of the currency."

"What then?" asked Harry, who'd slowly regained his composure.

"I am not sure," said the doctor, wagging his head back and forth. "I am a doctor, not the United Nations."

The four of them looked from one to the other for a moment, confused, unsure what to say next.

"What about ..." Andrew suggested.

"If we ..." chimed in Frances.

"And the children ..." added Harry.

"What about if we and the children all went to Britain? And slept at Kensington Palace?" finished the doctor, delighted with himself.

"What good would that do?" asked Harry.

"Travel is education," observed the doctor. "They will see something beyond their borders. If you show them something they like, they will bring an idea of it back to Mazar e Sharif. It might have a better effect on them than watching armed vehicles on their road and helicopters in their sky." He then

held up his hands in his conductor's gesture again. "And everyone would like to know where Hari sleeps."

"I think that's an excellent idea. Don't you, Andrew?" put in Frances.

"It might work," Andrew answered, "but only if he gets on the plane this afternoon. And there would have to be something for the children to do once they got there. They can't just go and be photographed on the London Eye. They've got to let people in the UK know that there's some community of interest between us all."

"Darling, won't you reconsider? Going back this afternoon, I mean." Frances didn't beg Harry exactly, but she asked it of him as if it were something that would especially please her. She said this with a small, ladylike cough behind her hand.

"I pronounce him fit for service," said the doctor nodding at Harry. He looked at Frances with the back of her hand still covering her mouth. "Now it is your turn, princess."

*

Harry and Cindy were standing just outside passport control at Kabul Airport. Though it was a high-ceilinged hall with tall windows, the exterior was made of the same cheap, raw concrete that had been used in many Soviet era buildings of

the 1970s. Harry and Cindy didn't care. They were holding one another in a tight embrace. They were also breathing in one another's smell. They wanted to remember it when the other one was gone. She smelled of the Tide she'd brought along with her to wash her clothes in bathroom sinks. He smelled of the English bar soap, Pears, that had been part of English officers' wash kits since the nineteenth century.

"Stop," said Cindy. She pulled away from him. "Now. Before we get any more of an audience." She nodded with her head to several groups of tourists, officials, and other passengers who were standing at a distance from them, watching. Several of them had their cellphone cameras out.

"Ignore them," said Harry, leaning back in and starting to kiss her.

"Harry! No."

"What's wrong?" He gave her a pirate's wink. "I know what you like."

Now Cindy took a definite step back and away from him. "Not when I say to stop."

"If you come with me, we don't have to stop."

"I've got a job, remember?"

"Sure. But come and do it in London, okay?"

"It's not like that. I have to go where they send me."

"Just like they embedded you out here, right?" He pulled her back into an embrace. "Like that was their idea?"

This time she allowed it. "I can't get away with stuff like that all the time."

"Hmm. Like the sound of that. What can you get away with? What can we get away with?"

"Stop. Let me go. We have to say goodbye now. It's late. You

have to get on the plane."

"Why don't you tell CNN you've got a story for them? That you're gonna fly to London and report on the Afghan kids? Follow them around with your camera. See what we can do for them?"

"Harry," she said with a note of decisiveness. She pushed him away, with both her hands spread apart on his shoulders. "There's something I have to tell you."

"I know you like it when I kiss you back here." He snuggled up his nose under her hair and began kissing her behind the left ear.

"Stop it. I mean it," she laughed. "This is serious." She resumed her grave face.

"What then?"

"We can't do this."

"Why can't we? Who says we can't?"

"I say. I can't do what you do. I want to be a journalist."

"I'm not stopping you."

"No, I mean in Atlanta. With CNN. It's the biggest job I've ever had. I can't quit now."

Harry looked back at her blankly.

"And I wouldn't know how to be with you. In public, I mean." She nodded at the people in a large semi-circle, still watching them. It had increased by a half dozen people. "I don't know how."

"I could show you."

"But not without giving up what I do. I can't do both. You know it. I don't want to be a celebrity girlfriend."

Harry looked back at her and swallowed. "I didn't ask to be this. I just woke up and I was it. I was born with it. I have to

make the best of it. Don't call me a celebrity."

"What then?"

Harry was a little angry that he should even have to put this into words for her. He'd thought she'd already understood. "What my grandmother does, what my dad does, what my brother will have to do one day—poor sod—is not the same as what Justin Bieber does. Don't you *get* that?"

Then a tall man came forward saying "Excuse me!" He managed to get through the circle of onlookers. It was Cindy's producer. With a friendly manner, and a big hand extended for a handshake, he gave Harry the self-assured smile an older man often gives to a younger one. "Great to see you, Harry!"

Harry unwillingly allowed his hand to be shaken. He did not squeeze back very hard.

Then the producer turned to Cindy. "You wouldn't believe it. What a little good reporting can do, huh?"

"What?" she said to him, uncomfortable with the interruption, unsure what he was talking about.

"I've been on the phone to Atlanta," said the producer. "They're considering giving you an anchor slot. In prime time! They're also talking about offering you your own show. With me to produce. It's fantastic. Not definite yet, but they want us both to come back and talk about it."

"What?" said Cindy again.

Harry looked crestfallen. "Well. That's that then."

"Wait a minute." She turned to him.

"No. I get it," said Harry, but he also felt wounded, as if he'd just been bested by the older man in an unfair fight. That's why he couldn't stop himself from adding a little insult. "And, maybe you just like older guys, hmm?"

Cindy felt this as if it were a slap to the face. He'd taken her secret, which she'd explained to him in confidence and let her producer know she'd told him everything. She felt exposed.

The producer was the only one who was utterly calm. "Hey, Harry. Pal. You've given her a hard enough time as it is. You put her in harm's way. Maybe you should back off." He reached out and put his arm protectively around Cindy's shoulders.

"Maybe I should," agreed Harry. He took a step backward and away from the two of them.

Then someone else came up saying "Sorry!" He elbowed his way through the circle of onlookers. It was the British ambassador. "Ah. Your Royal Highness. I'm glad to have caught up with you."

Harry was not happy to see him. It felt to him as if the military career he'd envisioned was suddenly over. That was what going back to London really meant. They'd put him behind a desk. This man was probably his future. He didn't return the ambassador's greeting.

"I've got one or two things in the diplomatic bag for you, sir." He held up a brown paper shopping bag and laughed at his own joke. "In here are two briefing books. A little light reading for the plane. Logistics of getting the Afghan children to the UK. Questions of where they should go and what they should do when they get there. Financial questions. Who's to pay for it? Media coverage. That sort of thing."

Cindy was feeling a little as if the threads of the situation had slipped out of her hands. She made a desperate effort to reassert control. She slid away from the producer so his arm fell away from her shoulders. She suggested to the ambassador, "Um, maybe that's something CNN could cover.

The kids. When they get to England."

"Sure," agreed her producer, easily. "We'll pitch it to the guys who decide that sort of thing."

The ambassador looked skeptically at the American producer. "Well, I can't guarantee that it would be approved on our end. Not until the plan's further advanced at any rate. Certainly, CNN wouldn't be allowed the sort of access you had before. The UK news media would have to come first, I'm afraid. I'm sure you understand that."

"Oh, we wouldn't even want exclusive access," answered the producer. "Too much trouble getting the pool film out to all the other news organizations. Right, Cindy?"

She looked at Harry and wouldn't look away from him. Her eyes spoke silent words of sadness, apology, and confusion. His eyes watched hers.

"And now, sir," said the ambassador checking his watch, "we just need to get you through passport control in time to meet a few people on the other side. People from the Afghan administration. My opposite number in their foreign ministry. One or two others. No more than five or six. They'd like to say goodbye. The departure time for your flight is coming up." He put his hand on Harry's elbow and pulled him gently in the direction of the glassed-in passport cabins.

"So long kid," said the producer. "It's been nice knowing you. You'll be glad to get back to the castle, I bet."

Harry ignored him. "Cind. Please. One last time. Come with me."

"I can't."

The ambassador began dragging Harry backwards toward passport control. One of the passport officers was already

smiling and on his feet waving them forward. Meanwhile, the producer took Cindy's hand and began pulling her in the opposite direction. "Come on, sweetheart. You'll see him again. There's Skype. There's email. There's Facebook."

Cindy, despite her producer's holding her hand held firmly, took a step in Harry's direction. He was already thirty yards away from her. The noise in the terminal building echoed off the walls. "Ha-ri!" she called out.

*

Although Harry flew back to the UK as he'd been ordered to, the reaction to his return in the press was hostile. Newspaper editors and reporters had all seen his press conference in Kabul where he'd promised to disobey the authorities. As a media event, this counted more with them, and had more reality, than his actual arrival back in the UK.

One thought it was an outrage that a young man from the Windsor clan should even think of disobeying the people's elected representatives, in this case the secretary of state at the Ministry of Defense, and the military authorities under him. They began to publish a series of articles that argued for the abolition of the monarchy.

Britain still had a large tabloid press too, with more

political influence than the equivalent newspapers had in the States. One of these took a more visceral approach. Its reporter made some calls to the hospital where Andrew and Mustafa had been treated for their injuries. She discovered that Mustafa's parents' money came from opium, and that Andrew Arbuthnot had probably been having an affair with Frances de Mornay. The newspaper ran a three-part series on Harry's deployment with the headlines "Harry Best Mate Is Son of Drug Lords," "Harry Commanding Officer Beds Former Royal Nanny," and "Cougar de Mornay Given the Sack for Drink." Those headlines were like French fries. If you had read that far, it was very hard to stop from reading further.

All the UK newspapers were secretly incensed that CNN had scooped them by reporting Harry's deployment to Afghanistan in the first place. They hadn't liked agreeing to the blackout on news about Harry in the first place. They felt it made them look foolish when their being parties to this agreement was brought to light.

The authorities acted swiftly in order to circumvent more criticism from the press. The army temporarily relieved Andrew Arbuthnot of his command and put him on an indefinite leave of absence without pay. Plans for his promotion to brigadier were shelved. Harry had been directly under his command. Colonel Arbuthnot ought to have been able to prevent a junior officer holding a press conference, or at the least he should have informed the army's media affairs division that it was taking place. The authorities hated ambushes.

Frances, who also returned to the UK because Andrew and Harry had been recalled, was miserable to see her past history

raked up. She felt humiliated that her relationship with Andrew had been discovered. It seemed twice as bad that this had happened in the early stages of their working out with each other what they wanted it to be. She was ashamed to see her name in the papers again. She felt partially responsible for Andrew's having been placed on a leave of absence. She went to live temporarily in the church basement in Staines. She did not answer telephone calls or emails from Andrew. She avoided passing near the local shops on her afternoon walk because there were several where she could buy whiskey. She began talking to the priest of the parish. Was it too late for her to take vows? Would it be wrong for her to try and join the Sisters of Mercy?

Cindy read all these newspapers in Atlanta. The promotion her producer had promised had indeed come through. He had for the first time a corner office with a round table and a sofa. Her office was smaller, but she was now featured on air just as he'd promised. This entailed their seeing more of one another rather than less. She was feeling lonely. She'd allowed herself to slip back into their old routine of sleeping together on nights they worked together late. She hated herself for it. She denounced herself for being weak, but the physical part of their being together was easy and comfortable and familiar. It was like slipping back into an old groove. The absence of Harry and the unsatisfactory way they'd left their relationship when he went back to London, made her more needy for physical contact than before, not less.

Nor did Harry respond to emails or friend requests or telephone calls from her. At first she'd tried not to contact him, but she wasn't strong enough to follow through on that

for more than a week. The switchboard at Kensington Palace started treating her as a nuisance caller and refused to take messages from her after her third try. The limbo of a non-reply was almost worse than his saying "Stop calling me," as at least then she would have known where she stood.

The army provisionally withdrew the commissions of Harry and Mustafa. This was pending an official investigation into their having left the camp against explicit orders to the contrary, their fraternizing with an Afghan militia, and their unauthorized interaction with Afghan civilians. There was no need for them to report for duty while the investigation was being conducted.

Harry reacted to all this by unplugging his devices and disabling his internet. The only exception was an old tablet that had some videos and games which he'd downloaded, and which he could play without being online. He wouldn't return his father's calls because what had happened was exactly what his father had said would happen. He didn't feel like talking to Cindy either, though the switchboard had forwarded her messages. Her goodbye to him in Kabul had felt too much like a rejection. He didn't shave. He didn't wash. He stayed in his apartment on his unmade bed. He slept a lot.

Nor was Mustafa on good terms with his parents. He stayed at home in his room with the door shut most of the time. His parents thought their son had destroyed all at once their patiently constructed edifice of Britishness and respectability. They were hurt and angry at him. They left him alone. On his part, Mustafa cared less about his parents than he did the media. How dare they ignore the humanitarian and cultural crisis taking place in Afghanistan? Every day Afghan villagers

were derided as medieval throwbacks in the press. Why had no one pointed out Afghanistan's history, its aesthetic heritage, its archaeological record, its resistance to invaders? All these were the equal, no, even the superior of Britain's. That was the way he saw it. The casual, and unthinking xenophobia of the Western media made him furious. What could he do? He didn't have Harry's resources. He couldn't fly back eighteen Afghan villagers on his own, as Harry had proposed to do, but perhaps he could do something. The warlord who was the cousin of his father had been put into prison in Kabul after their escape from the cave. Mustafa made arrangements to rescue the young warrior who'd been the warlord's underling. He'd done nothing wrong, and he had nowhere else to go, but back to his village. What would happen to him there if his former patron was disgraced? At least he might be brought to London and given some education in Britain, Mustafa thought. Beyond finding him a language course, however, Mustafa wasn't quite sure what he was going to do with him.

Mustafa also hatched a plan to move the media's attention away from Harry and put its focus on the reality of Afghanistan that was most meaningful to him. He wanted to stage a presentation on Afghanistan's cultural heritage at the British Museum. There were valuable relics there of Afghan history already. He thought there might be a lecture on these relics. Rory Stewart, a British diplomat, who'd returned from a walking tour of Afghanistan and written a bestselling book about it, might be one of the keynote speakers. Mustafa also thought of reading himself from some Afghan poetry of the seventeenth century, which he'd recently discovered. Someone

could also talk about Islamic fundamentalists destroying ancient Afghan treasures. If he could get Harry to attend, and maybe even Harry's father, it would shift the media debate to something more serious. Mustafa had a hard time proposing this to Harry, as he wouldn't reply to messages. So Mustafa went and presented himself at the security kiosk outside Kensington Palace. After he'd been permitted to pass that, he was waved through as far as the door to Harry's bedroom by a cleaner who came every week and refused to touch Harry's room. She thought it was a lost cause.

Mustafa stood at the doorway and sniffed inside. "It's rank in here. You stink, man."

"So do you," said Harry, without looking up from his tablet.

Mustafa regarded that as the equivalent of an invitation to enter. After half an hour of deriding his friend's hiding and refusing to deal with a crisis, he told him his idea for the British Museum. Harry agreed. He was tired of having nothing to do. He was tired of feeling sorry for himself. Half an hour later, he proposed the idea by phone to his father. His father also agreed to come.

That's how they all came to be in a dusty room at the back of the old British Museum. There were half a dozen display cases. In these cases were elaborate gold necklaces excavated from Tillya Tepe, or "the hill of gold," in Northern Afghanistan. They dated from the first century BCE. There were small bronze figures of Hercules and Dionysus from a different site. There were precious jewels made of turquoise and lapis lazuli. These had been mined and fashioned in Afghanistan at an era roughly contemporary with the early Roman Empire. They had been exported thousands of

miles away, using a sophisticated and extensive network of transport, throughout what later became the Islamic world. There were also fragments of gold bowls from two thousand years before the Roman Empire, an era that pre-dated even Homeric Greece. On the strength of Harry's father's agreeing to come, Mustafa had managed to gather together half a dozen curators, archaeologists, and historians to give brief introductions to these relics.

He was still angry at the way the army had treated him. He was angry at the way the press had injured his parents. The newspaper articles made him feel that no matter what schools he'd been to, or what regiment he'd joined, the British would never accept him as one of them. He wanted to rub British noses in the riches and glories of his country's cultural record as a way of wiping the smugness off their faces. He would show them who was civilized and who was not. Combined with this militancy was a feeling of insecurity. He was still unsure of himself and still uncertain of his sexuality. Harry might have seen it, and named it, but he hadn't entirely admitted to himself that he was gay.

Members of the press from the major British newspapers, as well as the cameras of media outlets from several other countries were all in the audience. In the front row sat Harry, his father, and his father's press secretary from St. James's. On the stage was the young warrior, recently arrived from Kabul.

An expert in the history of religions had just finished speaking about the Taliban's destruction of two stone Buddhas from the sixth century. They were immense statues that had been carved into limestone cliffs north of Kabul. Completed without steam-powered stone cutting machines, iron pulleys,

or modern chisels, they were testimony to the ingenuity of ancient sculptors, as well as to Afghanistan's place at the geographical crossroads of several different mobile religious traditions. This included not only Islam, but also Buddhism, Greco-Roman polytheism, and Hinduism. In defiance of this history, the Taliban had destroyed the Buddhas' faces in 2001 because they regarded them as anti-Islamic sacrilege.

Last in the program, the young warrior was called upon to read poetry in Pashto of Abdur Baba Rahman. Another young man played an authentic rubab, an ancient Afghan stringed instrument that resembled a lute or a guitar. Mustafa joined them at the rostrum to translate the poems into English. This was Mustafa's last militant surprise. He had slapped them all in the face with evidence of an Afghan civilization as old or older than anything to be found in the Britain. Now he would assault them further with these last poems. Their theme was the pointlessness of conflict. His last selections signaled a different, more humane approach. A last poem began "*I am a lover and I deal in love.*"

When all three of them had finished, the Prince of Wales stood up and approached Mustafa at the rostrum. He was wearing a bespoke flannel suit and a silk pocket square.

"Lieutenant Khan," said the prince, "that was fascinating. More than that, it was beautiful."

"Thank you, Your Royal Highness."

"You've taught us all so much about this lovely country's storied past, its moving literature, its ancient monuments. I want to go there. Will you take me? Will you show me?"

Mustafa took a surprised step backwards. He hadn't expected so favorable a reaction. He'd half expected to pick a

fight. "Um, sure. I mean, yes. I'd love to."

The members of the press in the room were less happy with a prince who was wearing what they regarded as suspiciously fancy clothes. They disliked Mustafa as a master of ceremonies whose commission had been suspended, and whom the army had under investigation. They also regarded the Prince of Wales as a kook when it came to questions of religion. They understood Mustafa's presentation as the attack on British stereotypes of Afghan culture that it was meant to be. They wanted to bring the discussion back to something that would appeal to their readers.

One freelance reporter stood up and directed a question to Mustafa, who was still at the rostrum. This reporter saw an irresistible chance to embarrass him. He thought he'd seen the young warrior speaking "*I am a lover and I deal in love*" directly to Mustafa. Was the kid wearing black eye makeup? "Thanks for the poetry and music. Aren't there troops of dancing boys in Afghanistan too? Isn't that wrong?"

"Thanks for keeping your questions on an elevated plane," answered Mustafa. "Let me ask you a question. What are you doing when you watch footballers running around in tight shorts? Let's not pretend admiration of young men is confined to Afghanistan, okay? By the way, it's also in Shakespeare."

"What? That old canard? Surely, Lieutenant Khan, you're not saying Shakespeare was gay, are you?"

"No. That's an anachronism. Gay didn't mean that in the seventeenth century. But at least some of the sonnets were written to a young man, or at any rate, to a man younger than the poet. That's roughly the same era as these poems in Pashto."

At this turn in the conversation, the prince's press secretary stood up to intervene. "That's all ladies and gentlemen. Thank you so much for joining us here today!"

Another reporter stood up. He was not going to be so easily shaken off. "Look! How old are those dancing boys?"

A third also stood up. He said, "Isn't there some funny business in *The Kite Runner*?"

Here Harry stood up. He was wearing a checked sport coat with an open-necked shirt over a pair of khakis and comfortable-looking pair of desert boots. "Hey, it's great you all could come. But I think we're getting off the subject here." He went over and put his arm around Mustafa. "The point of all this was to show that Afghanistan's not just a desert. It's not primitive people. It's not fighting over piles of rocks so far away that they don't count. It's a real place with real history. They're real people who're leading tough lives. They've got feelings too. And I'm no big fan of poetry, but my friend here is, and I thought it was all right. None of it was about sex, exactly, was it?" He gave Mustafa a comic smooch on the cheek. Mustafa reddened. "The banjo thingy in the background was cool, hmm?"

"With all due respect, Harry," resumed the first reporter.

"Let me translate that for everyone," said Harry with a bright expression and raised eyebrows. "You don't respect me at all." There was some appreciative laughter in the room.

"Harry, are you here to endorse Afghan abuse of teenage sexuality?"

"I don't know where you went to school, mate, but where I did, the guys were not exactly innocent when it came to sex."

"Yeah, well not all of us can go to Eton."

"Wait a minute! Wait a minute. You can't have it both ways. You just said that teenage sex was weird. Now you've got some kinda grudge 'cause you didn't go there. Which is it, mate?" There were more sympathetic murmurs in the room. "I mean, I admit, it's not exactly the Babylon of the Thames Valley, but we had our moments."

His father looked dismayed.

At this, Andrew Arbuthnot, who'd been sitting quietly at the back of the room, stood up. "I hope you'll all pardon me. And please excuse my interruption. But we have another event in the planning stages that may untangle a few of these knots. We will be exploring some of the ways the war-torn country that Lieutenant Khan, Lieutenant Wales, and I have just left sheds light on Shakespeare. And vice-versa, of course."

"We will, sir?" said Harry, surprised.

"The children from the village and their mothers, Lieutenant Wales. I thought we might rehearse them in that staged reading of *Henry IV*? When they get here."

"Oh that, sir."

"We have only to find a venue and appoint a time. But I think everyone here in this room will be favorably surprised."

The Prince of Wales's press secretary used Andrew's intervention as an opportunity to hustle the prince out of the room. Harry was grateful that his colonel was still speaking to him and had come up with an idea for the visit of the children. What he'd thought of for them so far had been beginning to look a little inadequate. The reporters left to write articles on Mustafa's presentation that implied, without directly saying so, that the whole Afghan war effort supported immoral practices. Mustafa continued standing at the front of the

room. He felt as if he'd made things worse rather than better. He was downcast. The young warrior came up to him and said in Pashto, "Are you all right?"

*

Cindy was in the bedroom of her producer's apartment in Atlanta. Because the producer's work occupied all his time and energy, he'd taken over without altering a single detail the decorating scheme proposed by the real estate developers of his condominium complex. It was an all beige room. There was no art on the walls and no clutter on the teak chest of drawers. The carpet was beige, the closed curtains were beige, and one of the walls was covered in a nubby beige fabric. Cindy disliked this room. It looked like dozens of others, and it refused to make any declarations about the occupant's personality. She was also reluctant to be where she was for other reasons. They'd had dinner after a late night at work. Talk at dinner had moved from work to the state of their relationship. She'd told him she didn't want to see him any more, not in a romantic way, at any rate. Nevertheless, he'd managed to play upon her nostalgia for the good times together of their relationship. He'd asked for one last hug. That and the wine had brought them both to the bedroom. It was

an unsatisfactory lovemaking that ended in his impotence.

"I guess it happens," he said. "To guys over fifty, I mean," he said, head on the pillow, looking up at the ceiling.

She was embarrassed.

He turned and reached out to her across a space between them in bed. "Cindy? I do still ..." he began.

"No," she said and moved further away from him on the king-sized bed with tufted headboard.

"I got an email from Arbuthnot. He's helping your boyfriend out."

"He's not my boyfriend."

"He was your boyfriend."

"He wasn't my boyfriend."

"I thought you were with me."

"Look. You know we shouldn't have. We both said so. It was a mistake. It went against everything."

"Sure. It broke the rules. But you felt it, didn't you? I did."

"What did Arbuthnot say?"

"I let you go out there."

"Is it something to do with Harry?"

"Right. That's what you really want to know, isn't it?"

She slipped out of bed. She found a pair of flowered bikini underpants on the floor and slipped them on. Then she picked up a silk top, more like a tee shirt than a formal blouse, also on the floor. She put that on too. "Don't be a jerk."

The producer looked over at her. He loved the way she looked in her underwear. She hadn't even walked out the door and he was already missing what they'd once had. "Yes. It's about Harry."

She looked at him now, directly.

"They want to put on this show. Some play Arbuthnot's pieced together. With the Afghan kids and their moms. But they can't get a stage for it."

"Why not?"

"C'mon Cindy. You saw the clips from the British Museum. The Brits think that Afghan guy with them's a weirdo."

"He's not Afghan. He's British. Mustafa. Mustafa Khan. And he's not weird."

"Tell that to them."

"It's all innuendo. And someone ought to call them on it. It's not news, it's gossip. They're trying to destroy him. That's the story."

"Anyway," said the producer looking away from her. "It's their news. Not ours. I told Arbuthnot CNN wasn't interested."

"Wait a minute. Don't you think there's an angle in this? I mean a more positive story? Something about the Afghan kids getting out of a war zone?"

The producer was losing interest. "We're not doing it."

"What if we did Harry on a tour of Muslim Britain? You know? With the kids? All of them together? Meeting the locals. You know? Talking about the war? Talking about what it's like to be Muslim in Britain today?"

The producer heaved a sigh. "Sounds like a lot of work. Not even sure we've got an audience for that, Cindy. That's not an American story."

"Oh come on! Anything with Harry in it is an American story. It'll do the same numbers as that film we ran before."

"I've gotta tell you the truth, sweetheart."

She stood and gave him an angry look. Then she began stepping into her pencil skirt and picking up the faun-colored

jacket she'd been wearing over it. She looked and couldn't find her shoes. If this was the way it was going to be, she was going to walk out.

"Here it is," continued the producer. "I'm just not sure you can be objective about this."

She looked under the bedskirt and pulled out one high-heeled shoe. She got up and began looking around the room for the other one.

"If we did do a story, and I'm not saying we are, you're supposed to be going in there with some impartiality you just don't have. When it comes to what's his name."

"Don't call me sweetheart." She was on the verge of deciding to leave. She'd just abandon the other shoe.

"You're gonna make the same mistake with him you made with me. Mixing work and play."

She was about to give him an angry reply, something he wouldn't forget, when, all of a sudden, she reconsidered. What if he was right? Maybe it was a mistake. Maybe it wouldn't help her become the sort of bitter-for-truth journalist she wanted to be. What if she wasn't even sure she wanted to be that anymore? Maybe she might like a different sort of life, one that didn't require her hair to be teased up, one that didn't require her to lie to the army to get a story, one that didn't require her to ask hostile questions of powerful people. Something in her relented. She just let go. She walked over to the bed in her skirt wearing a single shoe, clomping up and down across the carpet. She leaned down with her elbow on the pillow and spoke close to his ear. "Maybe it wasn't a mistake," she said quietly.

"What?"

"Us. Maybe it wasn't a mistake. Not all the time," she said to him. She leaned back where he could see her. She smiled into his eyes.

"I'm old enough to be your dad. I had responsibility for you. I decided what assignments you got. I was your boss. It was wrong."

"Yeah, okay. It was wrong. But you know?"

"What?"

"I learned stuff from you. I looked up to you. It was flattering. That you even paid attention to me. You taught me things."

"I did?"

"You did."

*

Mustafa and the young Afghan warrior were on the District Line. They were on their way to a college of further education in Hammersmith. Mustafa hoped to enroll the younger man in a course of English as a foreign language. He had to pass a test first. He also had to have an interview to demonstrate that he knew the English alphabet. Mustafa was not sure he did.

They were sitting on a bench of seats, separated by armrests, facing into the aisle of the train and looking toward

an identical bench on the opposite side. That part of London's underground railway dated back to the middle years of the nineteenth century. It had some of the slowest trains of anywhere on the entire urban network. Some of the signaling was still of Victorian vintage. The forward motion of the train was leisurely. It went at no more than thirty miles per hour, often with long delays in between stations. Mustafa supposed they waited on trains ahead of them. He was not sure. No explanations were ever given. They had an appointment with an admissions officer at two p.m. Mustafa hoped to be on time, but he was not sure they would be.

They were late because the young warrior had run low on black eye powder, surma. He applied it with a small brush that fit inside a small silk purse. Mustafa had found a shop on Brick Lane in East London that advertised surma for sale, but that was a considerable distance from his parents' flat. What had slowed them down even further was that, before leaving, the young warrior had insisted on applying the last of his surma under his eyes, and on his eyelids. When it was fresh, the effect was dramatic. It made him look both fierce and operatic. He looked like a diva backstage at Covent Garden. He also looked angrier and more capable of a violent act than he looked without it. When Mustafa made fun of him for it, they'd briefly wrestled on the floor of Mustafa's bedroom. The young warrior may have been younger than Mustafa, but he was also stronger. He overpowered him. Then the young warrior leaned over and patiently applied surma to Mustafa's eyes too. When he'd finished, there was no time for Mustafa to wash it off. So they'd both run out of the door still wearing it. Mustafa didn't feel out of place in

Brick Lane, where there was a South Asian community, but as they returned westwards again, underneath the Duke of Norfolk's land at the Temple, underneath Whitehall Palace, where Charles I had been executed, underneath the railway station named for Queen Victoria, Mustafa felt they were advancing into the depths of white London. Although he was a Londoner, and at ease in almost every part of town, he still felt self-conscious wearing what looked to him like women's eye makeup. He was having a terse conversation in Pashto with the young warrior.

"I can't believe I let you do this to me."

"Do what?"

"Put this bloody surma on, that's what."

"It's natural."

"In your village it's natural. In mine, it's not."

"It does many things for you."

"Oh yeah? Like what?"

"It strengthens your vision. It helps diminish the glare of the sun. It keeps God's eye upon you. It wards off the evil eye of your enemies."

"What nonsense," said Mustafa with a skeptical laugh

"If you wish to deny Pashtun wisdom about surma, you deny wisdom accumulated over centuries."

This made Mustafa pause. He had respect for history. He wanted to have more knowledge of his family's Afghan origins. He tried a different tack. "Here, though, men don't wear makeup. Women do. Men don't."

"Why not?"

"It's considered effeminate."

"That is too bad."

"Why?"

"Because surma also makes men look better. More desirable, more attractive. Like you, for instance."

Mustafa shot a look at the young warrior. What did he mean? Commenting on one another's appearance was new territory. He looked away. His command of Pashto was good, but he sometimes missed the underlying implications. The young man's gaze was also too intense for him.

"I'll tell you what the problem is," said Mustafa, determined to stamp out any ambiguities in the relationship between them. "Here you risk being called a poof if you're seen in public wearing it." He didn't know an equivalent word in Pashto for poof, so he used the English word.

"What is poof?"

"A poofter, a fairy, a queer, a nancy boy." He was delaying defining the word. He also felt a gloomy pleasure in reciting in English the names that, despite many decades of social progress, could still be used to brand a British homosexual.

"Why do you wish to stop me from understanding?"

"Okay," Mustafa resumed in Pashto. "It's a man who loves other men."

"What is wrong with a man who loves other men?"

"Um, nothing. But this is a man loving other men to sleep with. I mean sexually. Like in bed."

"What is wrong with that?"

Mustafa rolled his eyes. "Because men aren't supposed to like other men sexually. They're supposed to like women. You know, make babies?"

Here the young warrior's eyebrows became smoother and he stopped being puzzled. Something had become clear to

him. He had understood. "Yes. Men sleep with women to make babies. But for having fun? It is better for men to sleep with other men."

Mustafa relaxed too. It all seemed so preposterously easy and straightforward to the younger man. Of course he couldn't see how gay love, whatever progress might have been made recently, went against centuries of accumulated teaching about sexual morality in England. He laughed. "Yeah? Well, it's not like that here. If people think you're a poof, they beat you up."

"Why would they do that?"

"I don't know. They don't always. But it still threatens lots of guys, somehow. Maybe it exposes something in themselves that they're not comfortable with. Maybe they consider it a threat to society. Maybe it's just different and when you're a thug, different is bad. I'm not sure why. But believe me, it happens. It's not a myth."

"So this has happened to you, then?"

Mustafa was surprised at the young man's intuition. Mustafa had to explain all the most elementary rules of London life to the young warrior. When it came to something emotional and complex in Mustafa's own personal history, however, the younger man seemed to catch it in a second. "Yeah, like right here on this train. On this line. Between Earls Court and Gloucester Road. A few years ago."

While Mustafa and the young warrior were having this conversation, a group of American college students, all of them young women, boarded the train and sat on the bench opposite them. They were from a small liberal arts college in Wisconsin. Their professor was leading them on a month-

long course, which required them to attend the theatre. They also had to write several papers on the urban context of the London stage. This had meant their going to a series of painfully incomprehensible performances of mime and dance, chosen by their professor. He'd also taken them on dull walking tours of multi-ethnic, multi-cultural, modern London. They weren't interested. They wanted to see Diana's dresses, shop at Harrods, and meet some boys.

Right away, they noticed the two young men sitting across from them. They were having an intense conversation. One was wearing a tweed jacket, scuffed Pumas, and a pale blue shirt. The other had on a tee shirt that said "Fly Ariana, Afghan Airlines," a pair of jeans, and a white turban. They both had light brown skin. Both of them were wearing black eye shadow. One of the young women elbowed her friend sitting next to her.

"Look at them," she whispered.

"I know," said the other. "Hot."

They'd been at a bar the previous night where they'd met some Australian boys. They'd all had quite a lot of beer and the Australians had dared the two of them to kiss each other. They'd complied, but they'd also extracted their revenge. As part of a truth or dare game, they'd also managed to get the two Australian guys to kiss each other. Everyone had shouted and clapped and hooted when they'd done it. It was the best thing, and the most international thing, that had happened to them in London so far.

"Did you get the cell of that guy from last night?"

"Sure, I did. Are you kidding me?"

"Tonight, let's see if we can get him to put on mascara!"

Meanwhile, the conversation between Mustafa and the

young warrior had moved on to something that made the young warrior uncomfortable. Mustafa, on the other hand, was more at ease than he had been a few moments earlier.

"I may fail the test," said the young Afghan warrior.

"Well, you give it a try and we go from there. They're going to be looking for kids to fill their seats. They'll probably be looking for a way to let you in no matter what."

"If I do pass, I will not let you pay for my English language school."

"Who else is going to pay for it?"

"I will work for it."

"You don't have the papers to do that. In England you need special permission to work if you're not from here."

"I will get those papers. I will get that permission."

"It could take ages. Years, I mean."

The young warrior looked down into his lap. England was a series of surprises to him, and not all of them were wonderful. Before a week ago, he'd never been on an airplane. He'd never seen soldiers dressed in scarlet coats. He'd never seen a train that ran completely underground. He didn't intend to be a perpetual guest, a perpetual drag on Mustafa's parents' hospitality, a perpetual dependent. He intended to find a rooming house for himself. He intended to find a job to pay for his meals and his lodging. He hadn't anticipated that there might be obstacles to this that could take years to surmount.

Mustafa reached over, put his arm around the younger man's shoulders and gave them a shake. "Don't look so glum. I can pay your tuition out of my pocket money."

The young warrior looked up at Mustafa with raised eyebrows.

"And still have some left over. After your test is over, after we've done the interview, I know a place in Ealing Broadway where they do Kabuli Pulau."

"If so, I will take the money," said the young warrior, "but only as a loan. I will pay it back."

"No! You don't have to," said Mustafa.

"Yes, I do!"

"No, you don't."

To punctuate his final refusal the young warrior leaned forward without warning and kissed Mustafa on the lips. "Yes, I will!"

The American young women sitting across from them cried out. They'd seen the whole thing. Several gave appreciative screams. One squealed. There was a smattering of applause. The first young woman observed to the second, "And we didn't even have to buy them a beer to do that."

The young warrior looked up in surprise, and then gave them a broad smile.

Mustafa looked up in embarrassment. He rouged, sat back in his chair, closed his eyes, and said quietly, wonderingly, almost to himself, "All right then."

✻

Frances and Andrew were in the back seat of a London black cab. They were on their way to Staines from central London, a fair distance even under good conditions. The cab was stalled in traffic. They'd been sitting, not moving, for fifteen minutes. When the fare box gave a loud click, and the electronic digits turned over to read £40.00, Frances looked over at Andrew.

"Don't worry, my darling," said Andrew. "It's a billable expense."

"I very much doubt that, Andrew," said Frances. "The Ministry of Defense won't pay for a journey like this. Even at your rank."

"Oh not them. You're right. Whitehall won't. But *Hello!* magazine might. I'm thinking of writing an essay for them. *Which Characters in Shakespeare Most Resemble Members of Our Royal Family?* That sort of thing, anyway."

Frances smiled at this. He was going to do no such thing. She put her arm through his. It was easier to do things in pairs, she reflected. That was one of the things she'd forgotten in all her recent years of facing approaching age alone. She sighed. She missed having someone who could dispel her gloom every once in a while.

Andrew enjoyed her hand holding his lower bicep for a moment. Then he raised up the same arm and put it protectively around her shoulders. His hand felt the shoulder of her tailored jacket, but he could also feel the bone underneath. It made him think of frailty, which he never had with her before. "My dear, I am sorry to be indelicate, but I do wish you'd allow me to take you out and fatten you up. Like a Christmas goose. You seem thinner to me since we got back. Let me take you out tomorrow night. What about Wilton's?

Some potted shrimps? Some Dover sole? Some chocolate mousse? That'll put the color back into your cheeks."

"Oh Andrew," she smiled. "I'm fine. Don't worry. Wilton's is not a billable expense, whatever you say." She coughed again.

"And what about that cough? I'd feel easier if you saw a doctor about it."

"I have as a matter of fact."

"And?"

"Well, he didn't know. I'm to go and see a bronchial specialist about it next week. Really, I'm sure it's nothing. All those cigarettes I smoked in the '60s. We all did. He'll probably give me one of those wonderful asthma spray thimbles. I can go around taking a shot of it whenever the conversation becomes awkward." She said this lightly because she didn't want him to worry. She concealed from him that the doctor had detected an unusual loss of weight and a small, low-grade fever.

"What specialist? When next week? I could take you. It's always better to listen to doctors with two sets of ears rather than one."

"Now Andrew. It's all too boring for words. I refuse to have it spoken of. When I'm sitting in a taxi with a man, it's him I want to hear about. I was warned in school never to do it, of course."

"Never to do what?"

"Never to get in the back of a black cab with a man. And no chaperone."

"What did they say might happen?" Andrew asked her with a poker face.

"Well ..."

Before she could finish, Andrew reached over quickly and took hold of her lower thigh, just above the knee. He squeezed

her through the wool fabric of her charcoal gray skirt.

She was on the verge of shrieking and then she stopped herself. She pulled away and looked at him accusingly.

He looked back with feigned innocence.

The cab driver, a Sikh, looked back at them in his rearview mirror. He winked at Andrew.

Frances saw the wink and scooted further away from Andrew on the seat. "Now, Andrew, I will not have it! I am sitting here. And you are sitting there. There is an imaginary line between us." She pointed at a seam in the black upholstery of the seat. "Don't cross that line!"

"All right my dear," he said smiling, facing forward, not looking at her.

She smoothed out her skirt and crossed her arms over her chest, as if for protection. She moved the conversation firmly on to a safer topic. "As you already know, I'm thinking of joining an order. There's an abbess I've spoken to. She might take me. I'm not too old."

"Oh, Frances, why?"

"I had my fling. I can't take more headlines from the newspapers. If I go away, at least I'll be safe from all that."

"Here we are. The two of us. There's no disaster." Andrew didn't dare look at her when he said this, but he meant it. "On the contrary. I think it shows great promise. *Publish and be damned.* That's what the Duke of Wellington said. When he was threatened with the exposure of one of his girlfriends. We take his line. We ignore them."

"I will not continue to ruin your career. By entangling you in all my past history."

"I'm already entangled, darling. Of my own volition. It's

not just you. It's us. And," he thought for a moment, before he added, "I've had one or two offers to go and consult with some different armies. The Ukrainians have hired some chaps like me to come out and advise. In a private capacity. The Pakistanis too, I believe. If the Household Cavalry won't have me back, I could be a sort of mercenary. Soldiering is what I know how to do. If you stick to the idea of joining a holy order, I mean."

She looked at him. What he'd just said had just caused her the first genuine pang of the afternoon. "Oh Andrew! *Go not to these wars.*"

Andrew was taken off guard. He turned on the seat and looked at her. Then he reached over the imaginary line and took both her hands. He moved over to touch his knee to hers. "Why. But darling. That's from *Henry IV*. Maybe you really do care about me."

He leaned forward and gave her a kiss, on the lips. It was a soft kiss, and they both kept their eyes closed. They both allowed it to go on five seconds longer than might have been considered entirely chaste. The Sikh driver watched them in the mirror.

Frances broke the kiss and leaned back against the seat bench. She was feeling more relaxed, torn, and approved of than she had in a long time. "I don't know."

"I do," he said.

She looked him calmly in the eye. "All right," she said at last. It might as well have been "I do."

"I can scarcely believe it," he said looking back at her.

There was a microphone in the back seat that broadcast everything the passengers said to a speaker in the front.

At Andrew's words the Sikh cab driver slid back the clear plastic partition that divided the cab's front seat from the back. "Believe it, sir! Believe it. There is a registry office on the King's Road. Chelsea Town Hall. Newlyweds often pose on the steps. I have seen them many times. Shall I take you there? I will be your witness!" He was delighted.

"Would you Frances?" asked Andrew turning back to Frances. "Shall we?" He took both her hands again. "You heard the man. He'll stand up with us."

"There's nothing I'd like better. You saw that before I did."

Andrew swiveled away from her a moment, let her go, and slid up on the seat to speak through the open partition. "Yes please! Can you take us there right away? Before the lady changes her mind?"

The cab driver turned to face out the windshield at the long row of stopped cars in front of him. His smile dimmed. He held up his hands in an elaborate, apologetic shrug to Andrew.

"But Andrew!" said Frances, appearing to reconsider. "What if this beastly cough is, I don't know, of course it probably isn't, but what if it is? Something serious?" She'd been afraid, but she didn't like to say so, not before now. "You mustn't marry an invalid."

Andrew turned back to her on the seat again and took up one of her hands. He slid his other hand around her waist. "An invalid who makes me happy."

"But what if I take some looking after? You don't want to sign up for that."

"There's nothing in the world I'd rather do." He leaned forward to kiss her again. This time they both allowed ten seconds. When they parted, with reluctance on both sides,

Andrew said, "There is one thing I'd like to know, however."

"There's always a but," said Frances folding her arms and leaning back against the bench seat.

"What else did they tell you in school? You know? About getting into the back of a taxi with a man."

Her eyes sparkled. She repressed a giggle. "I'm not telling."

"Did they say he might do this?" Andrew leaned forward to kiss her collar bone. At the same time, the Sikh driver pulled the taxi around one hundred and eighty degrees from where he'd been at a standstill for almost a half hour now. He thumped over a curb on the right. He then pressed the accelerator hard, and the cab surged forward. This threw Andrew backwards. He kissed the seatback instead of Frances's neck.

She also was pressed back against her seat, her head tilting backward with the new forward motion of the taxi. She laughed at Andrew's kissing the seat. The schoolgirl she once was, who'd done much that she shouldn't have, also flashed into her mind. With the recovered eagerness of that schoolgirl, she said, "We're off!"

✻

On the Afghans' last day in the UK, following the staged reading, they were all set to attend a farewell banquet. They were going

to Mustafa's parents' apartment. It was true that they had grown more ashamed of their money since its origins had been exposed in the newspapers, but Mustafa was still their son and they forgave him. Further, it was not every day that a member of the royal family came to call. They were happy to host the banquet. It was not far from Kensington Palace, so Cindy and Harry were going to walk over from there.

Cindy and Harry were in Harry's bedroom. She'd been more curious to see its interior than Mustafa had been when he'd come to visit. The entrance was from an unmarked roadway off Kensington High Street. Past the security guard's kiosk, and through several locked outer doors was the foyer of Harry's place. Inside, the front door, to the left was a low antique side table with a basket where he tossed his keys and threw circulars from the agency which managed the flats. She thought it was funny that even he got junk mail. Against another wall was an African shield that had been made into a bar. It held a silver ice bucket, a jumble of liquor bottles, and many glasses. An opened wooden crate of Bordeaux was underneath the bar. There was also an umbrella stand that had a polo mallet and riding crops in it, but no umbrellas. Over the bar was a mirror, into one corner of which had been wedged a snapshot of Harry together with four soldiers in a tent. Their arms were around one another's shoulders. They were grinning. They'd all dropped their camouflage trousers to their boots and were showing off their brightly-colored underpants.

His bedroom, down the hall, was a boy's bedroom. It wasn't just the plastic fighter plane models hanging from the ceiling and the array of toy soldiers on the shelves. It was also the pile

of shorts, tee shirts, and socks tossed in a heap in the corner.
It was the wastebasket next to the computer full of Kleenex
tissues. Harry was only half dressed. He wore a pair of stretchy
boxer shorts and a striped banker's shirt. He was bouncing
a light foam ball off the walls of the bedroom. Cindy lay on
the bed. She already had on the white shirt she was wearing
to the Khans' apartment and a pair of pressed trousers she'd
found at a Gap on Regent Street. She'd left Atlanta in a hurry,
without giving CNN any notice, and she'd had to buy some
clothes to make up her outfit. She was reading with pillows
propped behind her head.

"Reading, reading, reading," he said watching the ball and
not her. "How can you? So boring."

"No it's not," she said, continuing to read and not looking at
him.

Suddenly he pivoted toward her, jumped forward, and
grabbed away the book from her hands. "Whoops! Don't drop
it!"

"Harry!"

"What's this anyway? He looked around at the cover. *The
Places in Between*. What's that?"

"Rory Stewart's book. He walked next to the Hari Rud."

"Don't start that."

"It's not you, it's a river. Hari's another name for Herat.
Rud is Persian for river."

"Whatever." He threw it over to her, the pages aflutter, and
she caught it, as if it were a bird. "Suit yourself." He went back
to bouncing his ball off the wall before he added, as if it were
an afterthought, "Page 132."

Suddenly, without warning, he turned around, just as he'd

done earlier when grabbing away her book, and launched himself toward the bed. He landed on top of her with both his hands pinning down her hands on either side.

Taken by surprise, she gave a muffled shout.

"I'll show you a little Hari rud," he said deepening his voice and looking into her eyes.

"Stop!" she said. She struggled underneath him with more resistance than he'd expected. They wrestled briefly and knocked over a small, silver-framed photograph that was standing next to the bed on a side table.

"No, you stop!" he said. He paused. He reached over and carefully set up the silver frame again. Then he angled the frame so she could see it. It was a picture of his mother. She was in a red dress. Her hair was in a short, blonde, pageboy haircut. She was giving the photographer an impish look.

"Oh," said Cindy.

"Yeah," said Harry, suddenly grave.

Cindy held her breath. She didn't speak. She watched him. After a while she said, "I can't be with you."

"Why not?"

"I can never be her." She nodded at the framed picture he'd just re-arranged on the bedside table.

"Who said you had to be?"

"And that's not all. Here it is. I don't wanna be a princess. I don't know how. Opening hospitals. Going on tours. Standing in a receiving line. I don't know how to do any of that."

"We don't have to do it that way."

"Yes we would. That's what it'd be like. Maybe CNN's not right for me anymore. But married to you? That'd be totally wrong."

"I don't think I asked you to marry me, did I?"

She looked into his eyes a moment. She was embarrassed. He was still on top of her. "Let me go."

He pretended he hadn't heard her. "But if I did ask you, or maybe, if you asked me, we could think up our own way to do it. We could make it up as we go along. We could help each other figure it out." Here he raised his fingers and began snapping them to an improvised tune "Hari, Hari, Hari!" He closed his eyes, sang, and grooved to the music, as if it was about him, but not quite him. He knew he looked silly. That was what he wanted.

She giggled unwillingly at his act.

"Hey," he said as if something new had just occurred to him. "What're you wearing to the Khans' tonight Princess? You're not going like that are you? I mean, just a white shirt and some khaki trousers?"

He said it "car-key" trousers and this made Cindy laugh. "Sure. It's fine."

"But tonight's special. It's the big send-off. For the kids. You've got to dress up. A little bit. What about a little bling?"

"I didn't bring any jewelry."

"That's a pity," he said. Then it occurred to him. "Maybe you could try this on?" He fingered the pendant around his neck. He reached up behind his neck to un-do the clasp. "Just for tonight I mean."

She looked back at him evenly, carefully. "Maybe. Just for tonight," she repeated.

"What if I were to open your shirt a button?" He now drew himself up to sit on top of her waist. He had the unchained pendant in his right hand. He held it up in the air to show

her. She was still lying on the bed underneath his weight. He reached down and unbuttoned a button of her shirt, which was already open one button at the collar. It was now open two buttons at her neck and exposed a flesh triangle of her upper chest. He threaded his pendant around and underneath her neck. She lifted her head so that he could bring it under her hair. Then he spent a long time furrowing his eyebrows and fumbling with the clasp to try and close it. He tried to do it with both hands and concentrated on it for several minutes. Finally, it snapped shut. He pulled the clasp around to the back and he patted it flat under her shirt. "There," he said, proud of his work. He leaned back to examine it. He narrowed his eyes. "I think it's okay. But I need to check it. You know?"

He leaned over from his sitting position and brought his head down toward hers. His descent was slow and she could see that he intended to kiss her. She lifted her head from the pillow to meet him and kissed him back. After a moment he leaned back and sat up again saying, "Maybe one more of these little buttons?" He reached down to open a third button, at the same time giving her a little comic grind of his hips on top of hers.

All at once, using a wrestling move she'd learned from her brothers, she pushed her waist in the air. It toppled him off her and on to the floor. He landed with a bump and a surprised shout on top of a sisal carpet next to the bed. She pressed her advantage. She jumped off the bed and on top of him, pinning him now to the floor with her hands on top of his. "No you don't," she said. She leaned over him, his pendant now hanging out of her white shirt. At first she held his hands and

arms down against the floor. Then she lifted herself up, took her hands away from his, and began to work at the neck of his shirt. "Let's try these buttons instead."

He put his hands behind his head as a cushion on the hard floor. He smiled at her. And he let her undo all his buttons, one by one.

About the Author

William Kuhn is a novelist, biographer, historian, scribbler, and dabbler. His debut novel *Mrs Queen Takes the Train* was a surprise (to him) bestseller. It has also been optioned for a film. His biography of Jacqueline Kennedy Onassis, *Reading Jackie*, tells the story of her life through the pages of the hundred books she edited at Viking and Doubleday. He has written on the British prime minister Benjamin Disraeli in *The Politics of Pleasure*. His book on a funny couple who lived in Windsor Castle, *Henry & Mary Ponsonby: Life at the Court of Queen Victoria*, was a BBC Radio Four Book of the Week. He wears antique military jackets around the house when no one is watching. He lives in Boston, Massachusetts, and whenever he can, in London too. For more, including audio files, stories, and pictures, please go to **williamkuhn.com**.

32463392R00192

Made in the USA
San Bernardino, CA
14 April 2019

ALSO BY

WILLIAM KUHN

FICTION

Mrs Queen Takes the Train

NONFICTION

Reading Jackie:
Her Autobiography in Books

The Politics of Pleasure: A Portrait of
Benjamin Disraeli

Henry & Mary Ponsonby: Life at the Court of
Queen Victoria

Democratic Royalism:
The Transformation of the British Monarchy,
1861-1914

4∞

PRASE FOR ***..n*** BY WILLIAM KUHN

"This is a novel, but no matter how you felt about the Queen before reading it, you'll come away thinking Her Majesty, at least this fictional one, charming, caring, thoughtful, and brave. William Kuhn's book is hard to categorize genre-wise. But its light comedy, romance, and royal sensibilities, mixed with subplots touching on aging, political correctness, and respect for sexual preferences, make for a delightful escape. We can only hope there are are more train rides in Her Majesty's future."

USA Today

"[A] charmer of a first novel ... This Elizabeth is delightful, slyly funny company. You'll never look at the real one the same way again."

People

"A witty, contemporary story of the ... tensions between servants and employers, the young and the old, and tradition and modernity."

Glamour.com

"Poignant and sweet, *Mrs Queen Takes the Train* is a comic study of the British class system, an unusual testament to the possibilities of friendship outside normal comfort zones and an affirmation of the humanity within us all."

Richmond Times-Dispatch

"A delightful read, a bit of fiction (the train journey) set into nonfiction (everything else), and a sly look at how the monarchy is changing along with—or maybe two beats behind—the rest of Britain."

Minneapolis StarTribune